MW00907036

Everyday
Diamonds

Articles of faith, hope and love

Ann H Nunnally

Everyday Diamonds

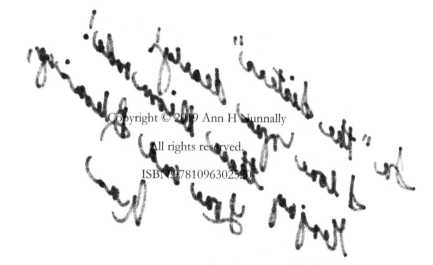

Source Notations

All stories shared in this book are from my own life. I have changed the names of people involved and added narrative details such as additional names and dialog as necessary for readability.

Unless otherwise indicated, all Scripture quotations are taken from the *Holy Bible, New Living Translation*, copyright 1996. 2004, 2007 by Tyndale House Foundation. Used by permission of Tyndale House Publishers, Inc., Carol Stream, Illinois 60188. All rights reserved.

Other versions of the Bible and their publication information are as follows:
The New King James Version (NKJV). Copyright © 1982 by Thomas Nelson. Used by permission. All rights reserved.

New Life Version (NLV). Copyright © 1969, 2003 by Barbour Publishing, Inc.

The Message (MSG), Copyright © 1993, 1994, 1995, 1996, 2000, 2001, 2002 by Eugene H. Peterson.

The Living Bible (TLB). Copyright 1971 by Tyndale House Foundation. Used by permission of Tyndale House Publishers, Inc., Carol Stream, Illinois 60188. All rights reserved.

The Amplified Bible (AMP) Scripture taken from the Amplified Bible, Old Testament copyright © 1965, 1987 by Zondervan Corporation. The Amplified New Testament copyright © 1958, 1987 by The Lockman Foundation. Used by permission.

Everyday Diamonds

Table of Contents

Everyday Diamonds

Dedication

This book is dedicated to the partners and friends who have stood with me since I started *An Encouraging Word with Ann Nunnally* in 2005. Your prayers, financial gifts, counsel and emotional support has sent me across America and around the world to preach the good news of Jesus Christ. I am forever grateful for all you have done to help me fulfill the call of God on my life!

This book is also dedicated to my family for sharing Ann, Mom and Meena with the multitudes! I love you dearly and thank you for loving me!

This book is also dedicated to the women who served and planned from 1996 – 2017, women's conferences that radically changed lives. *The Destiny Christian Women's Conference, The North Alabama Christian Women's Conference, the EWAN Christian Conference Cruise, and the Thomasville Christian Women's Conference* impacted so many lives for the kingdom of God!

This book is also dedicated to the *Victory Fellowship Church and Training Center, Inc.* family of God who called me "Pastor Ann" from 1997 – 2016. Wow! Twenty years! You will always have my heart!

Acknowledgements

I would like to thank my wonderful husband, Larry, and my sons,
Sam and Jamie for reading and correcting hundreds of articles
through the 10 years of writing and publishing. Your guidance has
been so valuable, and you have been the source of
so many wonderful life lessons.
Thanks also to my niece, Cassia, for an excellent title for this book.

I would also like to thank the many people who loved me and taught
me the word of God through the years so I could teach others. My
childhood Sunday School teachers, those who "grew me up" through
home Bible studies, those who had audio and video teaching
ministries that I gleaned from.
You will never know the impact you had.

I would also like to thank Lauren at *Adele Creative Marketing and
Design* for her genius in cover design. You have been a friend in this
journey.

A bird's eye-view

Several years ago, my family and I lived in a country subdivision. Nestled in the woods south of town we enjoyed living among the wildlife and having a bird's eye-view of the lifestyle of other creatures. While I despised the snakes we often found, I loved the various birds, raccoons, beady-eyed possums, various lizards and frogs and an occasional fox. Canopied by ageless water oaks, our little house was a tri-level design and provided window access to lots of happenings in the animal kingdom.

One morning I looked out the living room window which was set at ground level and I saw a mama Cardinal building a nest in the dense shrubbery. Without a concern, she looked at me through the window panes and continued to build her nest. Daily I watched her progress as she built a nest for her soon coming family. One morning I awoke to the sight of little eggs in mama bird's nest. She faithfully sat on the nest keeping her eggs warm and preparing them for birth. Her mate for life would bring her food during the incubation phase. They would momentarily touch beaks and transfer the food needed for her nourishment as she guarded her eggs. He would protect the territory and deliver the food to his hungry mate.

 I shared the miracle that was happening with my husband and my two young sons. Together we anxiously awaited the chirping of new life. Sure enough, one morning I looked out the window and there were four baby birds calling for mama and daddy to feed them. Laughter and joy overwhelmed our family as we watched their family develop. The babies got stronger, louder and more demanding of mama and daddy. Every day was an adventure watching the Cardinal family grow.

One day I was home alone, and heavy rain began to fall from the sky. Mama bird spread her wings and covered her chicks to protect them from the rain. Neither she nor I realized she had built her nest under the eve of the house and this unusual downpour was causing torrents of rain to pour directly down into her nest. Helplessly I watched as she weathered the spring rain, giving all she had to saving her brood.

She looked weary, cold, alone and helpless. I watched as the situation got worse. I was without options as I couldn't stop the rain, divert the downpour coming off the roof or move the nest. I could only peer through the window, hope and pray that this little family would make it through this ordeal.

In the whole process, from the first twig of the nest to the birth and growth of the baby birds neither mama bird nor I could see the storm coming. We were both unprepared for the reality of life and death. In my heart I was out in the rain, setting on the nest with her, hoping for a miracle that would save the Cardinal family. In tears I watched mama bird almost drown herself as the nest filled to overflowing and the babies chirped their final goodbye. She had given her best and almost her life to saving her little fledglings.

I was reminded of the time Jesus looked out over the city of Jerusalem and spoke these words, "O Jerusalem, Jerusalem, the city that kills the prophets and stones God's messengers! How often I have wanted to gather your children together as a hen protects her chicks beneath her wings, but you wouldn't let me. And now, look, your house is abandoned and desolate." Matthew 23:37-38 (NLT)

While mama Cardinal almost lost her life to protect her chicks, Jesus did lose his life to protect and cover his children during life's storms. We often make the mistake of building our lives in an unsafe place, not realizing the brewing storm and the potential for disaster that awaits us. But God's great love expressed in the person of Jesus Christ is always present to cover us with protection and care. There is never a storm in life that we suffer alone unless we are like the Pharisees and reject his help. He wants to love, protect and care for his children in this uncertain world we live in. With Jesus on our side, even the bad times are good. His comfort is limitless, and his word says he will never leave us nor forsake us no matter how strong the winds and rain. He is faithful.

2

A Merry Heart is Good Like Medicine

I sometimes get overwhelmed with the things that are happening in the world. I lose my joy and begin to worry about the things I have no control over. I know I am not alone in this place of confusion and anxiety. I must return to the basics of my faith which instructs me to walk in peace and have a merry heart knowing God is on my side. It's not easy when the world seems overbearing and loss seems monumental. *Lord, when did I forget you have always been the king of the world?*

In Proverbs 17:22 NKJV, states, "A merry heart does good, *like* medicine, but a broken spirit dries the bones." The NLT puts it this way, "A cheerful heart is good medicine, but a broken spirit saps a person's strength." It's important to laugh especially in the face of adversity.

Bi-weekly I post "Today's funny" on my Facebook page. It is often shared among friends and family members across the U.S. It's a variety of quotes and memes designed to put the world on pause and make a smile appear in the darkness.

The following story is written by an unknown author and exemplifies the struggle the Christian often experiences. It also demonstrates God's unrelenting grace and mercy in our lives when we just "try" to walk in obedience. It's called, "If Noah Lived in the 21st Century".

And we thought we had problems! If Noah had lived in the United States in the last ten years, the story may have gone something like this:

And the Lord spoke to Noah and said, "In one year, I am going to make it rain and cover the whole earth with water until all flesh is destroyed. But I want you to save the righteous people and two of every kind of living thing on earth. Therefore, I am commanding you to build an Ark." In fear and trembling, Noah took the plans and agreed to build the ark. "Remember," said the Lord, "you must complete the Ark and bring everything aboard in one year."

Exactly one year later, fierce storm clouds covered the earth and all the seas of the earth went into a tumult. The Lord saw that Noah was sitting in his front yard weeping. "Noah!" He shouted. "Where is the Ark?" "Lord, please forgive me," cried Noah. "I did my best, but there were big problems."

"First, I had to get a permit for construction, and your plans did not meet the building codes. I had to hire an engineering firm and redraw the plans. Then I got into a fight with OSHA over whether the Ark needed a sprinkler system and approved floatation devices. Then, my neighbor objected, claiming I was violating zoning ordinances by building the Ark in my front yard, so I had to get a variance from the city planning commission."

"Then, I had problems getting enough wood for the Ark because there was a ban on cutting trees to protect the Spotted Owl. I finally convinced the U.S. Forest Service that I really needed the wood to save the owls. However, the Fish and Wildlife Service won't let me take the 2 owls. The carpenters formed a union and went on strike. I had to negotiate a settlement with the National Labor Relations Board before anyone would pick up a saw or hammer. Now, I have 16 carpenters on the Ark, but still no owls."

"When I started rounding up the other animals, an animal rights group sued me. They objected to me taking only two of each kind aboard. This suit is pending. Meanwhile, the EPA notified me that I could not complete the Ark without filing an environmental impact statement on your proposed flood. They didn't take very kindly to the idea that they had no jurisdiction over the conduct of the Creator of the Universe. Then, the Army Corps of Engineers demanded a map of the proposed flood plain. I sent them a globe."

"Right now, I am trying to resolve a complaint filed with the Equal

4

Employment Opportunity Commission that I am practicing discrimination by not taking atheists aboard. The IRS has seized my assets, claiming that I'm building the Ark in preparation to flee the country to avoid paying taxes. I just got a notice from the state that I owe them some kind of user tax and failed to register the Ark as a 'recreational water craft.' And finally, the ACLU got the courts to issue an injunction against further construction of the Ark, saying that since God is flooding the earth, it's a religious event and therefore unconstitutional. I really don't think I can finish the Ark for another five or six years."
Noah waited.

The sky began to clear, the sun began to shine, and the seas began to calm. A rainbow arched across the sky. Noah looked up hopefully, "You mean you're not going to destroy the earth, Lord?"

"No," He said sadly. "I don't have to. The government already has."

Take your medicine today! Laugh a lot!

An afternoon that changed the world

We have all experienced moments in time when an event changed our world. Sometime those events are catastrophic and other times the event is the greatest blessing ever. Good or bad, the event changes our history forever.

I would like to share with you a story from the Book of Acts that changed the world forever. It's not the crucifixion or the resurrection, it's not the day of Pentecost nor is it Paul's missionary journeys. It is the story of one woman who sought God, received his grace and opened up a continent to the gospel.

Acts 16:13-15 NLT, "On the Sabbath we went a little way outside the city to a riverbank, where we thought people would be meeting for prayer, and we sat down to speak with some women who had gathered there. One of them was Lydia from Thyatira, a merchant of expensive purple cloth, who worshiped God. As she listened to us, the Lord opened her heart, and she accepted what Paul was saying. She and her household were baptized, and she asked us to be her guests. "If you agree that I am a true believer in the Lord," she said, "come and stay at my home." And she urged us until we agreed."

The banks of the river that flowed through Philippi to the Aegean Sea had been designated as a legal meeting place for Jews and God-fearers by the Roman authorities. There was no building, simply a grove where worshipers could gather in safety. It was not a place of preaching but a place of prayer and worship. Paul and his entourage approached those worshiping that Sabbath afternoon and shared the story of Jesus.

In church history, Lydia is Paul's first convert in Europe. Her faith in God and her hospitality to Paul and his preaching team opened the continent of Europe. One afternoon changed the world.

There are several things about this new convert, Lydia, that are worthy of noticing. First, the scripture says, her heart was opened. Salvation never comes to one with a closed heart. Romans 10:9-10 NLT tells us that we must believe with our heart to be saved. "If you openly declare that Jesus is Lord and believe in your heart that God raised him from the dead, you will be saved. For it is by believing in your heart that you are made right with God, and it is by openly declaring your faith that you are saved."

The second interesting thing of note about Lydia is that she was wealthy. Her purple cloth was sought after by the wealthiest people in the world and her enterprising spirit had rewarded her with a big house and statue in the community. She could invite, even compel Paul and his entourage to stay with her because there was room and food for her family and others.

Thirdly, Lydia was a leader. Not only did she believe and was baptized but her household also followed her into this new faith. She was such a leader that she immediately began to influence Paul, compelling and persuading him to stay at her house during their ministry time in Philippi.

Fourthly, according to church history Lydia was a widow. However, she never let life's circumstances define who she was or her ability to find God. Not being a "normal woman" of the day with a husband to provide for her and her children never kept Lydia from taking her place in the kingdom of God.

Today you can change the history of those around you. If your heart is open to the word of God, if you are willing to use what God has given you financially to further the cause of Christ, if you are willing to lead others and finally if you live your own life in your inheritance in Christ and not in your circumstances, you will change the world! The world needs your faith and your leadership. Be the influence God has called you to be!

Anti-aging Faith

No one likes looking old. The anti-aging market is estimated to be worth in USD 191.7 billion globally by 2019 per *Transparency Market Research.* We are willing to try anything and spend lots of money to stop the aging process. But what about spiritual aging? Are we as concerned about the effects of exposure to sin, wrinkles of unforgiveness, age spots of disappointment and facial lines of worry and fear?

While there are many products in the anti-aging market, there are three simple procedures that work against the wrath of aging. A regimen of daily skin care that includes cleansing, toning and moisturizing will work miracles using almost any product. Cleansing removes the environmental pollutants, makeup, and dead cells, allowing the skin to breathe and repair. Toning restores the ph. balance to the skin. Moisturizing supplies the emollients needed to nurture new growth where the skin has been exfoliated. It's more the process than the product that brings the results.

A daily spiritual regimen of cleansing, toning and moisturizing will work miracles in your faith walk also. The cleansing process is acquired by what the scripture calls the washing of the word. In John 15:3 KJV, Jesus says, "Now you are clean through the word which I have spoken unto you." In Ephesians 5:25-26 NLT, "For husbands, this means love your wives, just as Christ loved the church. He gave up his life for her to make her holy and clean, washed by the cleansing of God's word." Devotional time in the word is not for God's benefit but ours because the word cleanses us from the exposure to the world and sin. It allows us to breathe and repair.

Spiritual toning is the work of keeping us in balance with a ph. that is not too base or too acid. Spiritual tangents of worry and fear cause trouble and stress. When we are to the left of center, we become acid and when we are to the right of center, we become base. In the center, we are totally neutral, at peace and free from stress. Ephesians 4:6-7

NKJV, says, "Be anxious for nothing, but in everything by prayer and supplication, with thanksgiving, let your requests be made known to God; and the peace of God, which surpasses all understanding, will guard your hearts and minds through Christ Jesus." It is harder to age when you are in the peace of God!

Spiritual moisturizer is found in the healing properties of the Holy Spirit. Acts 10:38 NKJV, makes this clear. "How God anointed Jesus of Nazareth with the Holy Spirit and with power, who went about doing good and healing all who were oppressed by the devil, for God was with Him." Being anointed, smeared on, by the Holy Spirit is the oil, the emollients needed for healing and new growth. After cleansing and ph. restoration, the Holy Spirit brings healing from all oppression.

Too many Christians have become "old" in their faith because of not having a renewal process. The spiritual pathway of cleansing, toning and moisturizing is easy and simple to follow. It must be done daily so we can experience the promise of Isaiah 40:31 NLT, "But those who trust in the Lord will find new strength. They will soar high on wings like eagles. They will run and not grow weary. They will walk and not faint."

Start your spiritual anti-aging program today! Cleanse with the word, tone with the peace of God and moisturize with the healing power of the Holy Spirit.

Are you a bikini Christian?

The apostle Paul wrote a beautiful letter to the Ephesian church and encouraged them in many areas of their faith. In what we know as chapter six of that letter, Paul begins to talk about the whole armor of God, a concept foreign to most of us 21st century Christians. Here's what he says in Ephesians 6:10-13 NLT, "A final word: Be strong in the Lord and in his mighty power. Put on all of God's armor so that you will be able to stand firm against all strategies of the devil. For we are not fighting against flesh-and-blood enemies, but against evil rulers and authorities of the unseen world, against mighty powers in this dark world, and against evil spirits in the heavenly places. Therefore, put on every piece of God's armor so you will be able to resist the enemy in the time of evil. Then after the battle you will still be standing firm."

What a powerful scripture! We are told three things from this passage - you are in a battle, your battle is not against people and finally, you need to learn to fight properly.

I think most of us have problems in all three areas. First off, we don't realize we are in a spiritual battle. We think it's just life, circumstances or lack of luck. We also blame people, flesh and blood, instead of acknowledging a spiritual world that's set against us as Christians. Finally, most of us don't know how to fight properly. So, what should do we do?

Step one is to awaken to the spiritual battle. Know that if you are a Christian, the enemy of the cross, the devil is your enemy also. He will not be on your side and he will always be trying to defeat you. John 10:10 NLT, states, "The thief's purpose is to steal and kill and destroy. My purpose is to give them a rich and satisfying life." No matter how disingenuous the devil may appear, his goal is always the defeat and the disgrace of the children of God.

Step two in the battle is to acknowledge that people are not the enemy. It's so easy to fight with the person standing in front of you. To understand the spiritual forces behind what that person is saying and doing will enable you to move past the person to the real enemy. The strife, hatred and arguments between people are always spiritually motivated. While all we see are the people, we must open our eyes to the real, unseen forces trying to bring hurt and defeat to our lives.

Step three is to learn how to fight properly. I love the recently released movie, "War Room". It clearly defines the need to fight properly using prayer and the word of God. It also emphasizes that we are not fighting against people and it challenges us to wake up to the authentic battles in our life.

Learning to fight properly requires putting on every piece of God's armor as stated in Ephesians 6:13 it is not enough to put on part of our God provided armor – we need it all! Too many of us dress like bikini Christians, covering specific areas but leaving most of our life exposed to the attack of the enemy. Every day we need to suit up spiritually with the whole armor of God so we can move forward in victory, protected against all the fiery darts of the enemy.

What is the whole armor of God? Ephesians 6:14-18 NLT gives us this list of what to wear. "Stand your ground, putting on the belt of truth and the body armor of God's righteousness. For shoes, put on the peace that comes from the Good News so that you will be fully prepared. In addition to all of these, hold up the shield of faith to stop the fiery arrows of the devil. Put on salvation as your helmet, and take the sword of the Spirit, which is the word of God. Pray in the Spirit at all times and on every occasion. Stay alert and be persistent in your prayers for all believers everywhere."

Spiritual warfare is serious business and it's not to be done by bikini Christians. Victory comes to the fully dressed, fully prepared child of God. Your armor has been bought and paid for in full by the sacrifice of Calvary. Daily by the power of the Holy Spirit it is cleaned, repaired and ready for you to wear. Don't leave it in your spiritual closet. Don't be a defeated bikini Christian.

Are you a lazy lover?

Do you remember your first love? I do. He started calling me in the eighth grade and patiently waited until I was old enough to date my freshman year of high school. When the telephone rang, I ran to hear his voice and in all those weeks and months, he never failed to call. We developed a friendship and that survived the high school ups and downs because we weren't lazy about our relationship an attentiveness to one another.

After he left for college things began to change. Distance, lack of mutual life experiences and the influence of other people took its toll. His visits home brought back the friendship and love but when he returned to college, we both defaulted to other friends and activities. I clearly remember the summer night before my sophomore year when I gave back his fraternity lavaliere because our lives were going in opposite directions and we both had become lazy about our relationship. I didn't know how to make things right, so I quit trying. I didn't date the following year because I was full of memories of my first love but neither did, I take the necessary steps to restore our relationship. I was a "lazy lover".

We both eventually moved on to other boyfriends and girlfriends and we kept in touch through mutual friends. But as you know, second-hand relationships never bring satisfaction. During Christmas break of my senior year, the telephone rang and brought the horrible news of his death in a car accident. I was devastated. My first love was gone.

The word lover has a variety of meanings: boyfriend, girlfriend, beloved, sweetheart, devotee, admirer, fan, enthusiast and junkie. You can be a dog lover or love your sweetheart. You can be an FSU lover or a book lover. The identifying "lover" quality is defined by what you are actively passionate about. You love the things you give time, money, energy, effort and mental commitment too. Anything less would put you in the category of being a "lazy lover".

So how does this apply to faith and values and life as a Christian? It is the essence of your relationship with God. Consider Matthew 22:36-

40 NLT, "Teacher, which is the most important commandment in the Law of Moses?" Jesus replied, "You must love the LORD your God with all your heart, all your soul, and all your mind. This is the first and greatest commandment. A second is equally important: 'Love your neighbor as yourself.' The entire law and all the demands of the prophets are based on these two commandments."

Having a personal relationship with Jesus Christ is not a passive, one-time, walk down the church aisle event. It is an all-consuming daily pursuit of seeking and getting to know the creator of the universe. He asks that we love him with our heart, soul, mind and strength. In addition, he asks us to love his family, the body of Christ, as we would love ourselves.

If you are a CEO Christian who attends church on "Christmas, Easter Only" then you are "a lazy lover". If you attend every Sunday and Wednesday but don't pick up your Bible, pray or spend time meditating and worshipping the Lord privately then you are a "lazy lover"!

Natural relationships and spiritual relationships must be nurtured to survive. You never get to the end of knowing God because he is a forever, unending wealth of knowledge, wisdom and love. His plan has always been fellowshipping and having a relationship with you! Remember the story of the Garden of Eden in the book of Genesis? You have perhaps camped out in the part when Adam and Eve sinned, but before the disobedience occurred and brought separation, God came down every evening to walk and talk with Adam and Eve. As crazy as it may seem, God has always loved mankind and wanted to be friends. In John 15:15 NKJ, says, "No longer do I call you servants, for a servant does not know what his master is doing; but I have called you friends, for all things that I heard from My Father I have made known to you". God wants to share the secrets of the kingdom with you!

Just as there was no second-hand relationship between me and my high school first love, there are no second-hand relationships between you and Jesus. Your mother's, your father's, or grandmother's faith does not work for you! You must be your own lover of Jesus!

13

In Revelation 2:4, the gifted church that was so eager to serve the Lord and do good works was rebuked by the Lord "You have forsaken your first love". Let's be diligent and passionate to pursue and love the Lord with everything we are. Don't be a "lazy lover"!

Are you running anywhere?

In the early morning hours when my toddlers and their daddy were asleep, I would slip out and run. I loved the freedom and the exultation I felt when I ran. It gave me ownership of a piece of life that was solely mine. I didn't have the shoes and the outfits that runners have now days. I didn't do marathons or half marathons, just two or three miles every morning to declare my victory over life's demands. I loved running!

As I got older my running turned into walking, either outside, at a track or on my treadmill. Life and age moderated my running, but they couldn't take away the memories of the smells, the sites, and the feeling of accomplishment at the end of a good run.

Recently, as I have been studying the word of God, I have noticed how many people ran in their experiences with Jesus. There are many references in the Old Testament of excited characters running to tell others of the amazing thing God had done. But it is within the New Testament that I see people, and finally the church running because of their faith, love, hope and excitement for spiritual experiences. Here are some examples of reasons people ran to Jesus.

The crazy, demon-owned man of the Gadarene's ran toward freedom when he saw Jesus coming. Mark 5:6 NKJV, "Then they came to the other side of the sea, to the country of the Gadarenes. And when He had come out of the boat, immediately there met Him out of the tombs a man with an unclean spirit, who had *his* dwelling among the tombs; and no one could bind him, not even with chains, because he had often been bound with shackles and chains. And the chains had been pulled apart by him, and the shackles broken in pieces; neither could anyone tame him. And always, night and day, he was in the mountains and in the tombs, crying out and cutting himself with stones. When he saw Jesus from afar, he ran and worshiped Him."

The crowd was so hungry for the message and ministry of Jesus that they ran to the other side of the lake to get a front-row seat. Mark 6:33 NLT, "But many people recognized them and saw them leaving, and people from many towns ran ahead along the shore and got there ahead of them." So was   Zacchaeus in Luke 19:14 NKJV, "Then *Jesus* entered and passed through Jericho. Now behold, *there was* a man named Zacchaeus who was a chief tax collector, and he was rich. And he sought to see who Jesus was, but could not because of the crowd, for he was of short stature. So, he ran ahead and climbed up into a sycamore tree to see Him, for He was going to pass that way." The rich and the poor ran to see and hear Jesus.

In Mark 6:53-55 NKJV, those who knew people who were sick, ran to get them and bring them to Jesus. "When they had crossed over, they came to the land of Gennesaret and anchored there. And when they came out of the boat, immediately the people recognized Him, ran through that whole surrounding region, and began to carry about on beds those who were sick to wherever they heard He was."

At the resurrection of Christ, the witnesses of this amazing event ran. Luke 24:12 NKJV, "But Peter arose and ran to the tomb; and stooping down, he saw the linen cloths lying by themselves; and he departed, marveling to himself at what had happened." John 20:1-4 NKJV, "Now on the first *day* of the week Mary Magdalene went to the tomb early, while it was still dark, and saw *that* the stone had been taken away from the tomb. Then she ran and came to Simon Peter, and to the other disciple, whom Jesus loved, and said to them, "They have taken away the Lord out of the tomb, and we do not know where they have laid Him." Peter therefore went out, and the other disciple, and were going to the tomb. So, they both ran together, and the other disciple outran Peter and came to the tomb first."

The early church in the Book of Acts ran from miracle to miracle as they rocked the known world with a message of love and grace.

As Christians and as the Christian church we must ask ourselves, "Do we run anymore?" Do we feel an urgency to hear the teachings of Jesus, to bring those sick and in need to him, to see those addicted and bound set free?

The apostle Paul at the end of his ministry said this in 2 Timothy 4:6-7 NKJV, "I am already being poured out as a drink offering, and the time of my departure is at hand. I have fought the good fight, I have finished the race, I have kept the faith." Paul was a spiritual runner up until his race was complete.

Although I don't run in the natural anymore, I am a spiritual marathon runner! I don't intend to miss anything Jesus is doing in the earth. Will you join me and countless others who are running to see Jesus?

Be still and know

Sometimes, the Lord will speak a word of comfort and correction in the strangest places – like Walmart. I was picking up a few necessities when I rounded the aisle and encounter a daddy and daughter amid a major meltdown. She was crying, kicking and protesting her situation and he was gently trying to comfort her and reassure her that in a few moments they would be on their way home. She would not be comforted! As he tried to calm her and love her, she resisted with every fiber of her being. Daddy's face reflected concern and frustration because he couldn't get through to her. They were at an impasse. The daddy could not do what she would not let him do. She struggled in her own strength to obtain what she wanted, and her protests were heard throughout the store.

I immediately thought of the many times my heavenly father had tried to calm and comfort me in a situation of stress and panic, and how I had behaved as this little girl. This visual made me realize the importance of being still and letting God love, comfort me and fight my battle!

As I waited to checkout, my mind wandered to a story a woman had shared with me a few years back about her husband. He was always in charge, active, demanding and moving. She shared how hard it was to love and comfort him because he was constantly fighting to protect, defend and get his way in every stressful situation. I had asked her, "What do you do?" She responded, "I wait till he's asleep and still, then I snuggle up next to him and pray for him". Great love never gives up!

Sometimes, the love and comfort we need is right in front of us, but we miss it because we are not still enough to receive it! I imagine there are times when God is frustrated like the daddy in Walmart, and the wife who was not allowed to comfort her husband. His love is unlimited, but it must be willingly received. Sometimes we are just hard to love and protect!

In Psalm 46:1 NLT, we find this revelation. "God is our refuge and strength, always ready to help in times of trouble." In Psalm 46: 10

NLT, we find this admonition, "Be still, and know that I am God! I will be honored by every nation. I will be honored throughout the world!"

We are challenged to allow God to fight our battles in 2 Chronicles 20:17 NLT, "But you will not even need to fight. Take your positions; then stand still and watch the LORD's victory. He is with you, O people of Judah and Jerusalem. Do not be afraid or discouraged. Go out against them tomorrow, for the LORD is with you!"

Also, in Exodus 14:14 NIV, "The Lord will fight for you; you need only to be still". In Deuteronomy 20:4 NKJV, we find, "For the Lord your God is the one who goes with you to fight for you against your enemies, to save you!"

There are fifty-nine bible verses about fighting battles and all of them summarily say, "Be still and let God do it!"

Whether you are a child in the bowels of Walmart or an adult in the turbulence of life, your peace and calm will only come when you allow God to comfort and defend you. Will He win on your timetable? Probably not, but the win will be decisive and there will not be an enemy left standing!

Becoming a servant in a serve-me world

The world system conditions us to be selfish. The advertising industry promotes: "have it your way". It offers choices and entitlement. It teaches us, "you can get anything you want, and we will help you do it!" It advocates "charge now and pay later", so instant gratification can be achieved.

Most of us have more "stuff" than we have room for. The storage building industry has grown astronomically. According to *IBIS World*, annual self-storage revenue was estimated to be about 32.7 billion in 2016. That figure is expected to grow at an annual rate of 3.5 percent over the next five years. We have become hoarders of goods and services we will probably never use.

Digital hoarding has also become a pitfall. Subscriptions to Spotify, SiriusXM, electronic greeting cards, online magazines and newspapers, and numerous other "serve-me" items are just a mouse click away. Most of us have more order instantly online accounts than we would like to admit. We have the world at our fingertips and thousands of unknown faces serving our every wish.

While we are blessed to live in a country of abundance and innovation, we must have a self-inventory system that regulates our indulgences. That self-inventory system is free, and it's called servanthood.

In the Beatitudes, (I like to transliterate into the Be-Attitudes), in Matthew 6: 19-21 NLT, we find these words of wisdom. "Don't store up treasures here on earth, where moths eat them and rust destroys them, and where thieves break in and steal. Store your treasures in heaven, where moths and rust cannot destroy, and thieves do not break in and steal. Wherever your treasure is, there the desires of your heart will also be."

I was fortunate enough to learn this scripture as a child, and it has been an anchor for me through the years. Please understand, I am not against any of the above-mentioned conveniences. I think God wants us to have an abundant life. He also wants us to serve others spiritually and naturally. The balance is found in Matthew 6:33 NLT, "Seek the

Kingdom of God above all else, and live righteously, and he will give you everything you need."

Becoming a servant is a choice. Every day we can consciously pray, "Lord, please use me today to serve and bless another human being." The Lord will always answer that prayer and will bless you in return as you serve others. We don't have to qualify for service by taking a course and receiving a certificate. We simply must open our eyes to the needs of others and share what we have. Much of the time money is the least needed act of service. What most people need is friendship, wisdom, emotional and physical help. Your time and attention when it's not convenient.

As parents, we can model and teach servanthood in our homes. Our actions always speak louder than our words. Our children need to be exposed to a world where need is real and simple acts of love are valuable. Television and movies, even books will not teach servanthood but we as parents can.

A friend of mine recently shared about cutting his neighbor's yard. I thought "That's nice – we've all done that". Then I discovered the neighbor was a 93-year-old, World War II veteran and my friend's servanthood was more than nice, it was life-saving.

Servanthood makes us grow physically, spiritually and emotionally. It helps us cope with our own problems and centers us on the truth. Jesus is a great example of this. Literally hours before he was to be betrayed by one of his closest friends, beaten, despised, and crucified, Jesus became the servant to his disciples. He taught them this one great and lasting lesson of humility and servanthood. John 13:1-5, 12-17 NLT, reveals the servant heart of our Savior.

"Before the Passover celebration, Jesus knew that his hour had come to leave this world and return to his Father. He had loved his disciples during his ministry on earth, and now he loved them to the very end. It was time for supper, and the devil had already prompted Judas, son of Simon Iscariot, to betray Jesus. Jesus knew that the Father had given him authority over everything and that he had come from God and would return to God. So, he got up from the table, took off his robe, wrapped a towel around his waist, and poured water into a basin. Then he began to wash the disciples' feet, drying them with the towel he had around him. After washing their feet, he put on his robe again and sat down and asked, "Do you understand what I was doing? You call me 'Teacher' and 'Lord,' and you are right, because that's what I am. And since I, your Lord and Teacher, have washed your feet, you ought to wash each other's feet. I have given you an example to follow. Do as I have done to you. I tell you the truth, slaves are not greater than their master. Nor is the messenger more important than the one who sends the message. Now that you know these things, God will bless you for doing them."

Let's become servants in this serve-me world and walk in truth and love.

Christians should understand cults

Waco, the television mini-series on the *Branch Davidians* that has recently aired was a reminder of how real cult activity is in the United States. According to an article entitled, *The Ten Most Famous Cults in United States History*, many are deceived and lead astray by a charismatic leader who "hears from God" on a specific religious topic.

The article states, "The term "cult" is one disputed among theologians, authorities, and deprogramming experts. In fact, some use the phrase "new religious movement" or NRM, because they feel cult has too many connotations or isn't accurate enough. Most governments take a stance on legitimate churches and cult activities by the level of coercion and brainwashing used to maintain membership. Their distinctions are often for tax purposes, but also have a major bearing on whether a cult will face persecution. With that in mind, here are the most famous and infamous cults in American history. "

1) The Branch Davidians -Waco, TX founded by David Koresh
2) The Manson Family-San Francisco, CA founded by Charles Manson
3) Heaven's Gate-founded by Marshal Applewhite and Bonnie Nettles
4) Peoples Temple-Utah, Los Angeles and San Francisco founded by Jim Jones
5) Scientology-founded by L. Ron Hubbard and survives in many international locations as well as the United States. It is recognized by some nations as a church and by others as a cult.
6) Unification Church-founded by Reverend Sun Myung Moon located in New York.
7) Bhagwan Shree Rajneesh-The Dalles, Oregon
8) Children of God-Family International- Texas, founded by David Berg
9) The Fundamentalist Church of Jesus Christ of Latter-Day Saints-founded by Warren Jeffs
10) The Twelve Tribes-founded by Elbert Eugene Spriggs-Island Pond, Vermont and worldwide

In all the above-mentioned cults and others that did not make the top ten list, an extra-biblical revelation by the founder is central. The expansion of a Biblical truth is also central.

Mind control, manipulation of lives, sexual indulgencies by the leader with members, accumulation of wealth and the requirement that the leader has ultimate authority are all red flags that Christians should watch out for.

Most cults expand, and pervert Biblical truth developing a "perfect theology" on the subject. The bible teaches about the family of God, heaven and hell, the seven seals in Revelation, being a child of God, the second coming of Christ and the army of God but not to the exclusion of all other scriptures. A healthy Christian, studies and understands the scriptures in context and with reference to history, time and socially accepted norms. A pet doctrine is a sign of abandoning the whole counsel of God.

In Matthew 24:4-6 NLT, Jesus warned the disciples of the deception of the end times. "Jesus told them, "Don't let anyone mislead you, for many will come in my name, claiming, 'I am the Messiah.' They will deceive many. And you will hear of wars and threats of wars, but don't panic. Yes, these things must take place, but the end won't follow immediately."

Hebrews 9:27-28 NLT, "And just as each person is destined to die once and after that comes judgment, so also Christ was offered once for all time as a sacrifice to take away the sins of many people. He will come again, not to deal with our sins, but to bring salvation to all who are eagerly waiting for him." The scripture always points to Jesus Christ as the Messiah, not any man, woman or extra-Biblical revelation. Beware of any gathering, where someone other than Jesus Christ is exalted.

John 7:18 AMP, "He who speaks on his own accord seeks glory *and* honor for himself. But He who seeks the glory *and* the honor of the One who sent Him, He is true, and there is no unrighteousness *or* deception in Him." A true Christian leader will exalt, promote, praise Jesus Christ and not himself!

Let's be wise and listen to the apostle Paul's advice to the Colossian church. Colossians 2:7-9 NLT, "Let your roots grow down into him, and let your lives be built on him. Then your faith will grow strong in the truth you were taught, and you will overflow with thankfulness. Don't let anyone capture you with empty philosophies and high-sounding nonsense that come from human thinking and from the spiritual powers of this world, rather than from Christ. For in Christ lives all the fullness of God in a human body."

Christians should understand cults and their deadly influence on the unsuspecting!

Deal with the little stuff in your life

One of the physiognomies of our South Georgia area is the use of the "controlled or prescribed burn" to manage the underbrush, leaf litter and fallen limbs in the forests. To be honest, until I moved to Thomasville over 45 years ago, I had never seen it. My first reaction to the widespread, low-lying fire that seemed to cover acres of woodlands was panic. I thought for sure fire was about to consume me! With some laugher from the locals who had managed the bountiful plantations in the area for many years, I was soon enlightened to the benefits of the controlled burn.

I was told that by eliminating the fuel provided by leaf debris, tree limbs and small brush the likelihood of a hot, uncontrollable fire was minimized. Yearly cleaning of the forest bed with a smaller, cooler, controlled fire would preserve the stature, fertility and health of the tall Georgia pines, the water oaks and the other beautiful tree varieties in our area. Lesson learned. Deal with the small stuff so it doesn't become fuel for something potentially catastrophic.

One evening last week, I was driving in from Tallahassee and saw my first controlled or prescribed burn of the season. I was thankful that I understood what was happening and didn't feel the panic of earlier days. I began to think about what I was seeing and how applicable it was to our spiritual lives.

Even the most mature Christian, who has been growing in the grace of God for years, is subject to being burned during trials and temptations. The bigger the trial or temptation, the hotter the fire and the more potential there is for spiritual destruction. If we submit ourselves to the "prescribed or controlled burn" of the Holy Spirit on a regular basis we are safer when the uncontrollable fires of life hit.

Some common items that litter our personal forest are strife, unforgiveness, unfruitfulness, apathy, lust, self- justification, fear, anger and influence from others that is contrary to God's plan for our lives. As we are growing taller and stronger in the Lord, we may also be littered at the root with some of these things. The conviction of the Holy Spirit and the grace of God can expose and gently burn off these hindrances before a big fire consumes everything we are.

By example, King David was a mighty warrior and king of Israel for many years. He was triumphant from his youth against the lion, the bear and Goliath. He was faithful and had the love and favor of all the kingdom of Israel. He was in some respects the most mature and the greatest leader in the history of the nation. But he had some underbrush growing in his personal forest that fueled his demise.

When he was a young man the people sang, "Saul has slain thousands, but David has slain tens of thousands". He was fearless in battle. He was the first to seek God and first to walk in humility and repentance. As time passed David stayed home when other kings went to war, he contended with others, he lusted after Bathsheba and he justified himself when he committed adultery and murder. Most importantly, he lost his passion for seeking God. The result was catastrophic!

In Psalms 51: 1-17 NKJV, we find David's cry for healing and restoration after uncontrollable fire swept through his life.

Have mercy upon me, O God,
According to Your loving-kindness;
According to the multitude of Your tender mercies,
Blot out my transgressions.
Wash me thoroughly from my iniquity,
And cleanse me from my sin.

For I acknowledge my transgressions,
And my sin is always before me.
Against You, You only, have I sinned,
And done this evil in Your sight—
That You may be found just when You speak,
And blameless when You judge.

Behold, I was brought forth in iniquity,
And in sin my mother conceived me.
Behold, you desire truth in the inward parts,
And in the hidden part You will make me to know wisdom.

Purge me with hyssop, and I shall be clean;
Wash me, and I shall be whiter than snow.
Make me hear joy and gladness,
That the bones You have broken may rejoice.
Hide Your face from my sins,
And blot out all my iniquities.

Create in me a clean heart, O God,
And renew a steadfast spirit within me.
Do not cast me away from Your presence,
And do not take Your Holy Spirit from me.

Restore to me the joy of Your salvation,
And uphold me by Your generous Spirit.
Then I will teach transgressors Your ways,
And sinners shall be converted to You.

Deliver me from the guilt of bloodshed, O God,
The God of my salvation,
And my tongue shall sing aloud of Your righteousness.
O Lord, open my lips,
And my mouth shall show forth Your praise.
For You do not desire sacrifice, or else I would give it;
You do not delight in burnt offering.
The sacrifices of God are a broken spirit,
A broken and a contrite heart—
These, O God, You will not despise

The time to repent is when the forest bed of our life is slightly littered, and the firestorm is still a great distance away. Ask the Lord for a "prescribed or controlled burn" in your life so you can continue to grow tall and strong in His grace.

Do You Have a Dream?

I often find myself looking at the YouTube selection, "Paul sings Nessun Dorma". Let me share with you the story behind my indulgence and why it inspires me. Paul was a mobile phone salesman from South Wales. He decided, at the urging of his wife, to try-out for the television show, "Britain's Got Talent". When the judges asked him why he was trying-out for the show he said, "My dream is doing what I feel I was born to do". Then the judges ask him what that was, and he said, "To sing opera". They discreetly hid their amusement because Paul did not look like an opera singer. Paul looked like a shy, vocally untrained, mobile phone salesman with a missing tooth! When Paul opened his mouth to sing, the audience and the judges were amazed at the vocal quality and passion of performance that came forth from this unlikely contestant. Paul continued through the competition and won at the finale with a standing ovation from the audience and the judges. No one was more surprised than Paul Potts. His childhood dream had become a reality. The week following the competition he was in the recording studio laying down the tracts to an album that has sold over two million copies. Paul's YouTube video has been watched by 166 million viewers. It impacts me every time I watch it. It encourages me to dream. Paul, the mobile phone salesman, now has a net worth of 10 million dollars because he followed his dream. I believe everyone needs a dream.

In the story of Joseph in Genesis chapters 37 - 47 his dream got him into trouble. His dream also sustained him during the years of waiting for its fulfillment. His dream impacted his life and the life of thousands of Hebrews during a nationwide famine. Joseph's dream was larger than himself and greater than comprehension by those closest to him. That's the way dreams are. If you could simply reach out and acquire your dream it would not mature you in passion and purpose. If dreams were not defined by struggle and self-doubt, their fulfillment would

not be life changing.

I believe every family and every family member need to a have a dream. The dreams of the family unit will serve to unify and bring closeness. The dreams of the individual will bring personal satisfaction and touch a great number of people outside the family unit.

Dreamers are always inventing, making better, and changing the world they live in. Dreams protect you from making unwise decisions. When the reality of your dream is more real to you than the temporary pleasure of drugs, alcohol, and pre-marital sex, it becomes easier to say no. Mistakes will not keep you from realizing your dream, but they will frustrate and delay the process. Proverbs 29:18 states, "Where there is no dream the people cast off restraint; but happy is he who keeps the law".

I recently talked to a young man who made a surprise visit to the emergency room with chest pains. He told me that he knew his family was financially in good shape, that his wife and children were secure in their relationship with the Lord and that his life was in order. He said, "The thing I realized lying in the ER was that I had not fulfilled my lifelong dream of writing and recording songs. If I had died in those crucial moments, I would have not fulfilled my dream". He had an "ah-ha moment". I have watched him pursue his dream over the past few months. He has obtained financial backing and is planning a week of recording with a producer who has helped launched many Christian artists. He is pursuing his dream.

Sometimes in pursuing your dream, it changes, expands, redefines and becomes even greater than ever imagined. It takes courage and determination to chase a dream that only you believe in and only you can fulfill. It takes that first "baby step" to begin the journey of faith. It is never too late to start. Does your family have a dream? Have you encouraged each of your children to dream big dreams about their future? Do they have dreams that will help them say no to immediate temptations? Do you have a dream that awaits fulfillment? A healthy family is a dreaming family. A healthy individual is a dreaming individual. Sweet dreams!

Don't Forget the Eggs!

I've always enjoyed entertaining. Having family and friends over for a meal and fellowship is one of my favorite things to do. Even though I do my fair share of disposable plates and cups, I really enjoy the china, crystal, candles and table decorations. Bring on the holidays and the opportunity to be creative!

Several years ago, Larry and I invited a special couple over for dinner. He was the principal where our children attended school. She was a great teacher and storyteller. Both were part of our church community.

This couple had taught me a lot about life and family, and I wanted to make something special for dessert. Chocolate–pure and simple was the perfect choice! I set about to make my homemade brownies, timing it so they would just come out of the oven as our company arrived. The smell alone of decadent, homemade, chocolate brownies would set the mood for the entire evening. Quickly, I readied the last details and put the anticipated dessert in the oven.

Just before the doorbell rang, I opened the oven door to remove the brownies and found the shock of my life. Instead of the blue-ribbon brownies I expected, there was a dish of bubbling, black crude sitting in the oven. The smell was deceptive, masquerading as the real thing but the recipe itself looked like the stuff Jed Clampett, of *The Beverly Hillbillies* fame, discovered in his backyard! In all my years of baking this had never happened before. I quickly diluted the hot, bubbling crude and poured it down the disposal. Lucky for me I had a frozen turtle cheesecake I could sub-in for dessert.

The evening ended and I began to retrace my steps in the dessert process, and I realized I had forgotten to add the eggs! Eggs serve two purposes in recipes. First, they bind together ingredients and create consistency when used with a variety of ingredients as in a casserole. Secondly, they serve as a rising agent, developing body and volume as when used in a pound cake. Although I had added all the other ingredients, without the eggs it didn't work.

It didn't take me long to see the spiritual parallels. All of our Christian efforts cannot produce the right recipe if we don't make sure we add *God's love*. Love binds us together even though we may come from very different backgrounds and may have very different ideas that we bring to the mix. The love of God enables us to develop bulk and maturity as we grow in the heat of life's oven. Also, the egg is a source of nurturing and life. So is God's love, the very source of life and comfort.

In I Cor.13 we find these words from The Message Bible:

If I speak with human eloquence and angelic ecstasy but don't love, I am nothing but the creaking of a rusty gate.

If I speak God's Word with power, revealing all his mysteries and making everything plain as day; and I have the faith that says to a mountain, "Jump" and it jumps, but I don't love, I am nothing.

If I give everything, I own to feed the poor and even go to the stake to be burned as a martyr, but don't love, I have gotten nowhere. So no matter what I say, what I believe, and what I do, I am bankrupt without love.

When you make brownies, don't forget the eggs! When you live life, don't forget the love!

Don't talk to me Snow White!

Do you ever have trouble with temptation? Most of us will answer "yes" in a heartbeat to this question. Even Jesus was tempted to make the wrong decision, a decision that would put him on the side of Satan instead of on God's side. Our natural man always wants his way in this life, while our spiritual man wants the way of the kingdom of God. How do we overcome our desires and the temptation of disobedience presented to us by the enemy? The answer is simple, just say "No".

My friend, Claire shared a story about a struggle her daughter, Jill and granddaughter, Melanie had one night at bedtime. It seems bedtime arrived before the granddaughter finished playing with her dolls. She loved dressing her Disney doll collection in new outfits and pretending they were on their way to a glamourous ball. Mom went through the nightly bedtime routine, kissed Melanie goodnight and tucked her in the bed. Quietly, she slipped out the door thinking Melanie was almost asleep. A little while later, she heard an exuberant conversation coming from Melanie's bedroom. She opened the bedroom door to find Melanie in the middle of her dolls, laughing, pretending and dressing them for the imaginary gala they were going to attend. Mom was irritated but thought a little more explanation would work and Melanie would grasp the importance of a good night's sleep. She tucked her in bed again, snuggled and kissed her and walked out of the bedroom certain that this time Melanie understood the boundaries. Jill continued with her household chores confident that Melanie was sound asleep – but it was not so. As she walked down the hall to put away the newly washed and folded towels, she heard a repeat of the laughter and conversation she had heard coming from Melanie's room before. She opened the door to see Melanie once again in the middle of her dolls preparing for the fashion event of the century. "Young lady why are you not in bed?" a less than happy Jill asked. "Mom, all my dolls are asking me to dress them and fix their hair for the ball", Melanie replied. Jill gathered up the dolls and put them away in a flurry and ushered Melanie in bed for the third time. "Young lady if you get out of this bed again, you'll be on restrictions and you won't get to do the things you want to do tomorrow after school. I'm tired of your disobedience and I expect you to go to bed now!" A pouty Melanie buried her head in the pillow as if to drown out the imaginary cries of her dolls and said sheepishly, "Yes Momma". Not to be fooled again, Jill silently waited outside the bedroom door listening for the slightest sound indicating Melanie was out of bed. Moments passed and Jill heard Melanie saying in a stern voice, "Don't talk to me Snow White!" Jill knew the temptation to get out of bed and play was over when she heard Melanie say "No" to the princess.

Claire and I laughed and laughed at the creative desire Melanie had and the difficulty she had overcoming what she wanted to do. We could see ourselves in the same scenario and now years later we quote Melanie when we are faced with a temptation. "Don't talk to me Snow White!" has become a declaration of war against temptation in our lives.

This may sound overly simplified to you if you are facing a temptation, but I promise "no" works every time against every temptation. Whether it's no to your favorite ice cream, no to drugs or no to adultery, you can count on that simple two-letter declaration to work.

Let me share a statistical, national example with you concerning the power of "No".

"When the Reagans moved into the White House on Jan. 20, 1981, drug use, particularly among teenagers, was hovering near the highest rates ever measured. Of that year's graduating class, 65 percent had used drugs in their lifetimes, and a remarkable 37 percent were regular drug users. Eight years later, when the Reagans left Washington, only 19.7 percent of 1989's graduating class were regular drug users, a 47-percent reduction. And the trend that began under their leadership persisted until it reached an all-time low of 14.4 percent in 1992, 61 percent lower than 1981." (DailySignal.com)

According to research conducted by the *Institute for Social Research* at the University of Michigan, fewer young people in the 1980s were using illicit drugs. High school seniors using cannabis dropped from 50.1% in 1978 to 36% in 1987, to 12% in 1991 and the percentage of students using other drugs decreased similarly. Psychedelic drug use dropped from 11% to 6%, cocaine from 12% to 10%, and heroin from 1% to 0.5%. (Wikipedia)

Although Mrs. Reagan was harshly criticized by many elites for her simple approach to the temptation of using and abusing drugs, the results cannot be denied. Her "Just say no" campaign successfully changed the culture.

"This clear, unequivocal stand against drugs galvanized the nation by placing a moral stake in the ground: Illicit drug use is wrong, harmful, and not compatible with a free society. It provided an example parents, teachers, community leaders, and especially young people could follow when confronting drugs." (DailySignal.com)

Without the moral leadership Mrs. Reagan provided, our nation has slipped back into drug addiction with a high cost in lives lost, prisons filled and crimes against humanity at an all-time high. Perhaps it's time to "Just Say No" again.

In our personal life, we can take comfort in the scripture that says we are not alone when we face temptation and God is faithful to help us with our "No". I Corinthians 10:13 NLT, "The temptations in your life are no different from what others experience. And God is faithful. He will not allow the temptation to be more than you can stand. When you are tempted, he will show you a way out so that you can endure."

God has given us victory over every temptation we face. He's made a way of escape through the doorway marked, "No". It's time to make a stand and say, "Don't talk to me Snow White!"

Families Should Take Time to Play

The story-line echoed a hundred other prime-time television programs I had watched before. A family was in crisis: daddy had lost his job, mom was working overtime, the children were caring for themselves and the teenage girl was lonely having just started a new school. Arguments, blame and name-calling blared on the television screen. Though they were exaggerated, the issues were common ones — families often find themselves in similar circumstances in real life as well.

One part of the dialogue grabbed my attention: the children reminded the parents of the time they had to take shelter in the basement during a storm. "Remember?" the teenage girl said. "We popped popcorn and just talked. We used to be happy. I know you and mom can work things out. Let's pop some popcorn!" The child's simple request to her parents was to have fun, share and become friends again.

I was reminded of how important it is for families to play together. Precious, often hysterical memories occur when a family sets aside time for recreation. The schedules and demands of life make playing seem indulgent. But it is not. May I share a couple of pranks that are still the topic of conversation when our whole family comes together?

One summer we took a trip to the Opryland Theme Park. The hot, humid day was just the catalyst for a prank on Mom. While Larry and our two sons ran ahead to the next ride, I took the time to do some shopping. By the time I caught up with them, both sons came rushing towards me saying, "Mom, come quick! You've got to see this!" Like a lamb being led to the slaughter, I followed them to an observation deck just in front of a water slide. A twelve-passenger boat topped the hill and plunged down into the water just in front of me. But Larry and the boys had run for cover — a huge wave crashed over the observation deck, drenching me from head to toe! Everyone on the platform howled! My sweet, caring husband was bent over double laughing and my sons thought they had pulled the prank of the century. I laughed also and took a bow as the people who had safely stayed out of harm's way clapped for me. The hot sun would soon dry my hair and clothes, and all would be just a memory. Or so they thought!

Payback was already brewing, and I was sure sometime before too long I would know just how to show my "appreciation."

Several months passed and fall brought extended schedules with football practice and late-night suppers. It was hard to get the chores completed before dark, so we all pitched in once we arrived home. As I was preparing dinner, Larry and the guys were going out to feed the dog. We had heard a news report earlier that had warned us about some purse-snatchers who had been in our area. As Larry and the guys discussed their need to be cautious, a slight smile crossed my face. This was it – payback time! As they gathered the food and walked out of the kitchen door, I quietly waited for them to get several paces out into the darkness. Ever so carefully I opened the door and headed straight for the tall azalea bushes that flanked the dog pen. I could hardly wait for the moment of surprise. I snickered as I heard them casually converse not knowing terror awaited them. At just the perfect moment, I let out a blood-curdling scream then leaped toward then in the darkness. They jumped a mile high and started yelling, totally terrified. It was great – now *I* was the one bent over double laughing!

Playing board games, making goofy family videos, having a favorite family television program or just eating popcorn and trying to catch a few popped kernels in the air are some of the fun things we did as a family. We were active in church, school, sports, work and the community but we always made time to play. Family recreation is so important - the cost is free, and the ideas are endless. Began today to be a playing family!

Faux faith is created by fear

Life experiences often teach us spiritual lessons that change and shape who we are as a Christian. I had one such experience over thirty years ago. I learned the difference between "faux faith" and "faith", and the deceptiveness of fear.

Albert (not his real name) attended the same church I did. One day he noticed a scaly growth on the side of his face. As he examined it, the fear of cancer began to fill his mind. His wife encouraged him to go to the doctor, but he said, "No I am going to believe God for my healing." Days past and the growth grew, and additional friends and family suggested Albert go to the doctor. With each bit of advice, Albert dug his heels in deeper, declaring his supernatural healing. The scaly growth quickly turned into a full- blown, grotesque, tumor that covered most of the side of his face. He publicly continued to confess his healing but privately the fear of death consumed Albert and his family. He told me shortly before his death that he should have gone to the doctor in the early stages, but he was afraid. On the long drive to his funeral, I pondered the heart-breaking event I had watched and ask God to help me understand what I had seen.

Faux is defined as "made in imitation, artificial, not genuine, fake or false". Faux faith is an imitation of real faith. It is formed by fear and masquerades as genuine.

The scripture in Hebrews 11:1 NKJV, defines faith, "Now faith is the substance of things hoped for, the evidence of things not seen." Faith in God is a substance for building our dreams and a title deed to the promises of God. It is supernatural, powerful, and amazing in its results. Faith can move mountains that cannot be moved any other way. I have seen many miracles, healings and provisions come by faith. Faith is the substance that moves us into a salvation experience that totally changes our life and our eternity. Ephesians 2:8-9 NKJV, explains the born again experience as one accomplished by faith. "For by grace you have been saved through faith, and that not of yourselves; *it is* the gift of God, not of works, lest anyone should boast."

Fear on the other hand often masquerades as faith and brings deception into our lives. Fear and faith cannot occupy the same space. Consider what happens when you hold two magnets and press the opposite magnetic poles together. They strongly repel each other. So, it is with faith and fear – they will always oppose one another. Although both have power, one produces real faith and the other produces "faux faith".

Identifying the deceptiveness of fear is often difficult but here are a few signs to look for when you are discerning the difference between fear and faith in your life.

First, fear puts all the work on you. You must work to be strong enough, to believe hard enough to accomplish the thing you are hoping for. God is full of love and grace and He sent Jesus to do the hard work, the heavy-lifting in our walk of faith. If you must be good enough, work hard enough, confess long enough then you are in fear not faith. Jesus is the author and finisher of our faith according to Hebrews 12:2. We should look to Him, not our ability to believe hard enough.

Secondly, fear eliminates all other options. If you are believing for healing in your body, faith is not offended if you go to the doctor. It's not either faith or medicine, it is both. God gives wisdom to the medical community for our benefit. I personally believe that doctors and nurses are ministers to us. They are not the healer, but the healer's hands in many situations. Take every pill and every treatment while using your faith in the goodness of Father God.

Finally, fear gives you no exit strategy. At any point in time, my brother Albert could have decided to seek medical attention but fear masquerading as faith said "No!". Fear repels your faith and keeps you isolated in fear. Faith always makes a way of escape for every temptation. I Corinthians 10:13 AMP, makes it clear that God's faithfulness is always endeavoring on our behalf. "No temptation [regardless of its source] has overtaken or enticed you that is not common to human experience [nor is any temptation unusual or beyond human resistance]; but God is faithful [to His word—He is compassionate and trustworthy], and He will not let you be tempted beyond your ability [to resist], but along with the temptation He [has in the past and is now and] will [always] provide the way out as well, so that you will be able to endure it [without yielding, and will overcome temptation with joy].

Be discerning in your walk of faith and don't settle for "faux faith" when "real faith" has been given to you. Fear brings foreboding, but faith brings the consciousness of the goodness and love of God.

Feeding the hungry, body, soul and spirit

I was sitting on the tarmac in St. Louis, Missouri, waiting for my flight home when the captain came over the intercom and said, "Because of thunderstorms in Atlanta, our flight take-off will be delayed for a short period. We will advise you when we are ready to depart."

I sat back in my seat with an irritated sigh and began to do some mental gymnastics about my weekend of women's ministry. Once I had relived an amazing weekend, I began to look for something to read to pass the time while I waited my departure. After many articles and many advertisements for products from the "Sky Mall", I happened upon an article that changed my life and the life of my church.

The article I read concerned the number of Fortune 500 companies located in the twin cities of Minneapolis/St Paul, Minnesota. For six years, I had been traveling to Minnesota to teach at women's conferences, minister in area churches and work with youth and children through week long, summer camps. The summer camp ministry had crushed my heart, for I saw children and youth, so hungry that I couldn't begin to teach them about Jesus until they had eaten several meals. Their attention span, at the beginning of camp, was mainly driven by hunger. I had never seen this level of poverty in America. When I read about nineteen of the nations' wealthiest companies being located four hours south of such painful, life threatening poverty I became angry! Why were they not taking care of those who had such desperate need right in their backyard? How could they go to sleep in their fancy houses while children slept hungry, cold, and desperate?

The captain's message interrupted my anger, "Ladies and gentlemen, we have been cleared for departure and we should be in Atlanta shortly. Please prepare the cabin for departure." I stuffed the magazine back into the seat pocket and refocused on "going home". But deep in my heart a revolution had begun.

Several weeks later during my time of Bible study and prayer, I felt anger all over again for the Fortune 500 companies who were not meeting the basic needs of children, youth, and families in their area.

The inward prompting of the Holy Spirit gently asked this question of me. "What are you doing in your backyard to meet the needs of the hungry?" I was shocked. For weeks I had focused on the failure of others, not considering there might be the same failure within my own life. In tears, I repented before the Lord, and committed to His leading to make this right. I was not a Fortune 500 company with unlimited resources, and I had no idea how to begin this challenge from the Lord. I waited and prayed.

Friendship with God is something very special

Did you ever receive a note in elementary school that asked the question, "Will you be my friend?" The instructions were "check yes or no". No explanation of why or why not, just you will be my friend! In a moment of time you were asked to commit to a relationship with someone you didn't know very well. I remember saying "yes" to such a note and becoming friends with a wonderful, lifelong friend who walked with me through many life experiences. I somehow overcame the fear of "yes" or "no" and made the decision.

In James 2:23 NKJV, we find this profound statement, "And the Scripture was fulfilled which says, 'Abraham believed God, and it was accounted to him for righteousness. And he was called the friend of God." Included in the declaration of Abraham's right standing with God was the statement of his friendship status. Can you imagine how exciting it must have been for Abraham when God asked him to check "yes" or "no" to the friendship note?

In 2004, Israel Houghton wrote a song about friendship with God. The idea of a bond, companionship, and a relationship with God was radical, as most of Christianity perceived God as someone holy, to be revered, and off limits to the common man or woman. I remember hearing the body of Christ sing this song with great joy as they embraced the concept that they could become a friend of God. Please consider the lyrics to this amazing song.

"Friend Of God"
[Lead:]
Who am I that You are mindful of me
That You hear me, when I call
Is it true that you are thinking of me
How You love me
It's amazing

[Chorus:]
I am a friend of God
I am a friend of God

I am a friend of God
He calls me friend

{Bridge:]
God almighty Lord of Glory
You have called me friend"

In the last few moments Jesus had with his disciples before his crucifixion, he tells them of his love and friendship. He tells them they are no longer servants but his friends.

 In John 15:11-16 NKJV, "These things I have spoken to you, that My joy may remain in you, and *that* your joy may be full. This is My commandment, that you love one another as I have loved you. Greater love has no one than this, than to lay down one's life for his friends. You are My friends if you do whatever I command you. No longer do I call you servants, for a servant does not know what his master is doing; but I have called you friends, for all things that I heard from My Father I have made known to you. You did not choose Me, but I chose you and appointed you that you should go and bear fruit, and *that* your fruit should remain, that whatever you ask the Father in My name He may give you."

Many of us are willing to be the Lord's servant. We are willing to do what we feel is right and profitable for the kingdom of God. I believe what the Lord wants from us is not servitude but companionship, relationship, shared vision and life experience. He wants us to have the joy of his friendship and the intimacy of knowing all about him and his kingdom. We have been given the opportunity to love closeup instead of from a distance. We have been offered "insider" information about the kingdom of God. We have been given a relationship that will cause us to produce fruit in the kingdom of God.

What must we do to accept this intimate relationship? Simply check "yes" when Jesus ask, "Will you be my friend". A lifelong journey will begin and will continue throughout eternity. A joy that defies understanding will be ours when we say, "I am a friend of God"! Friendship with God is something very special!

Getting to know Millennials

Before I minister in a foreign country or a different region in the United States, I consider the influences that have molded my group of listeners. The customs and traditions of native American youth in Minnesota, the history of British colonization in India and the effect of apartheid in South Africa have been study points for me. Why should I share the gospel from the perspective of a middle class, white American, when my audience comes from a very different perspective? Only pride would require "them" to be like me!

In 1 Corinthians 9:21-23 NLT, the apostle Paul expresses my mindset, "When I am with the Gentiles who do not follow the Jewish law, I too live apart from that law so I can bring them to Christ. But I do not ignore the law of God; I obey the law of Christ. When I am with those who are weak, I share their weakness, for I want to bring the weak to Christ. Yes, I try to find common ground with everyone, doing everything I can to save some. I do everything to spread the Good News and share in its blessings."

I have always felt an ease in ministering to every demographic until recently. When it comes to the age group called Millennials, I have struggled to communicate. Perhaps it's my slow, southern thought process or maybe it's a lack of understanding a generation born at the turn of the century with its own world view. A millennial, also known as Generation Y is a person or group of people born between 1982 and 2004. They are the first born into the digital world, specifically the internet and social media. Technology touches every part of their lives. Generation Y is the most ethnically and racially diverse generation in U.S. history.

So here are a few things I have learned about millennials to communicate, love and share the good news of Jesus Christ. The following ten bullet points are excerpts from an online article by Tina Wells in December 2013.

1. Traditional values are still somewhat important to 20-somethings. Despite allegations regarding Millennials' lack of values, our research reveals the three most important things to this generation: being a good

family member and friend, living a religious or spiritual life, and finding a good partner for life.

2. Millennials are paying attention to their money. Per to our research, a little over two-thirds (64%) of Millennials feel financially secure, while 79% are completely financially independent. Over half (53%) are already saving for retirement, and 94% are aware of how much they spend.

3. Generation Y is on the move when it comes to employment opportunities. 94% of Millennials have actively searched for a new job while still employed – "Higher salary," "More growth opportunities," and "Higher sense of purpose" were listed as the main factors that would cause these Millennials to leave their current jobs for new positions. Furthermore, members of Generation Y are not afraid to try different things until they find the right fit, as 34% have experimented with two careers, and 39% have experimented with three or more careers before finding the most fitting one.

4. This generation has strong opinions on issues. We learned that 80% of those surveyed believe that marijuana should be legalized, 76% believe that same-sex couples should have the right to marry, and 95% believe there should be mandatory background checks before any firearm purchase. Although opinions may vary depending on the issue at hand, these Millennials are not afraid to express what is on their minds.

5. Media and technology continue to influence Generation Y. Almost half (49%) of survey respondents spend over six hours online per day, and about a third (31%) spend between three and six hours per day using the Internet. The majority (92%) owns a smartphone and a laptop. Although **Facebook** is not as popular as it once was, it is still the most popular among all social media sites, with 85% of Millennials checking in daily.

6. Social media and digital integration are key in capturing Generation Y's attention. Since they are spending so much time online, it comes as no surprise that the members of this generation are   influenced by the advertisements that are presented to them through online platforms.

7. Digital media doesn't always win out. Though Generation Y spends an incredible amount of time browsing the web, these young people do not necessarily always prefer online versions of media to traditional versions. For instance, 86% prefer in-hand magazines over online editions, and 89% prefer actual books over their online counterparts.

8. Millennials enjoy giving. Research shows that 86% donate to local charities and 74% are much more likely to purchase a product if the proceeds go to charity. The most popular types of charity organizations among 20-somethings are those dedicated to children's causes (47%), health-related issues (22%), and environmental matters (14%).

9. Value propositions matter in purchasing decisions. Millennials are looking for more than just another product to buy or another store to browse. They seek inspiration, which is why brands such as *Warby Parker* and *TOMS* are winning out over the once-popular brands like *American Eagle* and *Urban Outfitters*. The former offers a promise and an experience, while the latter simply do not.

10. Spirituality is on the rise, even if religion isn't. Only 9% of Millennials consider themselves to be religious, and 40% consider themselves to be less religious now than in the past. Although institutionalized religion is not as popular as it once was among Millennials, over 60% of surveyed 20-somethings consider themselves to be "spiritual".

This study has adjusted my thinking about Millennials. I am always the student, hoping to find new ways to share the old, old story! Join me in studying and influencing this challenging generation called "Millennials". Every generation needs the good news of Jesus Christ!

Give with joy this year!

I believe that all gifts should be wrapped in joy! Joy for the giver and joy for the receiver. I do like all the cute ribbons and Christmas wrappings, but if it's not given out of joy it's only an obligatory present. Retailers spend billions on Christmas TV ads per *CNN Money* to help us find the perfect gift. Yet most of us find ourselves insecure about many of our selections.

Recently, Larry and I were driving through our neighborhood looking for landscape ideas. We saw a young mom and her three children enjoying the beautiful sunshine and ideal temperatures of early November in the south. One child was eating an early supper on the screen porch, the youngest toddler was looking at everything with the inquisitive eye of a seventeen-month-old, and the oldest little boy was playing with brightly colored plastic Easter eggs. I loved seeing the happiness that comes from the simple things in life. I turned my car into the driveway to say "Hello" and to encourage this young mom of three.

It only took seconds for the young boy to run up to the car to show me his treasured Easter eggs. He was having a blast with these simple leftovers from spring. After I cooed over them, he took them away to a safe place while his mom and I talked. In a few moments, he returned with a smile on his face and a gleam in his eye and he offered me the gift of one of his Easter eggs. He enthusiastically said, 'you can pick any one you want!" I chose a hot pink egg and he was overwhelmed with joy! I cradled the plastic egg in my hand and held it close to my heart as if it were a five-carat diamond. He understood the feeling of joy we should have when we give. There was no insecurity and no fear on his part. I think children are often smarter than adults in gift-giving aptitude. I'll never forget the joy in his eyes as he gave me that simple, plastic egg.

Larry asked me what I was going to do with my egg. In seconds, I responded, "I'm putting quarters in it along with some of Michael's favorite candy. At the right time, I'll give it back when he least expects it and watch the joy as he receives it"! The hot pink egg is in my car at this moment waiting for that perfect encounter. I smile just thinking about it!

There were many people who gave during Jesus's three-year ministry here on earth. Some wealthy Pharisees and Sadducees gave a great amount with great splendor and ceremony. But the gift that brought joy to Jesus was the gift of a little widow who gave out of her need to the work of the kingdom of God. In Mark 12: 41-44 NLT, we find the story.

"Jesus sat down near the collection box in the Temple and watched as the crowds dropped in their money. Many rich people put in large amounts. Then a poor widow came and dropped in two small coins. Jesus called his disciples to him and said, "I tell you the truth, this poor widow has given more than all the others who are making contributions. For they gave a tiny part of their surplus, but she, poor as she is, has given everything she had to live on."

Impressing the son of God was not easy. He had seen it all. But this poor widow impressed him as she gave out of joy all she had. There was no insecurity and no fear. She knew that her gift would be received and her provision for life would flow from her heavenly Father. Her action brought great joy to Jesus, so much so, that he called his disciples and said, "Come look!"

I challenge you to give with joy this Christmas season. Don't worry about the amount you spend, wondering if it's good enough. Don't give out of fear and false hope of winning someone's heart. Give out of joy - a feeling of great pleasure and happiness, cheerfulness, and calm delight. If you do, this will be an amazing Christmas for you and those you love.

God is not afraid of the dark!

Do you ever feel like there's so much darkness in the world? The news reports of terrorism, global wars, political divisiveness, murders, rapes and economic crisis make me feel like I live in a dark and foreboding world. I'm not alone in considering the darkness I see around me but I'm also not alone in realizing there is a great light that can dispel the deepest darkness. That light is Jesus Christ.

When we think about the birth of Jesus, we rehearse the story of a young couple, stranded during a census without a place to give birth to their firstborn. We think of angels, shepherds and wise men who wanted to be a part of this miracle event. But contemplation of the world at the time of Jesus' birth can give us insight, hope and revelation that God is not afraid of the dark!

Isaiah 9:6 "For unto us…" is often quoted concerning the birth of Jesus but it is verses 1-5 that give us a peek into the world situation at the time of Jesus' birth.

Isaiah 9:1-5 NLT, "Nevertheless, that time of darkness and despair will not go on forever. The land of Zebulun and Naphtali will be humbled, but there will be a time in the future when Galilee of the Gentiles, which lies along the road that runs between the Jordan and the sea, will be filled with glory. The people who walk in darkness will see a great light. For those who live in a land of deep darkness, a light will shine. You will enlarge the nation of Israel, and its people will rejoice. They will rejoice before you as people rejoice at the harvest and like warriors dividing the plunder. For you will break the yoke of their slavery and lift the heavy burden from their shoulders. You will break the oppressor's rod, just as you did when you destroyed the army of Midian. The boots of the warrior and the uniforms bloodstained by war will all be burned. They will be fuel for the fire."

There are five areas of darkness during the time of Jesus that parallel our current darkness. The first is spiritual darkness. The word of the Lord had not been heard for four centuries, 400 years at the time of Jesus birth. After the last words of the last book, Malachi, of the Old Testament there was no prophetic revelation. The people wandered spiritually having a form of religion but no power to walk victoriously. The heavens were silent. The people walked in spiritual darkness.

Secondly, there was political darkness. Israel was under the oppressive rule of Rome. A puppet king named Herod represented them and their streets were filled with brutal Roman guards. Luke 2:1 speaks of the census to be taken by Rome and its purpose was to count the conquered subjects of Israel. The people walked in political darkness.

Thirdly, the nation of Israel was fracturing from divisiveness and man's desire for control. Four basic groups with their own agenda wanted to lead Israel. The Pharisees wanted to control by law and tradition. The Sadducees wanted the people to embrace a life without supernatural hope. Their ideology was "this is it". They believed there was no resurrection and no supernatural influence in the life of mankind. The Essenes were a sect of recluse scribes who separated themselves and prayed. They believed in enduring to the end and putting all responsibility on God to do something. The fourth and final group that caused fracturing and divisiveness in Israel was the Zealots. They wanted to develop the army and violently overthrow the Roman rule. Darkness permeated Judaism.

The birth of Jesus was shrouded in darkness by a virgin birth that was unheard of in Israel and by a dark pilgrimage, 100 miles from Nazareth to Bethlehem. There was no family, no money for a room, no hospitality committee to greet them and no baby shower for Mary's firstborn. It was a time of emotional darkness.

Finally, it was the darkness of a paranoid king who relentlessly sought to kill baby Jesus that filled the land with sorrow and grief. Herod ordered all the children under two years of age to be slaughter in case the wise men were right and a "new king" had been born. Matthew 2:16 NLT, gives this account "Herod was furious when he realized that the wise men had outwitted him. He sent soldiers to kill all the boys in and around Bethlehem who were two years old and under, based on the wise men's report of the star's first appearance." The darkness of insecurity and fear brought death of the land of Israel.

Deep darkness. composed of spiritual darkness, political darkness, the darkness of division, emotional darkness and the darkness of insecurity and fear filled the land where a helpless baby was born. He was not overcome by any of the darkness but was supernaturally protected and provided for as the "Light of the world".

We have been made joint heirs with Jesus through the finished work of Calvary. Although we walk in a world of darkness much like the one Jesus was born into, we walk in the light of His love and protection. We must acknowledge our helplessness, use the power and authority given to use in the name of Jesus and walk listening and obeying the Holy Spirit. But most of all, we must remember, "God is not afraid of the dark"!

God's mercies are new every morning

I was sharing with a friend this week a passage from Lamentations. Now this is a book of the Bible most of us pass over during our morning devotions or time of study. The prophet Jeremiah is lamenting over the problems of the nation of Israel. His despair pours through every chapter and every verse as he rehearses the sin of the nation and the distance that has grown between them and their God. I can feel Jeremiah's pain as I reflect on like circumstances here in America. I grieve over a country that has lost its way and has abandoned its foundations of faith, hope and love. But nestled in chapter three is one of the most profound truths of the faith. Let me share it with you.

Lamentations 3: 22-26 NKJV,

> *Through the Lord's mercies we are not consumed,*
> *Because His compassions fail not.*
> *They are new every morning;*
> *Great is Your faithfulness.*
> *"The Lord is my portion," says my soul,*
> *"Therefore I hope in Him!"*
>
> *The Lord is good to those who wait for Him,*
> *To the soul who seeks Him.*
> *It is good that one should hope and wait quietly*
> *For the salvation of the Lord*

I love this passage as it has the truth to take me from grief to faith; not because of me or my country, but because of the character of God. He is compassionate and full of mercy. His love which is new every morning is limitless. His faithfulness is abundant. He is the portion or serving of hope that we need in times of discouragement and trouble. The key to receiving his blessing is waiting and trusting in His timing and purpose.

Parallel scriptures in the New Testament include the following:

Hebrews 6:18 NLT,

"So, God has given both his promise and his oath. These two things are unchangeable because it is impossible for God to lie. Therefore, we who have fled to him for refuge can have great confidence as we hold to the hope that lies before us."

Hebrews 10:23 NLT,

"Let us hold tightly without wavering to the hope we affirm, for God can be trusted to keep his promise."

I am reminded of this eternal truth when I look out my kitchen window in the early morning and see a "Morning Glory" I planted a little over a year ago. As you know the Morning Glory blooms new every morning. It heralds the beginning of a new day with beautiful, lavender pink, trumpet style blooms.

When I first planted the Morning Glory it only produced one, maybe two blooms at a time even though it was a tall, beautiful specimen from a local nursery. I pruned it back severely at the end of the growing season last year so it would become healthy and prolific. It was a little scary to take the six-foot-tall bush down to two feet, cutting off all the previous foliage and blooms but I knew it had to be done. There were times when I looked out the window and thought, "Did I do the right thing?"

This summer the Morning Glory blooms new every morning with no less than a dozen beautiful fresh flowers. I had cut away the old and prepared for the new. We must do this in our spiritual lives also to receive the portion of hope God is waiting to give us. It's scary to purge our past accomplishments and seek God for new growth and fruit. But if we are willing to, His unending love, mercies and faithfulness will be new every morning in great abundance!

Allow God to purge you of past failures, regrets, false growth, grief and independence and then declare, "You are my portion and your mercies are new every morning!"

God's timing is perfect

As I write this article, I am watching the sun rise over the Picachos mountains that surround San Miguel de Allende, Mexico. I have been making my way to the airport through the dark mountains but now I can see their beauty and majesty. The sun brings peace to my hour and a half shuttle ride and day six of my ministry trip to Mexico. I am on my way home from a wonderful time of ministry to the women of Antioch Church and a visit with my longtime friend, Marsha. The sunrise seems to be saying "Amen" to a great awaking in the kingdom of God. I know the Word of God that was sown will bring much fruit in the coming year.

The sunrise is so perfect it is hard to image the fury of a category one hurricane that is approaching. By day's end landfall on the Yucatan Peninsula will bring torrential rain and mudslides to the very place where I am standing. I can only smile when I think of God's perfect timing.

The invitation to speak at the women's conference was issued during the Christmas season of 2016. Prayer and planning had set the dates for the August 2017 trip, including the very return flight just hours before the hurricane's arrival. God had ordered my steps as His word says.

In Proverbs 16:9 AMP, we read this declaration. "A man's mind plans his way [as he journeys through life], But the Lord directs his steps *and* establishes them."

In Psalm 37: 23 AMP, "The steps of a [good and righteous] man is directed *and* established by the Lord, And He delights in his way [and blesses his path]."

Proverbs 20:24 AMP, "Man's steps are ordered *and* ordained by the Lord. How then can a man [fully] understand his way?"

The God who sees the storms of life coming can safely navigate us through them if we simply ask and believe in His order and goodness. It takes a truly wise heart to submit your plans to Him. Most of us trust in our own abilities and strength, but the humility of submitting our plans to God brings protection and success.

The apostle Paul experienced this divine leading and direction during his missionary journeys recorded in the book of Acts. More than once he was directed by the Holy Spirit to change his route. In Acts 16:9-10, Paul was instructed in a vision to go to Macedonia and preach. The result was the conversion of Lydia, the first European convert to Christianity and the Philippian jailer and his household. An entire continent was opened to the gospel because Paul allowed God to order his steps.

In Acts 18:9-10 AMP, Paul is directed to preach the gospel in Corinth. "One night the Lord said to Paul in a vision, "Do not be afraid anymore, but go on speaking and do not be silent; for I am with you, and no one will attack you in order to hurt you, because I have many people in this city. So, he settled *there* for a year and six months, teaching them the word of God [concerning eternal salvation through faith in Christ]." The direction and leading of the Lord brought faith and comfort to Paul and helped established the church in Corinth.

In Acts 22:18, 21 AMP, Paul is warned to leave Jerusalem because of opposition and danger. "and I saw Him saying to me, 'Hurry and get out of Jerusalem quickly, because they will not accept your testimony about Me. And the Lord said to me, 'Go, I will send you far away to the Gentiles." Protection from the coming storm came because Paul was obedient to change his plans.

Paul was one of the most learned men in all of Jerusalem, but he sought God's timing and direction in his ministry. He didn't depend on his own wisdom, but he trusted God to order his steps. He was joined by Peter, Philip, the apostles, Cornelius and Ananias in the book of Acts as disciples who followed the leading of the Holy Spirit.

I challenge you to ask God daily to order your steps. Pray and ask for His wisdom and direction in all your plans. He will protect, prosper and lead you to greater success than you could ever obtain on your own. He sees the storms of life coming and He will orchestrate your journey to safety and blessing!

God's Math is 2 + 5 = 12

There's a great deal of controversy in the news concerning the U.S. Department of Education. Some say the new Secretary of Education will make sweeping changes that will benefit families across America. Others say her leadership will cripple the American education system forever. I am thankful God's education system will stand forever and cannot be changed by new leadership. I am so glad the controversy that erupts from His math, brings miracles and blessings to all who apply His principles.

He established His "common core" for the family of God that always gives provision in a supernatural way. Consider Ephesians 3:20-21 NKJV, "Now to Him who is able to do exceedingly abundantly above all that we ask or think, according to the power that works in us, to Him *be* glory in the church by Christ Jesus to all generations, forever and ever. Amen." This scripture indicates we cannot begin to comprehend the greatness of God's love and provision through the Holy Spirit for those who belong to the body of Christ.

There is a great example of this extravagant love and provision in the Gospels. Only two miracles are repeated in all four Gospels, the resurrection, and the feeding of the five thousand. In both we see miraculous provision. In the resurrection, we received spiritual provision for eternity, and in the feeding of the five thousand we see God's natural provision for the present. God is always extravagant with His children!

John 6:1-14 NKJV, *"After these things Jesus went over the Sea of Galilee, which is the Sea of Tiberias. Then a great multitude followed Him, because they saw His signs which He performed on those who were diseased. And Jesus went up on the mountain, and there He sat with His disciples. Now the Passover, a feast of the Jews, was near. Then Jesus lifted up His eyes, and seeing a great multitude coming toward Him, He said to Philip, "Where shall we buy bread, that these may eat?" But this He said to test him, for He Himself knew what He would do. Philip answered Him, "Two hundred denarii worth of bread is not sufficient for them, that every one of them may have a little." One of His disciples, Andrew, Simon Peter's brother, said to*

Him, "There is a lad here who has five barley loaves and two small fish, but what are they among so many?" Then Jesus said, "Make the people sit down." Now there was much grass in the place. So, the men sat down, in number about five thousand. And Jesus took the loaves, and when He had given thanks He distributed them to the disciples, and the disciples to those sitting down; and likewise of the fish, as much as they wanted. So, when they were filled, He said to His disciples, "Gather up the fragments that remain, so that nothing is lost." Therefore, they gathered them up, and filled twelve baskets with the fragments of the five barley loaves which were left over by those who had eaten. Then those men, when they had seen the sign that Jesus did, said, "This is truly the Prophet who is to come into the world."

It is this miracle that reveals God's math. Two fish and five barley loaves blessed by the Lord meets every need with twelve baskets full left over. That is God's math, $2 + 5 = 12$!

Sometimes we need to be reminded that earthly wisdom does not bind our God, but He is free to move in heavenly supply. The apostle Paul stated it this way. Philippians 4:19 NKJV, "And my God shall supply all your need according to His riches in glory by Christ Jesus".

The warehouses of heaven are filled with the supply we need here on earth. The power of the Holy Spirit supernaturally delivers all supply, to those who are seeking Him. Notice the five thousand men plus the women and children that were fed were actively seeking God. Just as a mother and father provide for their children and not the neighbors' children, so God has made His covenant promise of provision to His children. God's math is always based on multiplication not addition or subtraction. His math is always skewed to benefit His children abundantly and He will do whatever is needed to provide for us!

Begin to believe that the windows of heaven will open and pour out your blessing as promised in Malachi 3:10 NKJV, "And try Me now in this," Says the Lord of hosts, "If I will not open for you the windows of heaven And pour out for you such blessing That there will not be room enough to receive it." God's math is for you!

Hairballs and Cockroaches

My husband Larry has a Siamese cat named Bear. To say he loves that cat would be a gross understatement. There are times when I wonder if it came down to me or the cat, if I would lose!

If you are a Facebook friend with Larry then you have seen pictures, several times a week of Bear and what he is doing. Just last night while I was preparing supper, I heard Larry producing a video of "the six words Bear understands". It will probably show up on YouTube also!

Bear is a beautiful cat. Some of Larry's photos of him have appeared in regional ads for the Alabama breeder that helped Bear arrive in this world. You could say the cat is beautiful, spoiled and famous because of all the press he gets.

Bear does a great job of grooming himself. Most of his day is spent eating, grooming, sleeping and posing for Larry's photos. He is finicky in all these areas and could easily wear the "prima donna" title. Bear seems to be perfect, and he talks constantly in the characteristic Siamese screech to let you know that he is. Bear's public image is spotless.

Did I say that I love Bear too? He is an equal opportunity lover and snuggles with Larry or me depending on our availability. He is a loved member of our household.

In all of Bear's outward perfectness, recently he reminded me of what we as humans deal with often, the inner man. Bear came in from romping in the backyard and began to gag and throw up. Larry and I both ran to look for him to make sure he was not on the sofa or the carpet. Deposited on the floor was the contents of Bear's morning adventures. It was undeniably a dismembered cockroach draped in hairballs and slime. With disgust – I hate roaches –I said to Larry, "You should take a picture of that and post it on Facebook"!

In the same moment, the Holy Spirit reminded me that the outward man is not the true picture of who we are. It is what we consume during our romp through life and how we deal with our sin nature that is the true picture. We bathe, dress, have our hair and nails done and pose for "selfies" but it's the inner man that reveals our true character.

Jesus scolded the Pharisees, the perfect religious leaders of the day for the difference between their outward appearance and their inner man. In Matthew 23:1-28 NKJV, we find Jesus' teaching about the Pharisees. "Then Jesus said to the crowds and to his disciples, "The teachers of religious law and the Pharisees are the official interpreters of the law of Moses. So, practice and obey whatever they tell you, but don't follow their example. For they don't practice what they teach. They crush people with unbearable religious demands and never lift a finger to ease the burden.

"Everything they do is for show. On their arms they wear extra wide prayer boxes with Scripture verses inside, and they wear robes with extra-long tassels. And they love to sit at the head table at banquets and in the seats of honor in the synagogues. They love to receive respectful greetings as they walk in the marketplaces, and to be called 'Rabbi'

"Don't let anyone call you 'Rabbi,' for you have only one teacher, and all of you are equal as brothers and sisters. And don't address anyone here on earth as 'Father,' for only God in heaven is your Father. And don't let anyone call you 'Teacher,' for you have only one teacher, the Messiah. The greatest among you must be a servant. But those who exalt themselves will be humbled, and those who humble themselves will be exalted.

"What sorrow awaits you teachers of religious law and you Pharisees? Hypocrites! For you shut the door of the Kingdom of Heaven in people's faces. You won't go in yourselves, and you don't let others enter either.

"What sorrow awaits you teachers of religious law and you Pharisees? Hypocrites! For you cross land and sea to make one convert, and then you turn that person into twice the child of hell you yourselves are!

"Blind guides! What sorrow awaits you! For you say that it means nothing to swear 'by God's Temple,' but that it is binding to swear 'by the gold in the Temple.' Blind fools! Which is more important—the gold or the Temple that makes the gold sacred? And you say that to swear 'by the altar' is not binding, but to swear 'by the gifts on the altar' is binding. How blind! For which is more important—the gift on the altar or the altar that makes the gift sacred? When you swear 'by the altar,' you are swearing by it and by everything on it. And when you swear 'by the Temple,' you are swearing by it and by God, who lives in it. And when you swear 'by heaven,' you are swearing by the throne of God and by God, who sits on the throne.

"What sorrow awaits you teachers of religious law and you Pharisees? Hypocrites! For you are careful to tithe even the tiniest income from your herb gardens, but you ignore the more important aspects of the law—justice, mercy, and faith. You should tithe, yes, but do not neglect the more important things. Blind guides! You strain your water, so you won't accidentally swallow a gnat, but you swallow a camel!

"What sorrow awaits you teachers of religious law and you Pharisees? Hypocrites! For you are so careful to clean the outside of the cup and the dish, but inside you are filthy—full of greed and self-indulgence! You blind Pharisee! First wash the inside of the cup and the dish, and then the outside will become clean, too.

"What sorrow awaits you teachers of religious law and you Pharisees? Hypocrites! For you are like whitewashed tombs—beautiful on the outside but filled on the inside with dead people's bones and all sorts of impurity. Outwardly you look like righteous people, but inwardly your hearts are filled with hypocrisy and lawlessness."

Like Bear, we must to purge the inside to get rid of the hairballs and cockroaches or our Christianity is only a facade like the Pharisees lived. Lord help us to be real!

Handling the chaos of life

It's becoming increasingly harder to find a quiet place. With the demands of family life, work, friends and technology, most of us feel like we are on a nonstop roller coaster. We feel driven by the urgent instead of the important. In our minds, we have a concept of peace and rest and joy but in the activities of life the concept finds little freedom of expression.

Did you know Jesus had the same problem? Although he didn't have a cell phone or media blaring their opinions, he had the constant chatter of unbelievers, people in great need and religious hypocrites following him with every step he took. Not to mention his family members who had no idea how to deal with their natural brother who was turning the nation of Israel upside down. How did he handle the chaos?

Luke 5 draws this picture for us of a day in the life of Jesus. In verses 1-11 Jesus calls four of his disciples into full time service. In verses 12-16, Jesus healed a man from leprosy. In Verses 17-26, Jesus healed a paralyzed man who was brought to him by friends who believed Jesus could do the impossible. He also debated and defeated the unbelieving scribes and Pharisees who didn't like the way he did it! In verse 27-32, Jesus called another disciple, Mathew the tax collector, attended a dinner party at Matthew's house with other tax collectors and sinners, corrected the objecting scribes and Pharisees, and announced his mission statement of calling sinners to repentance. In verses 33-39 Jesus is questioned about fasting and chided about his disciples feasting. Concluding his day, Jesus gave one of his most important teachings about the need to have new wineskins to hold new wine. Jesus new how to pack out a day!

Nestled in all this activity is the key to Jesus' incredible focus and accomplishment. Luke 5:16 NKJV, simply says, "So, He Himself *often* withdrew into the wilderness and prayed."

Another translation, NLT says, "But Jesus often withdrew to the wilderness for prayer."

Pastor Rick Warren, from Saddleback Church stated the need to withdraw and pray in this statement. "If we want to fulfill God's vision for our lives, we must continually hear from God. We must believe that hearing from God daily is a requirement for us as we move forward toward our destiny. It is not just a nice add-on to our lives; it is a necessity for fulfilling our destiny."

The prophet Habakkuk says this about getting alone with God in Habakkuk 2:1 NLT, "I will climb into my watchtower and stand at my guard post. There I will wait to see what the Lord says and how he will answer my complaint. "

Every child of God has a sphere of influence to watch over. The climb up into the tower or out into the wilderness often seems an impossibility because of the daily life chaos. But we must admit none of us are busier than Jesus and none of us are strong enough to do it on our own. We need a quiet place to communicate with God. Often, we are tempted to complain that God didn't answer our prayers-on-the-run. Often, we are tempted to blame him when life doesn't work out. What we must do is ask ourselves if we have been to that quiet place where communion with God allows us to handle the chaos of life.

In closing I want to share one of my favorite humorous poems entitled "Jake the Rancher" that illustrates the need to "stay in touch".

Jake, the rancher, went one day, to fix a distant fence.
The wind was cold and gusty; the clouds rolled gray and dense.

As he pounded the last staples in and gathered tools to go,
The temperature had fallen; the wind and snow began to blow.

When he finally reached his pickup, he felt a heavy heart.
From the sound of that ignition, he knew it wouldn't start.

So Jake did what most of us would do, had we been there.
He humbly bowed his balding head and sent aloft a prayer.

As he turned the key for one last time, he softly cursed his luck.
They found him three days later, frozen stiff in that old truck.

Now Jake had been around in life and done his share of roaming.
But when he saw Heaven, he was shocked — it looked just like
Wyoming!

Of all the saints in Heaven, his favorite was St. Peter.
(Now, this line ain't needed but it helps with rhyme and meter)

So they sat and talked a minute or two, or maybe it was three.
Nobody was keeping score — in Heaven time is free.

"I've always heard," Jake said to Pete, "that God will answer
prayer,
But one time I asked for help, well, he just plain wasn't there."

"Does God answer prayers of some and ignore the prayers of
others?
That don't seem exactly square — I know all men are brothers."

"Or does he randomly reply, without good rhyme or reason?
Maybe, it's the time! of day, the weather or the season."

"Now I ain't trying to act smart, it's just the way I feel.
And I was wondering, could you tell me — what the heck's the
deal?"

Peter listened very patiently and when Jake was done,
There were smiles of recognition, and he said, "So, you're the one!"

"That day your truck, it wouldn't start, and you sent your prayer a
flying,
You gave us all a real bad time, with hundreds of us all trying."

"A thousand angels rushed, to check the status of your file,
But you know, Jake, we hadn't heard from you, in quite a long
while."

"And though all prayers are answered, and God ain't got no quota,
He didn't recognize your voice, and started a truck in Minnesota."
Unknown

Do you have a Godly pattern for your life?

I had been selected to be Mrs. Santa Claus in my second grade Christmas play. My Mom told me she would make me a red dress with white trim, and it would be large enough to stuff with the needed curves for jolly Mrs. Santa. I was so excited! I watched her lay out the red fabric on the dining room table. She placed a well wore pattern for a girl dress strategically on the fabric and weighted it down with cutlery as she had no pins to secure the pattern. Then she began to cut out what would become my costume for the Christmas play. It took weeks for her to complete the red dress, barely finishing in time for the school play. She agonized over every sewing session and was so distraught she didn't attend the play.

I had watched my Aunt Margaret create many pieces of clothing and many patchwork quilts. She was an excellent seamstress and had the confidence to tackle any task and accomplish it. It seemed effortless for her to whip up a dress for me during my visits with her. She made applying a pattern to fabric and creating a garment look so easy.

Two very important women in my life approached applying a pattern and creating a living product in two very different ways. For my Mom, applying the pattern was a struggle and for my Aunt Margaret it was a joy.

In later years, I realized that was the way they both lived their lives. My mother made excuses, was filled with self-doubt, procrastinated based on her emotions and blamed life for her lack of creativity and accomplishment. My aunt had many difficulties in her life, including a severely disabled husband but her faith and the application of God's pattern for her life caused her to be victorious.

I am convinced that joy and accomplishment come in our lives when we apply God's pattern. He weaves the fabric of our life, creating many garments so we can be clothed in His goodness and grace. Our responsibility is to apply the pattern He has selected for us.

I decided in the seventh grade to learn how to sew. I read the instructions and applied my limited wisdom to a blouse. It was dreadful! So, I tackled a dress and it too was terrible. I decided no matter how many times I failed; I would apply the pattern until I succeed in creating something beautiful that I could be proud of. I decided that hand-me-downs would not be my only clothing, poverty would not be my garment and excuses would not be my song. By the time I entered high school, I made a new outfit a week, starting on Monday and finishing in time for the football game on Friday night. I learned to apply the pattern to the limited resources I had and with God's help I became victorious.

God has a life pattern for you. You may think it's too difficult to apply. You may think you need more than what you possess to start the development. You may feel extremely limited in your ability. But God's patterns always work when we use our faith in Him to cut away the fabric of the world and structure a life in Christ.

In Exodus 25:8-9 NLT, Moses was instructed by God to build a dwelling place, a tabernacle where the presence of God could dwell. "Have the people of Israel build me a holy sanctuary so I can live among them. You must build this Tabernacle and its furnishings exactly according to the pattern I will show you." He had a pattern for the original dwelling place and He has a pattern for you, His new testament dwelling place.

Paul admonished the church to follow his pattern of life. Philippians 3:17 NLT, "Dear brothers and sisters, pattern your lives after mine, and learn from those who follow our example."

Hebrews 12:2 NLT exhorts us, "Don't copy the behavior and customs of this world, but let God transform you into a new person by changing the way you think. Then you will learn to know God's will for you, which is good and pleasing and perfect."

Don't pattern your life after the world's way of doing things but pattern your life on God's perfect plan and structure for you. Lay your life down like fabric on God's cutting table and ask Him to create something beautiful. He's a master creator and a perfect seamstress!

Honoring Mom

Celebrating motherhood can be traced back to the ancient Greeks and Romans who held festivals in honor of the mother goddesses Cybele and Rhea. The Christian faith established the precedent for our Mother's Day celebration by establishing an early Christian festival called, "Mothering Sunday".

President Woodrow Wilson proclaimed the second Sunday in May as America's official Mother's Day in 1914. The US is not alone in recognizing mothers, as forty plus countries worldwide celebrate motherhood in the months of March or May. Spring brings new life and it is thought to be the perfect time to honor those who bring new life - children into the world.

There are many ways to celebrate Mother's Day, but the giving of cards and flowers is the most common. Churches and schools encourage children to write poems and present plays honoring their Mothers. One of my favorite keepsakes is a poem written by my oldest son where he clearly states, "My Mom almost never makes me mad!" Now that's a tribute!

I've noticed on Mother's Day the memories shared are the "good ones". There are no perfect Moms, but this day of remembrance brings the grace and love needed to magnify the good and dismiss the bad. Even the neglectful, abusive mom is honored with forgiveness and the words, "she gave me life". This amazing display of grace is a life lesson for all of us. What if every day we gave honor and not judgment, gratitude not itemized failures, and love instead of hate? What a wonderful world this would be.

The New Testament word for honor, "time' (tee-may) is defined as "a price, properly perceived value in the eyes of the beholder." It is a measured look at something or someone to determine its value or price. When we dishonor someone, we are figuratively saying, "You are of no value to me". What a deeply, wounding experience that can be.

In the Bible, we find this commandment in the old and new testaments multiple times. Exodus 20:12 NLT, "Honor your father and mother. Then you will live a long, full life in the land the LORD your God is giving you".

Deuteronomy 5:16 NLT, "Honor your father and mother, as the LORD your God commanded you. Then you will live a long, full life in the land the LORD your God is giving you."

Ephesians 6:2-3. NLT, "Honor your father and mother." This is the first commandment with a promise: If you honor your father and mother, "things will go well for you, and you will have a long life on the earth."

We are challenged by God to determine a value, a price of honor for our parents so we can have a long fruitful life on this earth. I honestly don't know how that works but I have repeatedly seen it come to pass in the life of families. There is something supernatural about honor!

In our relationship with Christ, we can see the fulfillment of honor as Jesus set the price, the value of mankind, and obtained it with His death. He looked at us and said, "they are worth my life"!

Philippians 2: 6-8 NLT, "Though he was God, he did not think of equality with God as something to cling to. Instead, he gave up his divine privileges; he took the humble position of a slave and was born as a human being. When he appeared in human form, he humbled himself in obedience to God and died a criminal's death on a cross. Therefore, God elevated him to the place of highest honor and gave him the name above all other names, that at the name of Jesus every knee should bow, in heaven and on earth and under the earth, and every tongue declare that Jesus Christ is Lord, to the glory of God the Father." You will notice that highest honor was given to a Savior who was willing to look at us through the eyes of love and set our value as worth His life.

Ellis Crum authored a song in 1977 that speaks of the price that was paid for our becoming honored, valued sons and daughters of God. The first verse says, "He paid a debt He did not owe; I owed a debt I could not pay, I needed someone to wash my sins away. And now I sing a brand-new song, Amazing Grace, Christ Jesus paid a debt that I could never pay."

Jesus Christ honored us by placing a value on our lives and paying the price for our redemption. We didn't deserve it but in the eye of the beholder, Jesus, we were worth every pain, sorrow and even death.

Could we on this Mother's Day 2019 begin to give honor and not judgment, gratitude not itemized failures, and love instead of hate? What a wonderful world this would be!

Hope does not disappoint

On New Year's Eve, 1,000,000 plus will gather in Times Square in New York to cheer in the new year and watch the crystal ball drop. It has been a tradition since 1907. Only two years, 1942 and 1943, because of World War 11 "dim-out" restrictions have the ceremony been suspended.

This year, the "ball-drop" will experience the coldest weather on record for many years. 3,000 pounds of confetti will shower the crowd once the ball drops and 2019 officially begins. What does all this tradition represent? I believe it heralds two things – a new beginning and a new hope.

It is a new beginning because a new calendar year starts. A new beginning where one can walk away from the mistakes of the previous year and start "new". A fresh look at what might be overcome and what might be accomplished. It is metaphorically a "clean slate' on which to write and create the future. Gone are the failures, the disappointments, the brokenness of a year gone by. Gone also, are the accomplishments and praise of yesterday. One is issued a new challenge to achieve. New Year's Day offers freedom from the past and exciting encounters for the future.

This tradition also offers new hope. While new beginnings are an offering governed by man's ability, hope comes from a spiritual ability one can only find in God.

In the scripture Romans 5:1-11 NKJV, "Therefore, having been justified by faith, we have peace with God through our Lord Jesus Christ, through whom also we have access by faith into this grace in which we stand, and rejoice in hope of the glory of God. And not only *that,* but we also glory in tribulations, knowing that tribulation produces perseverance; and perseverance, character; and character, hope. Now hope does not disappoint, because the love of God has been poured out in our hearts by the Holy Spirit who was given to us. For when we were still without strength, in due time Christ died for the ungodly. For scarcely for a righteous man will one die; yet perhaps for a good man someone would even dare to die. But God demonstrates His own love toward us, in that while we were still sinners, Christ died for us. Much more then, having now been justified by His blood, we shall be saved from wrath through Him. For if when we were enemies we were reconciled to God through the death of His Son, much more, having been reconciled, we shall be saved by His life. And not only *that,* but we also rejoice in God through our Lord Jesus Christ, through whom we have now received the reconciliation."

In verse five of this passage, it speaks of a hope that does not disappoint or make ashamed. This is a hope dependent on what God has done through Jesus Christ not on what we can do. A hope that is set in eternity.

Joseph Prince Ministries puts it this way, "But "hope" in the Bible is a confident and positive expectation of good. God wants you to have a confident expectation of good because as His child, He favors you."

One of my favorite old testament stories presents a great visual of hope. The Hebrew word for hope is "tikvah" which means hope, expectation, something yearned for and anticipated eagerly; something for which one waits. Its original meaning was "to stretch like a rope".

In Joshua 2, the story of the spies that entered Jericho, we find a woman named Rahab. She hides the spies from the king of Jericho and then request sanctuary for herself and her family members when the armies of Israel take the city. She is told by the spies to lower a scarlet rope, a "tiqvah" outside the window of her home on the city wall. She is promised protection and deliverance for all inside the home when the armies of Israel attack. The scarlet rope was her hope for rescue. So literally hope "tiqvah" is a rope to our freedom and protection. Rahab couldn't see her deliverers coming, but she had the promise that they were there at the end of her "rope of hope".

Hope works the same way in our life. We live knowing when we hold on to hope, God is on the other end of the rope waiting to deliver us supernaturally from any war that rages. Psalm 71:5 KJV, states that "Yahweh" himself is the hope of the godly.

In 2019, enjoy the new beginnings you are promised. Do everything to the best of your ability to enjoy a better life. But also, grasp the supernatural "rope of hope" that God has given those he loves. It will not disappoint!

Hopelessness is not God's plan

There are many silent souls who will go to work today, run their households or volunteer at a local charity while bearing the pain of hopelessness in some area of their life. What is the root of this quiet pain and is there a Biblical answer?

The word hopeless is defined as "having no expectation of good or success" or "incapable of solution, management or accomplishment: impossible."

Hope is the expectation or blueprint for good or success. Just as a builder reads a carefully prepared blueprint before he starts laying the foundation and erecting walls for a building, hope serves as life's blueprint. Hope helps us see the big picture or final product.

In their book, "Hope in the Age of Anxiety" authors Anthony Scioli and Henry Biller   list the following nine areas where we experience hopelessness. (Google.books.com)

1. Alienation - Alienated individuals believe that they are somehow different. Moreover, they feel as if they have been cut loose, no longer deemed worthy of love, care, or support. In turn, the alienated tend to close themselves off, fearing further pain and rejection.

2. Forsakenness - The word "forsaken" refers to an experience of total abandonment that leaves individuals feeling alone in their time of greatest need. Recall Job in the Old Testament, crumpled over and covered with sores, pleading with a seemingly indifferent God.

3. Uninspired - Feeling uninspired can be especially difficult for members of underprivileged minorities, for whom opportunities for growth and positive role models within the group may be either lacking or undervalued.

4. Powerlessness - Individuals of every age need to believe that they can author the story of their life. When that need is thwarted, when one feels incapable of navigating one's way toward desired goals, a feeling of powerlessness can set in.

5. Oppression - Oppression involves the subjugation of a person or group.... The word "oppressed" comes from Latin, to "press down," and its synonym, "down-trodden," suggests a sense of being "crushed under" or "flattened."

6. Limitedness -When the struggle for survival is combined with a sense of failed mastery, individuals feel limited. They experience themselves as deficient, lacking in the right stuff to make it in the world. This form of hopelessness is all too common among the poor as well as those struggling with severe physical handicaps or crippling learning disabilities.

7. Doom - Individuals weighed down by this form of despair presume that their life is over, that their death is imminent. The ones most vulnerable to sinking into this circle of hell are those diagnosed with a serious, life-threatening illness as well as those who see themselves worn out by age or infirmity. Such individuals feel doomed, trapped in a fog of irreversible decline.

8. Captivity - Two forms of hopelessness can result from captivity. The first consists of physical or emotional captivity enforced by an individual or a group. Prisoners fall into this category as well as those help captive in a controlling, abusive relationship. We refer to this as "other-imprisonment." An equally insidious form of entrapment is "self-imprisonment. This occurs when individuals cannot leave a bad relationship because their sense of self will not allow it.

9. Helplessness - Helpless individuals no longer believe that they can live safely in the world. They feel exposed and vulnerable, like a cat after being declawed or a bird grounded by a broken wing. Trauma or repeated exposure to uncontrolled stressors can produce an ingrained sense of helplessness. In the words of one trauma survivor, "I was terrified to go anywhere on my own ... I felt so defenseless and afraid that I just stopped doing anything."

Most of us have experienced one or more of these areas of hopelessness during our lifetime. How do we as Christians rise above hopelessness?

The Bible says many things about the importance of hope. Here are a few scriptures that will help us understand hope and hopelessness.

"Hope deferred makes the heart sick, but a dream fulfilled is a tree of life." Proverbs 13:12 NLT

"Through Christ you have come to trust in God. And you have placed your faith and hope in God because he raised Christ from the dead and gave him great glory." 1 Peter 1:21 NLT

"Even when there was no reason for hope, Abraham kept hoping-- believing that he would become the father of many nations. For God had said to him, "That's how many descendants you will have!" Romans 4:18 NLT

"Three things will last forever--faith, hope, and love--and the greatest of these is love." 1 Corinthians 13:13 NLT

"I pray that God, the source of hope, will fill you completely with joy and peace because you trust in him. Then you will overflow with confident hope through the power of the Holy Spirit." Romans 15:13 NLT

In the preceding verses we can determined four things: God is the source of hope, hope and trust in God work together, having no hope will make you sick and finally, hope is an anointing that remains forever just like faith and love.

It's time to reconfigure your blueprint for life by using the ink of trust and the paper of God's faithfulness and love toward us.

How Do You Eat an Elephant?

Often when I am teaching on overcoming life's obstacles, I pose the question, "How do you eat an elephant?" Of course, the only reasonable answer is, "One bite at a time!"

Every overwhelming situation in our life must be addressed "one bite" at the time. Often patience, diligence, courage and an indomitable spirit are the seasonings for our elephant meal. There is no easy, quick way to dispose of a 12,000-pound elephant, aka a problem.

Several years ago, I experienced an elephant in my own life. After surgery I found myself unable to walk and dependent on a walker. After several weeks of physical therapy, I was "sprung" from the inside of my house and given the go ahead to begin walking in my neighborhood. I had two wheels and two tennis balls adorning my walker and I was off to the races! I was delighted to be free but embarrassed to be hobbling down the road. I found myself hoping the neighbors thought I had been in a car accident instead of in recovery from a surgery that happens to "old people"! When there's an elephant in your life there is usually embarrassment and humiliation too.

I had made progress on my one-mile goal and I invited the grandchildren to walk with me one afternoon following a family gathering. Larry and one of my sons came along to keep seven children from having too much fun with "Meena". My son whipped out his new Droid and measured the rate of speed we were traveling. With great laughter he announced that I was going one mile per hour! How humiliating was that! It would take me a whole hour to walk one mile when I used to run a mile in eight minutes.

I wanted to make this elephant my companion for life by giving up, retreating to the inside of my house, gorging on chocolate and whining to my friends about how unfair life was! But instead, I sought strength and courage from God's Word that says, "Yet in all things we are more than conquerors through Him who loved us." Romans 8:37 KJV.

I made the journey down the road every day for four weeks, whether I felt like it or not. I increased the distance traveled every two days, struggling from street light to street light. I talked to my body and encouraged it to be strong. I prayed for others as I walked. Sometimes I just enjoyed the company of family members. Finally, I hit the one-mile mark with calluses on my hands from gripping the walker, a gait that suggested I had never had surgery and an a confidence that good things would happen when I visited my doctor in a few days.

The x-rays revealed the fracture was healed and after watching me walk the doctor totally released me with no limitations and no return visits! I was so thankful for the grace God had given me to eat my elephant "one bite at a time".

Lord, when I feel overwhelmed and I am in the shadow of the elephant, please transfer me into the shadow of your love and protection. Infuse me with strength, faith and determination that are beyond my ability. Help me to be victorious for you have purchased my victory through your shed blood on Calvary's cross! Amen

How will they hear?

For about a month I have been "hearing" this passage of scripture at random times during the day. I think the Lord is reminding me how important it is to share the gospel and to teach others how to share the gospel.

Romans 10:8-15 NKJV, "But what does it say? "The word is near you, in your mouth and in your heart" (that is, the word of faith which we preach): that if you confess with your mouth the Lord Jesus and believe in your heart that God has raised Him from the dead, you will be saved. For with the heart one believes unto righteousness, and with the mouth confession is made unto salvation. For the Scripture says, "Whoever believes on Him will not be put to shame." For there is no distinction between Jew and Greek, for the same Lord over all is rich to all who call upon Him. For "whoever calls on the name of the Lord shall be saved." How then shall they call on Him in whom they have not believed? And how shall they believe in Him of whom they have not heard? And how shall they hear without a preacher? And how shall they preach unless they are sent? As it is written: "How beautiful are the feet of those who preach the gospel of peace, who bring glad tidings of good things!"

Our churches are filled with programs and events to help us grow up in the Lord and to survive the trauma of everyday living. I am thankful for the comfort and support of the local church in my life. I am a fan of church attendance and involvement for it keeps us anchored on the importance of Christian fellowship. It causes us to depend on our brothers and sisters in Christ and does not allow us to be an island unto ourselves. It makes us accountable.

However, I am being personally provoked to go beyond the four walls of the church and to consider those who have never heard the gospel or who have little knowledge of the good news of Jesus Christ. For the past 3 years, I have been training ministers to go out into the highways and byways and bring people into a saving knowledge of Jesus Christ. Because as the above scripture states, "How shall they believe in Him of whom they have not heard?". The world needs to hear the gospel of Jesus Christ. The world needs men and women who are equipped to share the knowledge and wisdom of God.

Currently I am working locally with eighteen regional students on a curriculum for ordination. At the same time, I am working with ten students in South Africa who will be ordained Easter weekend. During the Easter conference at *Victory In Fellowship Church* in Bronkhorstspruit, Gauteng, SA, I and a team from the USA will be conducting a women's conference, an ordination service, a baptism and a resurrection Sunday service. It is going to be an amazing, powerful weekend of sharing. The students who are ordained will continue the work of "bringing glad tidings of good things" long after I return to the United States. I am thrilled with the multiplication of the gospel through these dedicated students.

Are you sharing the gospel as part of your everyday lifestyle? Do you understand the great gift, the opportunity you have, to bring good news to a lost, dying, hurting world? I believe these scriptures are being whispered to the hearts of men and women across the world as the Holy Spirit is seeking those who are willing to "preach the gospel". According to the scripture, it's a way to have beautiful feet in the kingdom of God. You may say, "I don't know what to do or how to start". The answer is simple, be a witness. Share what God has done in your life. Testify as a witness of his mercy and grace to someone who needs to know that mercy and grace. You will be surprised how spiritually hungry people are.

We spend a great amount of time within the church walls. I believe it's time to reach out and touch the world for Christ!

I don't live there anymore

One of the most embarrassing moments of my life happened during the summer after the seventh grade. My family had moved across town and I had been invited back to the old neighborhood to a party. The party happened the week of the move and my whole life was still in boxes and piles. My brother dropped me off at my friend's house and she and her boyfriend would be bringing me home.

I was familiar with everything about my old neighborhood – the smells, the houses, the people and the memories both good and bad. Although I was excited about my new home, there was comfort in the old neighborhood as I knew how to navigate it and honestly it was all I had ever known.

When the party was over, I hopped into the car with my friends and headed home. I told them I lived on Highpoint Drive and I assumed that would be enough information. As we turn down the drive to my new house I heard from the front seat of the car, "Which house is it?' A wave of panic crossed my face as I realized I didn't know my new address. Confident I would recognize the little two-bedroom white house I replied, "It's just down the road a bit". I didn't understand almost every house in the neighbor was white, small and looked the same except for a few distinguishing features. It was dark and I had no idea how to find my way home. We drove up and down the street with the embarrassing glow on my face becoming brighter and brighter. Finally, after what seemed like an eternity, I spotted my new house. I couldn't get out of the car quick enough. I could only imagine the conversations that would follow about the dumb kid who didn't know where she lived!

I wished I had never moved. I wished I was back home in the old neighborhood where I knew what to do. I wanted to go back much the same way the children of Israel wanted to go back to Egypt after facing difficulties in the wilderness on the way to the Promise Land. I couldn't see the blessing of a better home, new friends, a new church family and a new school that would nurture me into adulthood. I could only feel embarrassment and insecurity.

That experience taught me how people feel when they try to leave the past behind and embrace their new life in Christ and in the world that has changed. Every person who decides to repent, and turn away from their old life, goes through times of wondering and insecurity. The old is always easier than the new.

I have often thought of the apostle Paul and the dramatic change he experienced when he came to Christ. His pathway as a Hebrew scholar was established. He had power and authority. He had respect and knowledge of how life was done. Then Jesus appeared and everything changed. I'm sure there were times when he longed for the old neighborhood, the familiar, and the established.

In Philippians 3:12-14 NLT, we hear Paul's heart, "I don't mean to say that I have already achieved these things or that I have already reached perfection. But I press on to possess that perfection for which Christ Jesus first possessed me. No, dear brothers and sisters, I have not achieved it, but I focus on this one thing: Forgetting the past and looking forward to what lies ahead, I press on to reach the end of the race and receive the heavenly prize for which God, through Christ Jesus, is calling us."

This passage has become my personal life scripture. Understanding that the past is the easier route through life, like Paul I must press forward through change in order to finish the race God has called me to. The past composed of good and bad life experiences is not the place to live. It's over!

Danny Gokey, third place finalist in season eight of America Idol, has recently released a new contemporary Christian song, "Tell your heart to beat again." I love the lyrics, "yesterday is a closing door, you don't live there anymore, say goodbye to where you've been and tell your heart to beat again." You can catch the entire song on YouTube and the story that was the inspiration for it.

The Christian walk is a life of forward motion. Look backwards and say, "I don't live there anymore!" Your new address is free from failure, addiction, regret and pain. It is waiting for you to occupy it with joy and expectation!

I had no idea!

When I attended Girl's Auxiliary (GA's) as a first grader at a local Baptist church in Tuscaloosa, Alabama, I had no idea God was preparing my heart for this adult season of my life. I memorized scriptures and learned about foreign and home missions during those formative years. I read about women in ministry in China, India and other dreamy, distant places. From first grade through ninth grade, I faithfully attended GA's and learned so much about the Bible, God's kingdom on this earth, and His great love for mankind. The song of the GA's, "We've a story to tell to the nations" still floats across my mind regularly and brings to me a smile of agreement. Here are the lyrics.

We've a Story to Tell to the Nations : The United Methodist
Hymnal Number 569
Text: *H. Ernest Nichol, 1862-1928 (CWH attrib. to Colin Sterne)*
Music: *H. Ernest Nichol, 1862-1928*

1. We've a story to tell to the nations,
that shall turn their hearts to the right,
a story of truth and mercy,
a story of peace and light,
a story of peace and light.
Refrain:
For the darkness shall turn to dawning,
and the dawning to noonday bright;
and Christ's great kingdom shall come on earth,
the kingdom of love and light.

2. We've a song to be sung to the nations,
that shall lift their hearts to the Lord,
a song that shall conquer evil
and shatter the spear and sword,
and shatter the spear and sword.
(Refrain)

3. We've a message to give to the nations,
that the Lord who reigneth above
hath sent us his Son to save us,
and show us that God is love,
and show us that God is love.
(Refrain)

When I taught myself to sew in the eighth grade, I had no idea God was preparing me naturally for this season in my life. I thought sewing would provide me with those new clothes my family could not afford. It would also provide income as I could sew and mend for others who had needs. I must admit I never wore those first few items I created, but I was diligent and eventually made most of my clothes including prom and pageant dresses. I learned to tackle almost anything with a needle and thread!

When I had that "aha" moment as a sixteen-year-old and said, "Lord I will go where ever you want me to go and do whatever you want me to do...even Africa", I had no idea God was preparing me for this season of ministry in Africa. I was sure this vow would be the end of my teenage life and I would be an "old maid missionary" on some distant shore with a thatched hut for a home and no bank account. How I underestimated the love and care of God in my life, thinking sacrifice and punishment, instead of an amazing, front row seat in the journey of God's redemption power.

And now many years after that "aha" moment, I am preparing myself and a team to travel to South Africa on Tuesday for a nine-day ministry trip to six churches who are hungry for the word of God and spiritual growth. I had no idea the threads of preparation and surrender were being woven into a garment to praise for my savior and friend, Jesus Christ.

The study of the Bible in those early years positioned me for the training and teaching I have been doing with eleven students since February of this year. Eight men and three women will be ordained at a special service and dinner during the team's visit. I will challenge them to make disciples and build the church into a power-house of grace in South Africa. They will be wearing caps and gowns and I have been sewing a special sole for each person to wear with the cross and my *An Encouraging Word* logo embroidery on it. The sewing preparation in my teen years has equipped me to make this special gift of recognition and love. And because I had answered the "call at sixteen", when the due date came a full fifty years later, I was ready to go.

So often we wander through life with no idea of our destiny and assignment in the kingdom of God. Yet, God has had a plan for us since before we were born. He has been weaving life experiences into a destiny of purpose.

Jeremiah 29:11 AMP, says, "For I know the plans *and* thoughts that I have for you,' says the Lord, 'plans for peace *and* well-being and not for disaster to give you a future and a hope."

Psalms 37:23 AMP, says, "The steps of a [good and righteous] man are directed *and* established by the Lord, And He delights in his way [and blesses his path].

Psalms 119:133-135 AMP, says, "Establish my footsteps in [the way of] Your word; Do not let any human weakness have power over me [causing me to be separated from You]. Redeem me from the oppression of man; That I may keep Your precepts. Make Your face shine [with pleasure] upon Your servant and teach me Your statutes."

I had no idea…. but God had a big idea for a little girl who loved him and believed she had a story to tell to the nations. He has a big idea for you too!

I love my country!

I love my country! I have always been a flag waving patriot. I have always believed that despite the selfish ambitions that often fuel the actions of political leaders, America is a country that will triumph. America is a country destined by God to preach the gospel of the kingdom of God. America is a country that has abundance and blessing because there are those citizens who believe in the power of prayer and the call to do justly, love mercy and walk humbly as found in Micah 6:8.

One of my prize treasures is a crayon drawing from a 5-year-old church member presented to me many years ago. It portrays a simple house draw in red, white and blue, lighted by a bright yellow sun, dressed in pink flowers and green grass. The artistic creation proudly states, "I love God" and "I love America". It was bordered in alternating stars and crosses. Somehow this preschooler had been able to look into my heart and see the love I felt for my God and my country.

When I minister in foreign countries, I am always awed when I return - setting foot on American soil and seeing the abundance and beauty that epitomizes our land. I can't explain the thankfulness I feel. When I fly across the vast Mississippi River, the Plains and the Rockies, I am always amazed at the diversity and beauty of the country I call home.

As I celebrate Memorial Day weekend, I am reminded of the joy of freedom, the cost of freedom and the value of freedom. Many men and women have made the ultimate sacrifice for freedom and a future of hope for American citizens. The value of their actions is priceless. The joy they have secured for us cannot be expressed.

I am also reminded of the joy of freedom, the cost of freedom and the value of freedom I celebrate spiritually as a Christian. Jesus Christ made the ultimate sacrifice for my freedom and my future hope. The value of His action is priceless as He laid his life down so I could be free. He gave me joy, freely without measure and without limits. I am daily thankful to also be a citizen of the kingdom of

God. Although I can't view the heavenly landscape like I do this country, I am sure it is more beautiful than anything I have ever seen in America. I know from the scripture that heaven is a beautiful place filled with His glory and grace. I look forward to the day when I see Jesus face to face and when I can explore the countryside of heaven.

Our spiritual freedom is expressed so well in this scripture in Titus 2:14 NKJV, "He gave himself for us to set us free from every sin and to cleanse us so that we can be his special people who are enthusiastic about doing good things".

I love the admonition in Psalm 33:12 NKJV, "Blessed is the nation whose God is the Lord, and the people whom He has chosen for his own inheritance." 2 Corinthians 3:17 NKJV, declares the source of ultimate freedom: "where the Spirit of the Lord is, there is liberty".

You can be a Christian and not be an American. You can be an American and not be a Christian. However, the perspective of George Washington one of our founding fathers, intrinsically ties the two together. He says, "It is impossible to rightly govern a nation without God and the Bible." He was a wise man, a man of commitment and a man who loved America. Let's consider his wisdom and remain a country of freedom that loves the God who has given us spiritual freedom.

As a tribute to the brave men and women who paid the ultimate price for my freedom as an America, I say "Thank you!" May this special weekend be a time of remembering the brave.

I will never leave you

Of all the promises in the Bible, my favorite as to be found in Hebrews 13:5-6 NKJV, "Let your conduct be without covetousness; be content with such things as you have. For He Himself has said, "I will never leave you nor forsake you." So, we may boldly say: "The Lord is my helper; I will not fear. What can man do to me?"

God's promise to never leave me or forsake me has sustained me through the years. Like most of you, I have had family members, friends and acquaintances who have decided to "leave" when something didn't go their way. It is always painful and presents many questions when "leaving" or abandonment happens. When someone promises their undying love and commitment then walks out the door on a whim, it shatters self-worth and hope. Recovery must be deliberate and with great effort.

Sometimes abandonment is without intention and is not as it appears. At family gatherings through the years, one of my nieces has shared this story often. The day I packed up and left for my dorm room at the University of Alabama, she was watching out her living room window just across the street. She says, "I thought my world had come to an end. My Aunt Ann was leaving!" It didn't take her long to realize, although I had changed locations, I would be at church with her and all the family gatherings. I would call and drop by often. I would always love her and be a part of her life. Through the years that has been true. From the birth of her children, their graduations, their weddings, her surprise fortieth birthday party, tornadoes, funerals and the extended sickness of other family members, I have been there. Her love and friendship are one of my most prize possessions. I would never leave her nor forsake her.

God spoke to Abraham in Genesis 28:15 KJV, and said, "Behold, I *am* with you and will keep you wherever you go and will bring you back to this land; for I will not leave you until I have done what I have spoken to you." God is not a quitter. His promises are always fulfilled.

Jesus' last words to his followers before he ascended to heaven were, "Go therefore and make disciples of all the nations, baptizing them in the name of the Father and of the Son and of the Holy Spirit, teaching them to observe all things that I have commanded you; and lo, I am with you always, *even* to the end of the age." God's commissioning always comes with the promise of his presence. He never intends for us to be alone or to feel abandoned by him.

In John 14:17-19 NKJV, Jesus promises the Holy Spirit, so we would never be alone. "the Spirit of truth, whom the world cannot receive, because it neither sees Him nor knows Him; but you know Him, for He dwells with you and will be in you. I will not leave you orphans; I will come to you. "A little while longer and the world will see Me no more, but you will see Me. Because I live, you will live also."

It seems that this fear of abandonment is an issue God the Father, Jesus the Son and the Holy Spirit all take seriously. We should too! Feelings of rejection and abandonment are never from God. He loves you and will never forsake you.

Taking the time required to sort out feelings of abandonment is well worth the effort. Understanding "the why" brings the opportunity to be set free. There are many good books addressing this topic. One of my favorites is, *Healing the Orphaned Heart* by Casey Treat. Biblical counseling is also valuable in overcoming the feelings of abandonment, rejection and desertion in relationship to others and God. Having someone to hold your hand and challenge you not to give up makes recovery much easier.

As we approach a new calendar year, a worthy goal for 2019 would be freedom from the fear of rejection, abandonment and being orphaned. Are you ready? Make the decision and begin a new life of freedom from the pain and fear of rejection and abandonment.

Immanuel, God with us

The gift of someone's presence can be an amazing thing. I can think of two examples in my personal life where the gift of someone's presence was life sustaining for me. From these two examples we can better understand the Christmas name of Jesus, Immanuel.

As a sophomore in high school I was notified that my father was up for parole and could possibly be released within weeks. I was terrified. For a few years of my life I had lived free from the fear and threats of his alcohol and drug induced actions. The news of his possible release from prison was overwhelming. My best friend, Margaret, attended school and church with me and she knew the violent history that had defined my young life. She sat with me on the front steps of the church, handed me tissues and held me as I cried through the fear and pain of my father's possible parole. There were no words to "make it better" but the very presence of someone who understood how I felt made life bearable. She gave me the greatest gift, her presence, and I survived that life crisis.

As a minister and conference speaker, I was scheduled to begin a women's conference in north Alabama several years ago on a Friday afternoon. My sixth grandbaby decided to make her appearance on the Thursday before which was usually my travel day. With joy I welcomed her into the family and realized the travel day would now be a travel night. It would be at least midnight before I made it to the hotel. The option to wait until the morning was not possible if I was to make the conference opening. I started the trip with an "I can do this attitude", but as the journey progressed, I became exhausted emotionally and physically. In the darkness a thunderstorm had rolled in and the rain and lightning added to my burden of driving. My brother was aware of the situation and he called to check on me. He could tell I was struggling, and he said, "I'll stay on the telephone with you until you get there so you won't be alone". For over an hour he was my virtual traveling companion. The gift of his presence kept me from being alone and from a possible accident. He gave me the greatest gift, his presence, and I survived the long trip to my destination.

In Matthew 1:22-24 KJV, we find the revelation of the name Immanuel/Emmanuel, "Now all this was done, that it might be fulfilled which was spoken of the Lord by the prophet, saying, Behold, a virgin shall be with child, and shall bring forth a son, and they shall call his name Emmanuel, which being interpreted is, *God with us*. Then Joseph being raised from sleep did as the angel of the Lord had bidden him and took unto him his wife."

In Isaiah 7:14 KJV, we find the prophetic announcement of Immanuel, "Therefore the Lord himself shall give you a sign; Behold, a virgin shall conceive, and bear a son, and shall call his name Immanuel."

When God considered the need of mankind, he saw not only a people who needed redemption from sin but a people who needed the presence of God in the flesh. Jesus's advent, his coming into the world, his presence with us, is a loving key to understanding the Christmas story. After the birth of Jesus, mankind would never be alone during the crisis of life.

John 1: 1-5 and 10-14 KJV, puts it this way. "In the beginning was the Word, and the Word was with God, and the Word was God. The same was in the beginning with God. All things were made by him; and without him was not anything made that was made. In him was life; and the life was the light of men. And the light shineth in darkness; and the darkness comprehended it not. He came unto his own, and his own received him not. But as many as received him, to them gave he power to become the sons of God, even to them that believe on his name: Which were born, not of blood, nor of the will of the flesh, nor of the will of man, but of God. And the Word was made flesh, and dwelt among us, (and we beheld his glory, the glory as of the only begotten of the Father,) full of grace and truth."

Immanuel, *God with us*, is the greatest gift you will receive this Christmas. It will sustain you during every life crisis. The darkness, the storms, the fear, the pain, the terror, the loneliness, the pressure to arrive at your destination, and the fatigue of life is all overcome because Jesus came as Immanuel to be with you. Open your heart to his unfailing love and presence this Christmas.

In times of crisis, trust in the Lord

Like everyone else I have been preparing for the arrival of Hurricane Irma. While it seems, a direct hit will be averted, we will be impacted by the wind and rain associated with a weakening but major tropical storm. This is not a fun scenario!

In addition to water, paper products, meds, gas for the generator and canned goods I have been preparing spiritually for the storm. Strength and spiritual sustenance are as important as any commodity I might purchase. I have prepared with my eyes open and with my eyes closed, focusing on God's faithfulness. I would like to share a few of my staple scriptures with you today. Store them in your heart for the approaching storm and don't be afraid!

Philippians 4:6-8 NLT, "Don't worry about anything; instead, pray about everything. Tell God what you need and thank him for all he has done. Then you will experience God's peace, which exceeds anything we can understand. His peace will guard your hearts and minds as you live in Christ Jesus. And now, dear brothers and sisters, one final thing. Fix your thoughts on what is true, and honorable, and right, and pure, and lovely, and admirable. Think about things that are excellent and worthy of praise."

Isaiah 41:10 NLT, "Don't be afraid, for I am with you. Don't be discouraged, for I am your God. I will strengthen you and help you. I will hold you up with my victorious right hand."

Psalms 91:1-2 NLT, "Those who live in the shelter of the Most High will find rest in the shadow of the Almighty. This I declare about the Lord: He alone is my refuge, my place of safety; he is my God, and I trust him."

Psalms 34: 17 NLT, "The Lord hears his people when they call to him for help. He rescues them from all their troubles."

Psalms 56:3 NLT, "But when I am afraid, I will put my trust in you,

Joshua 1:9 NLT, "This is my command—be strong and courageous! Do not be afraid or discouraged. For the Lord, your God is with you wherever you go."

Psalm 55:22 NLT, "Give your burdens to the Lord, and he will take care of you. He will not permit the godly to slip and fall."

There have been many storms in my life that I have had to ride out, but God has always, always been faithful. He knows everything about me, and you and His desire is for good for His children. One of the scripture passages I learned as a child and I taught my children is found in Matthew 6:19-33. It always "centers" me when I am afraid. It's my generator in the storm, providing power and perspective.

Matthew 6:19-33 NLT, "Don't store up treasures here on earth, where moths eat them and rust destroys them, and where thieves break in and steal. Store your treasures in heaven, where moths and rust cannot destroy, and thieves do not break in and steal. Wherever your treasure is, there the desires of your heart will also be. Your eye is like a lamp that provides light for your body. When your eye is healthy, your whole body is filled with light. But when your eye is unhealthy, your whole body is filled with darkness. And if the light you think you have is actually darkness, how deep that darkness is! No one can serve two masters. For you will hate one and love the other; you will be devoted to one and despise the other. You cannot serve God and be enslaved to money. That is why I tell you not to worry about everyday life— whether you have enough food and drink, or enough clothes to wear. Isn't life more than food, and your body more than clothing? Look at the birds. They don't plant or harvest or store food in barns, for your heavenly Father feeds them. And aren't you far more valuable to him than they are? Can all your worries add a single moment to your life? And why worry about your clothing? Look at the lilies of the field and how they grow. They don't work or make their clothing, yet Solomon in all his glory was not dressed as beautifully as they are. And if God cares so wonderfully for wildflowers that are here today and thrown into the fire tomorrow, he will certainly care for you. Why do you have so little faith? So, don't worry about these things, saying, 'What will we eat? What will we drink? What will we wear?' These things dominate the thoughts of unbelievers, but your heavenly Father already knows all your needs. Seek the Kingdom of God above all else, and live righteously, and he will give you everything you need."

God is faithful and He loves you! Trust Him in times of crisis!

Kindness is a fruit of the spirit

I have had two experiences recently that started me pondering the meaning of kindness. The first was a compliment from a precious lady on my recent trip to South Africa. As she approached me after the weekend conference, she extended her hand and said, "You are so kind". She didn't compliment my teaching, my ministry or my clothes. She complimented what had touched her heart. The second experience came this week as I attempted to help another lady and she exploded in anger and told me what a hypocrite I was and how much she resented me! Wow! It was two totally different experiences. So, what is kindness and how do we develop it?

The Bible list kindness as one of the fruits of the Spirit in Galatians 5:22-23 NLT, "But the Holy Spirit produces this kind of fruit in our lives: love, joy, peace, patience, kindness, goodness, faithfulness, gentleness, and self-control. There is no law against these things!"

Kindness is a fruit that is grown through the work of the Holy Spirit in our lives. We are not born with it, but it begins to grow as we yield to Christian values and as we allow change to occur in our lives. It is often mimicked or used interchangeably with being nice. The difference between being nice and being kind is simple. The nice person is externally motivated. The kind person is internally motivated. The kind person has good self-esteem and isn't looking for approval or praise. The action receives the compliment when you are nice, - "That was a nice thing to do". But with kindness comes that personal identification of "You are so kind".

Please let me share some quotes that will express the breadth and depth of kindness.

"Human kindness has never weakened the stamina or softened the fiber of a free people. A nation does not have to be cruel to be tough." -Franklin D. Roosevelt

"Kindness is the language which the deaf can hear and the blind can see." -Mark Twain

"You cannot do a kindness too soon, for you never know how soon it will be too late." -Ralph Waldo Emerson

"Guard well within yourself that treasure, kindness. Know how to give without hesitation, how to lose without regret, how to acquire without meanness." -George Sand

"A warm smile is the universal language of kindness." -William Arthur Ward

"Constant kindness can accomplish much. As the sun makes ice melt, kindness causes misunderstanding, mistrust, and hostility to evaporate." -Albert Schweitzer

"Love and kindness are never wasted. They always make a difference. They bless the one who receives them, and they bless you, the giver." -Barbara de Angelis

"Remember there's no such thing as a small act of kindness. Every act creates a ripple with no logical end." -Scott Adams

"There is overwhelming evidence that the higher the level of self-esteem, the more likely one will be to treat others with respect, kindness, and generosity." -Nathaniel Branden

"The level of our success is limited only by our imagination and no act of kindness, however small, is ever wasted." -Aesop

"Wherever there is a human being, there is an opportunity for a kindness." -Lucius Annaeus Seneca

"Because that's what kindness is. It's not doing something for someone else because they can't, but because you can." -Andrew Iskander

"You can accomplish by kindness what you cannot by force." -Publilius Syrus

"Always be a little kinder than necessary." -James M. Barrie

"Kind people are the best kind of people." -author unknown

"Three things in human life are important. The first is to be kind. The second is to be kind. And the third is to be kind." -Henry James

"A single act of kindness throws out roots in all directions, and the roots spring up and make new trees." -Amelia Earhart

"One who knows how to show and to accept kindness will be a friend better than any possession." -Sophocles

In the cruel world we live in, let it be our goal to grow in kindness through the tutelage of the Holy Spirit. Let the self-confidence of who we are in Christ become the vine on which much kindness fruit grows!

Let it be - the process of healing

Last night I finished the PBS series entitled, "The Vietnam War". I had recorded the 10 - part series and it has taken me about a month to finish the twenty plus hours of history. I was moved to tears many times as I watched the story of war and its casualties. I was also taught many life lessons by the Holy Spirit as I digested the thirty years of war rehearsed before my eyes.

I was a teen during the war, but I was impacted because my brother served two tours in Vietnam during the mid-sixties. Also, because I watched the news and saw the pictures of a cruel battle that raged amid political corruption, lies and civil unrest. I also had friends, boyfriends, cousins, uncles and aunts who crossed the ocean to another world to fight for my freedom and the halt of communism. I will forever be thankful for their sacrifice and their love for this country.

While there are many things I gleaned from the series, I think the greatest spiritual lesson for me came during the last segment when veterans shared their experience of returning to Vietnam and receiving healing. The courage to visit their worst nightmare, to bring hope to the indigenous people of Vietnam and to help rebuild a country devastated by war was no less than amazing. The rebuilding of Vietnam has come from the veterans who fought there on both sides of the war. It has not come from the politicians who started it and funded it but from those who suffered through it.

It's hard to put into words but I am going to try to share the healing process I watched using three phrases: re-visit, re-vision, redeem. I have used these steps in counseling for many years, but I have never seen it work as I did for tens of thousands of wounded warriors.

To accomplish healing from pain and suffering there must be a time when you re-visit the event. Most of us would rather deny it, minimize it and not talk about. Opening the past often opens shame, condemnation, fear and the feeling of failure. But the wound only heals when it is opened and scrubbed clean by the Holy Spirit. A dirty wound may heal on the outside, but it never heals deeply without cleansing. King David revisited his moral failure with

Bathsheba in Psalm 51: 1-3 NKJV, "Have mercy upon me, O God, According to Your lovingkindness; According to the multitude of Your tender mercies, Blot out my transgressions. Wash me thoroughly from my iniquity and cleanse me from my sin. For I acknowledge my transgressions, and my sin *is* always before me." In the new testament this promise found in 1 John 1:9 NKJV, is foundational in the process of healing. "If we confess our sins, He is faithful and just to forgive us *our* sins and to cleanse us from all unrighteousness." Acknowledgement and cleansing, not denial and blaming others, is the first step in the healing process.

The second step is to re-vision. The Vietnam veterans who returned saw a country side that had recovered from Napalm, bombing and the blood of comrades. They saw green fields, rice paddies, working people and rebuilt dwellings that helped them re-vison their memories. They understood the war that raged in their minds was over. It had happened but it was over. They began to re-vision Vietnam as a place of life and hope not death and destruction. Re-visiting and re-visioning the past put our memories in perspective. Our memories are often bigger than the event and need to be adjusted by the current truth. Not forgotten nor denied, but re-missioned with love, hope, healing and forgiveness.

The third step in the healing process is redemption. Redemption can best be illustrated as a trade. As a child, I pasted S & H green stamps into a book. I collected a certain number of books and marched down to the redemption store and traded them in for something my family wanted and needed. It took work and tasting a lot of awful glue, but I could receive something new and valuable by trading in something as simple as pages of stamps. I didn't want the stamp books, a necessary and real part of the experience, but I wanted the prize of redemption. It was exciting to hand over what I had for what I could receive through the redemption process. My actions impacted all those around me, not just me.

Many veterans, in the process of redemption, have started schools for the children of the Vietnam war. Many have relocated to Saigon/Ho Chin Minh City to teach English and life skills to the fatherless. Many have traded hate for the enemy into friendship. Many veterans are using their medical expertise to redeem those maimed by the war and to start clinics for the citizens' health needs. They are trading in their pain for something extraordinary that changes them and those around them.

So, it is with God's redemption and healing of mankind. It's a trade in; our sin for His forgiveness and healing. When we are willing to honestly re-visit, in faith re-vision and in humility receive redemption, the war in our minds and hearts is over. Peace and purpose replace the devastation of the enemy and we can be free.

Is there a war zone in your life you need to re-visit, re-vision and redeem?

Listening is not easy

Once a week I post on social media a meme meant to encourage my friends in their relationship with others. I call it simply "relationship wisdom". This week it was a message about listening. You may think listening is a natural part of life since we have two incredible ears, but it has become a lost art in our hustle, bustle world.

This week's meme was a simple statement that said, "The biggest communication problem is we do not listen to understand. We listen to reply." Every time I read this I am challenged about my relationships because I am guilty. Before an expression is complete, I have often formulated my reply. I don't want to appear slow of thought or not to have a comeback if needed. It seems to be what we do in the 21st century.

In the Bible there are two hundred and twenty-six verses translated listen and they all have to do with our relationship with God or our relationship with others. They also address who not to listen to!

The Hebrew word for listen is "shama" and can be translated "hear" or "to perceive sound". Biblical Hebrew includes only about 4,000 words, far less than our English language that boasts 100,000 or more words. Therefore, every Hebrew word is like an overstuffed suitcase, bulging with extra meanings that must be unpacked, steamed and hung before wearing or understanding. "Shama" unpacked means "listening, taking heed and responding with action to what one has heard". The concept of hearing God's word and not obeying or responding with action is unbiblical, based on the fullness of the word. Modern-day Christians like the option to obey but this is an erroneous concept. It's like replying before you have listened; you don't really know how to reply because you haven't listened for understanding.

As a Mom, I had to learn to listen to my children's requests with understanding not simple comprehension of the words. For instance, "I'm hungry" might mean "I need food" or it might mean "I'm tired and sleepy and I can only keep going if I get some carbs". Replying before I listened and unpacked the real meaning always produced conflict. I had to consider all the extenuating circumstances of my child's request and respond accordingly. So, it is with all relationships – we have to hear the heart of the message and then respond accordingly.

The following are a few of my favorite humorous quotes about listening for I feel it is important lighten-up this serious topic!

A good listener is a good talker with a sore throat – Katharine Whitehorn.

Congress is so strange. A man gets up to speak and says nothing, nobody listens and then everybody disagrees – Will Rogers.

Make sure you have finished speaking before your audience has finished listening – Dorothy Sarnoff.

The older I grow the more I listen to people who don't talk much – Germain G. Glien

The right to be heard does not automatically include the right to be taken seriously – Hubert Humphrey

In relationship with God and man there is no action more important than listening. Talking to God in prayer using your "give-me" list will produce a shallow, one-dimensional relationship. But listening through the teaching ministry of the Holy Spirit and the word of God will produce an eternal bond that no circumstance in life can break. It develops in you a listen and obey mentality that produces great spiritual fruit. Likewise, listening and really hearing the thoughts of your spouse, your children and your friends will produce lasting relationships that will not easily be broken. Unpack the art of listening today and watch your relationships change!

Living in the Blue

Over the past decade I have spent more time flying than I ever thought I would. I have learned many lessons during those "sky hours" about myself and others. One of my favorite experiences involved a little four-year-old boy. From the moment I boarded the plane he was screaming and resisting his Mom's request that he sit down and buckle up. As I passed his row of seats, I breathed a sigh of relief that my seat was not next to his. Several rows back were still not far enough from the toddler to enjoy the five-hour flight to Denver. I wondered if we would survive as I saw passengers all over the plane roll their eyes, insert ear buds and scowl in the direction of the toddler and his mom.

Take off brought the normal hush, even from the toddler. With the engines roaring and most passengers clutching the arm rest, the silence of take-off was deafening. Several minutes into the assent, the rambunctious toddler spoke for all of us. In a shrill, emotion filled voice he said, "I want down"! The entire plane burst into laughter as the toddler expressed what we all were feeling. We all wanted down! The idea of sitting in a metal tube next to a stranger, traveling in access of 500 miles per hour, six miles above the surface of the earth for five hours didn't make sense, yet, here we were. The toddler went from public enemy number one to everyone's friend. He had expressed in his unguarded behavior what we all felt. Throughout the flight, people read to him, shared stories with he and his mom, provided toys from their children's backpack and rallied to make this flight a pleasant experience for the honest little boy. Love triumphed over judgment because of truth.

Another flight that impacted my life was early in my travel experiences. I noticed when the plane made its ascent through the clouds, on top of the billowing cover was a clear sky of the most magnificent crystal blue. It was breath-taking to see such a pure expanse of sky. Immediately I understood the scripture in Ephesians 2:4-6 NKJV, "But God, who is rich in mercy, because of His great love with which He loved us, even when we were dead in trespasses, made us alive together with Christ (by grace you have been saved), and raised us up together, and made us sit together in the heavenly places in Christ Jesus."

God's grace and His great love for us provide us with the opportunity to live above the storm clouds of this earth - the privilege of "living in the blue". The Greek word for "heavenly places" does not refer to heaven in the sense of it being the destined home of the redeemed. Rather, it refers to the invisible realm that surrounds our present daily situation, the arena or sphere of spiritual action and activity.

If all we can see in life is the earth-bound storm clouds, then we feel disappointed and depressed. If we can see beyond these daily obstacles by faith, there is a realm where we are seated in heavenly places in Christ. Our joy is not based on the clouds we see, but the understanding that regardless of life's difficulties there is a place of peace and rest when we allow ourselves to be seated in heavenly places in Christ Jesus! There is a place of "living in the blue".

In John 16:33 NKJV, the scripture says, "These things have I spoken to you, that in Me you may have peace. In the world you will have tribulation; but be of good cheer, I have overcome the world." The Greek word for tribulation means to put a lot of pressure on that which is free and unfettered. The word is used of crushing grapes or olives in a press.

Christ has made us free and invited us to spiritually sit with Him in heavenly places, but the pressures of this world try to keep us earthbound, disappointed and depressed. I encourage you to take flight, rise above life's clouds and begin "living in the blue"! Your seat has been reserved and the view is amazing!

Love one another with wisdom

The moment I saw him I knew we were meant for one another. As I looked into his eyes, I could tell the attraction was mutual. I had desired a special companion for years, but only recently had I discovered the courage to seek a new love. The excitement was unspeakable as I acknowledged he was the one for me. It was love at first sight! I asked his owner about his pedigree and the selling price. I wrote the check and scooped up the small, furry golden retriever as he kissed my hands in gratitude.

I began polling the family for their ideas of the perfect name. I made the appointment with the veterinarian and started the eleven-year journey of loving and caring for my special pet. I spent many hours serving his needs for food, shelter and attention. He has spent many hours giving me affection and a listening ear without interruption or criticism. He has reinforced my belief that nurturing, and loving is time consuming and often confusing. But it is always well worth the effort.

We truly live in a "throwaway" world: where replacing something is easier and quicker than applying the time and energy to fix a situation or the relationship. This disposable mentally has invaded our marriages and families to such an extent that new spouses and new children are becoming the norm. According to research from the National Stepfamily Resource Center, almost half of marriages each year are remarriages for one or both partners. Most involve children. Half of Americans today are presently or will be in a step relationship in their lifetime. No matter what your status — married or remarried, children or stepchildren, the need to express love and nurturing requires knowledge and dedication.

One of the best resources for understanding how to give love and nurturing to your family is a book by Dr. Gary Chapman, titled *The Five Love Languages*. My oldest son shared this book with me during his college years. It has become a favorite resource for our family and I'm careful to use it with my seven grandchildren. Larry and I both use it in pre-marital counseling and in our personal relationship. Let's take a quick look at each of the five languages discussed in Dr.

Chapman's book. They are words of affirmation, quality time, receiving gifts, acts of service and physical touch.

Words of affirmation are best described as encouraging words, kind words and humble words. For the recipient who is emotionally built up by words of affirmation, a day filled with criticism and fault-finding is almost overwhelming. To feel nurtured and loved, this person needs simple, straightforward statements of affirmation. Nothing fake or unbelievable, just share a truth and watch your relationship change for the better.

Quality time simply means giving undivided attention. Some couples think that they are spending quality time if they are in the same room, sitting next to one another while watching television or flipping through a magazine. That's not quality time – that's quality proximity! Quality time means your spouse or child has your attention, without cell phones, iPads or work lists for a determined period. It usually doesn't take hours and hours but just a few minutes of undivided attention. If spouses and children must compete for your time and attention, eventually they will give up on receiving your love.

Receiving gifts is a love language fundamental to all cultures. For the spouse or child who receives love in this manner, the simplest gift will bring joy and contentment. The price tag doesn't matter as much as the thought behind the gift. When my children were growing up, I had the occasion one day to explain why a four-leaf clover was considered valuable. I explained how rare it was to find one and how fragile the tiny leaves were. In just a few minutes, my youngest son returned with a four-leaf clover as a present for me. I couldn't believe he had found one. I was so touched by his gift that I pressed it, dried it and to this day have it in a little round frame with the date on it. As a mom I felt loved and special because of a gift that literally cost nothing.

Acts of service can be a demanding love language. The spouse or child who needs acts of service to feel loved often smiles when the dishes are done, or the clothes are cleaned and neatly stored. Where we might think of it as a chore or obligation, they perceive someone taking care of their natural needs as an expression of love.

Physical touch is the fifth love language. Research data in child development has shown that babies who are held, hugged and kissed are healthier emotionally than children who are given no physical expressions of love. The adult whose love language is physical touch needs a touch on the hand, a pat on the back, a hug or a kiss every day to feel loved.

Determining the love language of your spouse and your children and applying it diligently will help each family member thrive. It will promote a safe and nurturing environment that will secure the boundaries of your marriage and family. It will make the confusing task of loving and caring for each other much easier. Love one another with wisdom!

Loving people is the plan of God

A few days ago, I returned from a nine-day ministry trip to South Africa. My heart is still full of the joy of sharing Christ with seven churches at their yearly Easter conference. I ordained ten new ministers dedicated eleven babies to Christ. Twenty were baptized on Saturday and sixteen gave their heart to Jesus on Easter Sunday morning. Hundreds received ministry through the preaching of the word of God and through the laying on of hands. I'm not a numbers person but they are important as they represent people – and God loves people!

Somewhere along the Christian road, I think we lost that understanding, becoming more judgmental and more willing to be satisfied with feeling superior in our own eternal safety. Yet God's plan has always been centered on loving people and bringing restoration and healing to all people. All people, even the ones who look different or act different than we do.

Romans 5:8 states "God showed his love for us in that while we were still sinners, Christ died for us." The plan of redemption was a plan of love. A strategy from God to and for the creation he loved. God is no respecter of persons and his heart is to pour love and healing on all mankind.

Now I know you have heard things like "God's going to get you for that", or maybe "God's mad at you for the mistakes you have made" or "God put me flat of my back so I would have to look up" but none of that is true. His primary goal in your life is not punishment but to love you into his kingdom and bring healing to your body, soul and spirit. He's not mad at you!

The following are a few scriptures from the entirety of the Bible that declare God's promises of love and restoration.

Deuteronomy 7:9 NKJV, Know therefore that the LORD your God is God, the faithful God who keeps covenant and steadfast love with those who love him and keep his commandments, to a thousand generations.

Psalm 86:15 NKJV, *But you, O Lord, are a God merciful and gracious, slow to anger and abounding in steadfast love and faithfulness.*

Psalm 136:26 NKJV, *Give thanks to the God of heaven, for his steadfast love endures forever.*

Zephaniah 3:17 NKJV, *The LORD your God is in your midst, a mighty one who will save; he will rejoice over you with gladness; he will quiet you by his love; he will exult over you with loud singing.*

John 3:16 NKJV, *For God so loved the world, that he gave his only Son, that whoever believes in him should not perish but have eternal life.*

John 15:9-17 NKJV, *As the Father has loved me, so have I loved you. Abide in my love. If you keep my commandments, you will abide in my love, just as I have kept my Father's commandments and abide in his love. These things I have spoken to you, that my joy may be in you, and that your joy may be full. This is my commandment, that you love one another as I have loved you. Greater love has no one than this, that someone lay down his life for his friends. You are my friends if you do what I command you. No longer do I call you servants, for the servant does not know what his master is doing; but I have called you friends, for all that I have heard from my Father I have made known to you. You did not choose me, but I chose you and appointed you that you should go and bear fruit and that your fruit should abide, so that whatever you ask the Father in my name, he may give it to you. These things I command you, so that you will love one another.*

Romans 5:2-5 NKJV, *Through him we have also obtained access by faith into this grace in which we stand, and we rejoice in hope of the glory of God. More than that, we rejoice in our sufferings, knowing that suffering produces endurance, and endurance produces character, and character produces hope, and hope does not put us to shame, because God's love has been poured into our hearts through the Holy Spirit who has been given to us.*

Romans 8:37-39 NKJV, *No, in all these things we are more than conquerors through him who loved us. For I am sure that neither death nor life, nor angels nor rulers, nor things present nor things to come, nor powers, nor height nor depth, nor anything else in all creation, will be able to separate us from the love of God in Christ Jesus our Lord.*

Galatians 2:20 NKJV, *I have been crucified with Christ. It is no longer I who live, but Christ who lives in me. And the life I now live in the flesh I live by faith in the Son of God who loved me and gave himself for me.*

Ephesians 2:4-5 NKJV, *But God, being rich in mercy, because of the great love with which he loved us, even when we were dead in our trespasses, made us alive together with Christ— by grace you have been saved.*

1 John 3:1 NKJV, *See what kind of love the Father has given to us, that we should be called children of God; and so we are. The reason why the world does not know us is that it did not know him.*

1 John 4:7-8 NKJV, *Beloved, let us love one another, for love is from God, and whoever loves has been born of God and knows God. Anyone who does not love does not know God, because God is love.*

1 John 4:9-11 NKJV, *In this the love of God was made manifest among us, that God sent his only Son into the world, so that we might live through him. In this is love, not that we have loved God but that he loved us and sent his Son to be the propitiation for our sins. Beloved, if God so loved us, we also ought to love one another.*

The love of God is the most powerful force on earth. It moves mountains and changes lives. It makes the impossible possible. Let 2019 be your year to walk in the love of God and see lives changed.

Mary needed a friend

One of the most important facets of the Christmas story is the relationship between Mary and Elizabeth, two women caught in the whirlwind of spiritual change. Two women who had been chosen by God to usher in the forerunner of the Messiah and the Messiah himself! It's the relationships we have that sustain us through the unbelievable circumstances of life. Like Mary, the mother of Jesus we all need a friend.

In the first chapter of Luke we get a look at the supernatural events happening in the lives of Mary and Elizabeth. Luke 1:26- 45 (NLT)

"In the sixth month of Elizabeth's pregnancy, God sent the angel Gabriel to Nazareth, a village in Galilee, to a virgin named Mary. She was engaged to be married to a man named Joseph, a descendant of King David. Gabriel appeared to her and said, "Greetings, favored woman! The Lord is with you!" Confused and disturbed, Mary tried to think what the angel could mean. "Don't be afraid, Mary," the angel told her, "for you have found favor with God! You will conceive and give birth to a son, and you will name him Jesus. He will be very great and will be called the Son of the Most High. The Lord God will give him the throne of his ancestor David. And he will reign over Israel[1] forever; his Kingdom will never end!" Mary asked the angel, "But how can this happen? I am a virgin." The angel replied, "The Holy Spirit will come upon you, and the power of the Most High will overshadow you. So, the baby to be born will be holy, and he will be called the Son of God. What's more, your relative Elizabeth has become pregnant in her old age! People used to say she was barren, but she has conceived a son and is now in her sixth month. For the word of God will never fail." Mary responded, "I am the Lord's servant. May everything you have said about me come true." And then the angel left her. A few days later Mary hurried to the hill country of Judea, to the town where Zechariah lived. She entered the house and greeted Elizabeth. At the sound of Mary's greeting, Elizabeth's child leaped within her, and Elizabeth was filled with the Holy Spirit. Elizabeth gave a glad cry and exclaimed to Mary, "God has blessed you above all women, and your child is blessed. Why am I so honored, that the mother of my Lord should visit me? When I heard your greeting, the baby in my womb jumped for joy. You are blessed because you believed that the Lord would do what he said."

When God is doing something in your life, you need a friend to share it with. You need someone who is spiritually sensitive and is also walking in obedience to God's will. You need a friend to affirm the impossible not criticize or challenge it! Mary ran to Elizabeth, an older woman she felt like she could trust, and she stayed with her three months. Mary gained strength and comfort from Elizabeth and likewise, Elizabeth gained strength and comfort from Mary. We have no record of their conversations during Mary's visit, but we know when she made her way back to Nazareth, she was ready for the miraculous journey ahead. She was ready to become the mother of Jesus, the Messiah.

Friendships are so important. In our busy world, we trade facetime with our best spiritual friend for activities that seem important. During this holiday season, I encourage you to focus on people not presents. Make a visit with a friend who is also experiencing the supernatural power of God. Find wisdom in your friendships. Find strength and courage in your friendships. Find a greater faith through your friendships.

Helen Keller, blind from birth, wrote this concerning friendship – "Walking with a friend in the dark is better than walking alone in the light," Friendship illuminates the darkness and confusion in our lives.

Walter Winchell, an American newspaper and radio commentator wrote this, "A real friend is one who walks in when the rest of the world walks out." For Mary, a young, unmarried, pregnant girl who was claiming a supernatural assignment from God, finding a friend who would understand was paramount.

Mary needed a friend and so do you! Share what God is doing in your life with someone special today!

Money Matters

The little boy was given the job of sharing a roll of quarters with his two younger siblings. He counted, "One for you and one for me" to his sister. Then he counted, "One for you and one for me" to his younger brother. He had figured out the way to get two quarters to everyone he gave away to his siblings! While you probably laughed at his creative ability, if you had been one of the siblings, you would not have been so impressed!

The top three problem areas in marriage sited by counselors and pastors are communication, sex and money. Money matters keep marriages and families in all social and economic strata in turmoil.

You have often heard the scripture in I Timothy 6:10 NKJV, quoted as "money is the root of all evil". The scripture really says, "For the *LOVE* of money is *A* root of all kinds of evil for which some have strayed from the faith in their greediness and pierced themselves through with many sorrows".

Money is not a living thing; it is merely a tool for living life. It is not inherently evil, but its application can be. Just as a hammer is a great tool for building a house or simply hanging a picture, used improperly it can become a weapon of death.

My nephew, Lance who lives in Alabama is a senior financial planner. He often shares four areas of financial consideration that families need to address. With his permission I want to share these four areas with you to help strengthen your marriage and family.

- The first category, financial position, is probably the hardest because it takes discovery and work on your part. You must take a detailed look at what is coming in and what is going out. You must assess where you are financially and consider changes that need to be made. You cannot progress to the next three categories until this honest evaluation is complete. This is the site of most arguments and strife in families.
- Protection planning is category two. Parents must consider the unthinkable, "What if I don't make it home tonight"? Is there enough provision in savings and insurance to meet the needs of your family and retire any outstanding debt should you no longer be there?

- Categories three and four are so closely related that it's hard to separate them. Taxes, investment planning and retirement are areas where most families need financial counseling from a professional, they trust. Remembering grandma's saying, "Don't put all your eggs in one basket" is not a bad idea either. Diversification and professional planning in today's economy is a must.
- Estate planning is the final category of consideration. In Psalm 37:25 we find a scriptural reference to estate planning, "I have been young and now am old; yet, I have never seen the righteous forsaken, or his descendants begging bread". You want to plan so your children and grandchildren are blessed. A scripture my father-in-law considered one of his "life principle scriptures" is found in Proverbs 13:22, "A good man leaves an inheritance to his children's children." Estate planning, no matter how large or small the volume, is an important consideration for each family. It is an expression of continued love and care.

In the New Testament Jesus has more to say about money than any other topic other than the "Kingdom of God". He talked more about money than he did about heaven and hell combined. Of the thirty-nine parables, Jesus used eleven to share wisdom concerning finances.

In Matthew 6:19-21 NKJV, Jesus says, "Do not lay up for yourselves treasures on earth, where moth and rust destroy and where thieves break in and steal; but lay up for yourselves treasures in heaven, where neither moth nor rust destroys and where thieves do not break in and steal. For where your treasure is, there your heart will be also."
Jesus is admonishing us to have the right heart perspective concerning money! He's not against money. He's for using it as a tool in the kingdom of God to accomplish eternal dividends.

There is no greater blessing than to be financially solid, have your house in order and to be ready to give into the projects of the kingdom of God! Recently my husband and I gave to ministry outreaches in Pakistan and South Africa. In addition, we give to our local church weekly and to individuals as the Lord leads. If we had not decided to live on a budget and manage our finances in a Godly manner, we could have only watched on the sidelines as the kingdom of God grew in these countries.

Money matters can strengthen or destroy your family. Be proactive and tackle those financial issues – today! Plan for your future, your children's future and the kingdom of God.

Name me

I posted several photos of family members with my new puppy on social media. Under the puppy's solo photo, I posted "name me". Little did I know that the posting would receive 109 responses and 95 comments naming my new little friend! Many who posted told me why they chose the name they did. The event reminded me of how important a name is.

Through the years you have probably heard comments like, "she looks like a Sally" or "he looks like a Billy". We give identity and meaning to a person by giving them a specific name. We often nickname a person if their formal name seems too formal or if their personality morphs it. Names are important in any language and any generation. When a waiter or someone in the service industry who wears a nametag approaches me, I often ask them if they know what their name means, especially if it's a biblical name. Usually, they respond with a smile and information about who named them and what the name means. Names are important as they represent purpose, identity, mission, character and personality.

In the bible when the angel appeared to Joseph and told him Mary would conceive a child by the Holy Spirit, the angel also told him what to name the new baby. Matthew 1:18 – 25 NKJV, *"Now* the birth of Jesus Christ was as follows: After His mother Mary was betrothed to Joseph, before they came together, she was found with child of the Holy Spirit. Then Joseph her husband, being a just man, and not wanting to make her a public example, was minded to put her away secretly. But while he thought about these things, behold, an angel of the Lord appeared to him in a dream, saying, "Joseph, son of David, do not be afraid to take to you Mary your wife, for that which is conceived in her is of the Holy Spirit. And she will bring forth a Son, and you shall call His name Jesus, for He will save His people from their sins." So all this was done that it might be fulfilled which was spoken by the Lord through the prophet, saying: "Behold, the virgin shall be with child, and bear a Son, and they shall call His name Immanuel," which is translated, "God with us." Then Joseph, being aroused from sleep, did as the angel of the Lord commanded him and took to him his wife, and did not know her till she had brought forth her firstborn Son. And he called His name Jesus."

Every day of his life, Jesus declared his mission on this earth as "savior" and "God with us" when he introduced himself. As his ministry developed, he became known by at least fifty other names that represented his character and his relationship with mankind. King of kings, good shepherd, bread of life, counsellor, lamb of God, mediator and redeemer are only of few of the names from this extensive list.

One of my favorites "name scriptures" is found in Proverbs 18:10 NKJV, "The name of the Lord *is* a strong tower; The righteous run to it and are safe." Many times, in my life I have run for safety and protection into the name of the Lord. He has never failed me!

People respond to their name. It's easier to get someone's' attention if you call them by name instead of "hey you"! So, it is in our relationship with the Lord. What does He mean to you? How do you communicate with Him? Do you call Him Lord, Savior, Deliver, Redeemer or do you hesitate when you approach him? I encourage you to begin to "name" your relationship with the Lord. Search out His character, purpose, mission, identity and personality in your life. He is waiting to respond!

No Imitations Allowed!

I love sitting on the screen porch listening to the birds as they converse. I usually start and end my day with coffee and this "mini vacation" where I release my cares. I watch the freedom of the birds as they ride the winds and chat with their friends.

I have learned to imitate the cry of the crow and can usually get a shouting match started as I call out from my seat on the porch. The flock of crows gathered in the pecan tree in the adjacent lot always respond to my imitation "caw-caw"!

While working on Thanksgiving dinner yesterday, I hear a loud "caw-caw-caw" and I thought one of the crows had somehow entered my kitchen. My eyes frantically scanned the ceiling, looking for the presumed visitor making such a ruckus. My husband who was standing across the kitchen bar from me was bent over with laughter as he watched my panicked search. He had downloaded a "crow ringtone" on his cell phone and was enjoying every moment of my confusion.

It was a great Thanksgiving Day joke, but it led me to think about how often we fall for the imitation. We are surrounded by imitations that satisfy our five senses. The raspberry tea has imitation flavoring instead of real raspberries. The cool whip is not real whipping cream. The pumpkin spice candle is not made with real pumpkin. The leather sofa is not real but faux leather. The music we hear is often synthesized instead of composed on real instruments. And places you see in the movies, they are constructed sets not real places most of the time. We live in an artificial world, bombarded by imitations that deceive our five senses.

In Hebrews we are admonished to have our senses trained to know the difference between the real and the fake, what is good and what is evil. Hebrews 5:13-14 NKJV, "For everyone who partakes *only* of milk *is* unskilled in the word of righteousness, for he is a babe. But solid food belongs to those who are of full age, *that is,* those who by reason of use have their senses exercised to discern both good and evil."

There is a lot of imitation Christianity going around. It looks like the gospel, smells like the gospel, taste like the gospel, and sounds like the gospel and feels like the gospel but it is an imitation with no power to change the lives of those who meet it! It is marketed as the real thing but lacks the substance and originality of the truth of the word of God.

Your theology should not be based on song lyrics, someone's best-selling book or what a television personality might say. Christianity is not a sound-bite or a meme off Facebook. Christianity is a personal relationship with a living God who has revealed himself in the word of God. There is no substitute for the scriptures which is God's autobiography. It is the express image of the Father, Son and Holy Spirit when studied in its totality, in historical context and in the original languages of Hebrew and Greek. The scripture says of itself in II Timothy 3: 15-17 NLT, "You have been taught the Holy Scriptures from childhood, and they have given you the wisdom to receive the salvation that comes by trusting in Christ Jesus. All Scripture is inspired by God and is useful to teach us what is true and to make us realize what is wrong in our lives. It corrects us when we are wrong and teaches us to do what is right. God uses it to prepare and equip his people to do every good work."

It has never been easier to read and study the Bible. Your smartphone, tablet and laptop provide you with amazing apps for reading the Bible anywhere you go. In a world of imitations, we must be careful to guard our faith and boldly say, "No imitations allowed"!

No longer slaves

I was visiting with an out of town guest yesterday. She asks me what my favorite praise and worship song was. I laughed because I love music and my mental hard drive is filled with song lyrics from every decade. In the Christian file there are hymns from my childhood that mean so much to me. "Great is Thy Faithfulness" and "In the Garden" to mention just a few. The contemporary Christian music explosion that began in the early 1970's provided me with a whole new genre of worship songs to love, memorize and sing. You won't be around me for long before you hear me humming, singing or even whistling the music that's in my heart for the Savior I adore.

I find music allows me to 'cocoon" into the presence of the Lord no matter what circumstance surrounds me. Am I a wonderful singer? No! But the word of God says, "Make a joyful noise unto the Lord" in Psalms 100:1 (KJV). I often qualify in the joyful noise category!

I love music because it helps define and give dimension to my theology. Because of that, I guard my heart and only listen to lyrics that agree with the word of God. I don't sing songs that diminish the character, love and forgiveness of God. My worship stays aligned with what God says about himself and about me!

In response to my guest's question, I told her next week there could be a new favorite but for some time my song of praise has been a work out of Bethel Music, entitled "No Longer Slaves". I can remember hearing Jonathan David and Melissa Helser sing this wonderful song for the first time as I was driving. I pulled off the road and listened with tears streaming down my face. I was touched at the very core of my existence. Here are the lyrics but you can find the video on YouTube if you would like to hear it.

"No Longer Slaves"

You unravel me with a melody
You surround me with a song
Of deliverance from my enemies
'til all my fears are gone

[2x]
I'm no longer a slave to fear
I am a child of God

From my mother's womb
You have chosen me
Love has called my name
I've been born again
Into your family
Your blood flows through my veins

[4x]
I'm no longer a slave to fear
I am a child of God

I am surrounded
By the arms of the father
I am surrounded
By songs of deliverance

We've been liberated
From our bondage
We're the sons and the daughters
Let us sing our freedom

You split the sea
So I could walk right through it
My fears were drowned in perfect love
You rescued me
And I could stand and sing
I am a child of God...

You split the sea
So I could walk right through it
You drowned my fears in perfect love
You rescued me
And I will stand and sing
I am a child of God

Yes, I am
I am a child of God
I am a child of God
Yes, I am
I am a child of God
Full of faith
Yes, I am a child of God
I am a child of God

[3x]
I'm no longer a slave to fear
I am a child of God

In my life and in the lives of countless Christians I have counseled over the years; fear is always at the top of the list of things that hold us back from the fullness of God. Fear is the number one stumbling block in most Christians' lives. We are even afraid of God at times! Nothing could be more opposite from God's plan for us. He wants us to approach as His children, without fear or hesitation.

In Jesus' mission statement on this earth, He says this in Luke 4: 16-21 NLT, "When he came to the village of Nazareth, his boyhood home, he went as usual to the synagogue on the Sabbath and stood up to read the Scriptures. The scroll of Isaiah the prophet was handed to him. He unrolled the scroll and found the place where this was written: "The Spirit of the Lord is upon me, for he has anointed me to bring Good News to the poor. He has sent me to proclaim that captives will be released, that the blind will see, that the oppressed will be set free, and that the time of the Lord's favor has come." He rolled up the scroll, handed it back to the attendant, and sat down. All eyes in the synagogue looked at him intently. Then he began to speak to them. "The Scripture you've just heard has been fulfilled this very day!"

The captives or slaves have been released through the finished work of the cross! It's time to sing the song of deliverance! It's time for Christians to walk free of fear, especially the fear of God. The Father's arms are open wide, and we are called to come in without fear, caution or hesitation. Choose freedom instead of slavery to the bondage of fear!

No thanks! I don't eat apples

Excess has become a lifestyle in America. We are so abundantly blessed with natural resources and technology that there is an unlimited cache of temptations at our disposal. Wealth, authority and freedom brings with it the necessity to know how to overcome temptation. Imagine what would have happened in the garden of Eden if Adam and Eve had simply said to the serpent, "No thanks! I don't eat apples". The fall of mankind and the separation between God and man would have been averted.

Adam and Eve had wealth, authority and freedom but they did not know how to resist temptation. Genesis 2: 15-17 NLT, "The Lord God placed the man in the Garden of Eden to tend and watch over it. But the Lord God warned him, "You may freely eat the fruit of every tree in the garden— except the tree of the knowledge of good and evil. If you eat its fruit, you are sure to die."

Then God created Eve and she became Adam's companion and joint ruler of the beautiful garden God had created. Genesis 2: 18-20 NLT, Then the Lord God said, "It is not good for the man to be alone. I will make a helper who is just right for him." So, the Lord God formed from the ground all the wild animals and all the birds of the sky. He brought them to the man to see what he would call them, and the man chose a name for each one. He gave names to all the livestock, all the birds of the sky, and all the wild animals. But still there was no helper just right for him."

Genesis 2:21-25 NLT, "So the Lord God caused the man to fall into a deep sleep. While the man slept, the Lord God took out one of the man's ribs and closed up the opening. Then the Lord God made a woman from the rib, and he brought her to the man. "At last!" the man exclaimed. "This one is bone from my bone, and flesh from my flesh! She will be called 'woman,' because she was taken from 'man.' This explains why a man leaves his father and mother and is joined to his wife, and the two are united into one. Now the man and his wife were both naked, but they felt no shame."

Companionship and joint authority were God's plan for His new family. When temptation came, they both yielded and disobeyed the Lord who had given them life, one another and the beautiful, lavish garden to enjoy.

Genesis 3:1-6 NLT, "The serpent was the shrewdest of all the wild animals the Lord God had made. One day he asked the woman, "Did God really say you must not eat the fruit from any of the trees in the garden?" "Of course, we may eat fruit from the trees in the garden," the woman replied. "It's only the fruit from the tree in the middle of the garden that we are not allowed to eat. God said, 'You must not eat it or even touch it; if you do, you will die.'" "You won't die!" the serpent replied to the woman. "God knows that your eyes will be opened as soon as you eat it, and you will be like God, knowing both good and evil." The woman was convinced. She saw that the tree was beautiful, and its fruit looked delicious, and she wanted the wisdom it would give her. So, she took some of the fruit and ate it. Then she gave some to her husband, who was with her, and he ate it, too."

Please note that this was not just Eve but a joint rebellion by Adam and Eve. They had both heard the temptation, knew God's will but had walked to the middle of the garden to act on it.

So, it is in our lives, we hear the temptation then we take steps to act on it. At any point we can stop, turn around and walk away if we choose to.

Even arriving at the threshold of temptation we can still choose to stop. Can we do this in our own strength? No, we can't, but God is faithful and always makes a way of escape. I Corinthians 10:13 NKJV, "No temptation has overtaken you except such as is common to man; but God *is* faithful, who will not allow you to be tempted beyond what you are able, but with the temptation will also make the way of escape, that you may be able to bear *it.*"

What would the story of mankind look like if Adam or Eve had resisted the temptation of pride and had simply said to the serpent, "No thanks! I don't eat apples". What will your story look like if you resist temptation and simply declare to the serpent, the tempter, "No thanks! I don't eat apples".

It's time to put God at the center of our garden not temptation. It's time to gravitate to His wisdom and life instead of the temporary fulfillment of our lust. It's time to put the tempter in his place and declare our freedom from the sins that separate us from God.

One generation to another

I was wandering through the store, diligently checking off my list of things to purchase. Out of the corner of my eye I saw a familiar parent in the distance. I smiled as I remembered her beautiful daughter and the charm class, we shared many years before. She was my first student in what would be years of teaching table manners, etiquette and kindness. I doubted the parent would remember me, so I kept my musings to myself.

I proceeded with my shopping list and shortly rounded the corner to the checkout counter. Momentarily, I heard, "Ann?" and I turned to see the parent smiling at me. 'I just wanted to say 'Hi' and thank you again for the impact you had in my daughter's life." We reminisced and enjoyed a few moments of history.

I thought often during the remainder of the day about the importance of teaching young people the social basics and other life lessons. It seems that life is so fast and furious we miss teaching values to the next generation. Between watching television, playing digital games, talking on cellphones, internet surfing and texting there is very little time for "values training". Are we missing something important here? Is society decaying because we have not taught the next generation the importance of a moral compass? Would a nineteen-year-old in Normandy, France have slit the throat of an 85-year-old priest during mass if there had been a moral code instead of internet radicalization?

"Values" is defined as, "a person's principles or standards of behavior; one's judgement of what is important in life". As Christians we have a biblical charge to teach our children and our environment the values of life. I have often heard Christian people say, "Well, this is what I believe but I wouldn't want to tell anyone else what to believe." We have failed to realize that ISIS and other ideologies will gladly recruit and teach our children what to believe.

As Christian parents, we must take a stand and train our children to know God and to know his grace, love and kindness to all mankind. We must help our children to define their life values or a drug dealer, a porn-promoter, a cult leader or a radical terrorist will instruct them in his perverted value system. God gave parents the commission to teach their children how to live. He did not ordain "a village" but godly parents to set the moral compass for their children. Parental teaching and training is not only by words but by example, for children mimic what they see.

Titus 2:1-8 NLT, speaks to the need for generational teaching. *As for you, Titus, promote the kind of living that reflects wholesome teaching. Teach the older men to exercise self-control, to be worthy of respect, and to live wisely. They must have sound faith and be filled with love and patience. Similarly, teach the older women to live in a way that honors God. They must not slander others or be heavy drinkers. Instead, they should teach others what is good. These older women must train the younger women to love their husbands and their children, to live wisely and be pure, to work in their homes, to do good, and to be submissive to their husbands. Then they will not bring shame on the word of God. In the same way, encourage the young men to live wisely. And you yourself must be an example to them by doing good works of every kind. Let everything you do reflect the integrity and seriousness of your teaching. Teach the truth so that your teaching can't be criticized. Then those who oppose us will be ashamed and have nothing bad to say about us.*

The apostle Paul wrote to his disciple Titus, a Greek believer and church leader on the island of Crete, these words of instruction in the New Testament. Taken in context, this passage is invaluable to the Christian family. Don't zero in on a pet doctrine like submission but take the whole text as a "values pattern".

Psalm 78:1-7 shares the wise council of Asaph, a psalmist appointed by King David. *O my people, listen to my instructions. Open your ears to what I am saying, for I will speak to you in a parable. I will teach you hidden lessons from our past—stories we have heard and known, stories our ancestors handed down to us. We will not hide these truths from our children; we will tell the next generation about the glorious deeds of the Lord, about his power and his mighty wonders. For he issued his laws to Jacob; he gave his instructions to Israel. He commanded our ancestors to teach them to their children, so the next generation might know them—even the children not yet born—and they in turn will teach their own children. So, each generation should set its hope anew on God, not forgetting his glorious miracles and obeying his commands.*

We teach and train in our businesses and in education. Let's do it in our homes too, so each generation will have Godly hope and wisdom!

Only Correct the Wise

Have you ever wanted to give advice or correction to someone about their work, their marriage, their children, their finances or perhaps their character? An even more crucial question is "did you do it"? And as Dr. Phil would say, "How did that work out for you?".

I hope you are laughing right now because we have all walked down that slippery slope of good intentions! Giving unrequested advice and having to deal with the repercussions is a lifestyle for most of us. There is a drive within all of us to share our opinion or solution with someone who is struggling in an area where we have "self-perceived expertise".

One of my favorite advice-giving stories happened in a church I attended. The pastor had one of those haircuts where the part was about two inches above the left ear and his hair had grown long enough to be combed completely, yet thinly over the balding area on the top of his head. He was a tall man so I supposed he thought no one could see the bald spot since it was covered with long hair. When the wind blew, he would palm the top of his head and press down to keep the long hair from flying up, revealing the onion smooth top of his head. Although I was fully aware and amused by this choice of hairstyle, I was not about to give advice on an alternate style. However, there was a rather wealthy member of the church who was dying to give advice and correct the situation.

"Don't do it" his wife told him, but it became the only thing he could think of during the church services. One day he approached the pastor and offered to buy him a toupee. The pastor reply, "What do you mean brother? Why would I want a toupee?" Although, full blown denial was driving the conversation, the church member pursued the logic of a nice toupee and a new hairstyle with a part at the correct location on the pastor's head. I think if they had not been in the church, a fist-fight would have developed as both men were offended and certain they were right! The wealthy church member was "just trying to help", and the pastor didn't want help and was completely happy with his hairstyle. He was amazed that anyone would think a change was needed.

Many friends have been separated because of advice that contradicted what the friend wanted to hear. Many arguments and fights have started because of the clash of opinions. Yet, we still share expecting a different outcome from our well-intentioned advice.

Some astounding concepts that will bring relief to this conundrum can be found in Proverbs 9:7-9 NLT, "If you try to correct an arrogant cynic, expect an angry insult in return. And if you try to confront an evil man, don't be surprised if all you get is a slap in the face! So, don't even bother to correct a mocker, for he'll only hate you for it. But go ahead and correct the wise; for they'll love you even more. Teach a wise man what is right, and he'll grow even more wiser. Instruct the lovers of God and they'll learn even more."

We need to seriously consider whether our advice is needed and whether it will be received. We can't thread into another person's life and expect a good outcome when our doing so is motivated by pride. Humility, love, and relationship procures us a voice into another's life. It's not a right but a privilege.

Even a good idea must be sown into a wise heart. We must realize that not everyone wants change. Sometimes it looks like a person wants lifestyle change but what they really want is temporary relief. Only God can give us the wisdom to discern the difference, keep quiet and pray.

Because a person is talking about a problem they have, doesn't mean they are asking you for the answer. Only correct the wise and your life will be so much more peaceful!

Papa, can you hear me?

In the 1980's Barbra Streisand captivated movie goers in *Yentl*, a poignant portrayal of a young Jewish girl who had a passion for studying the word of God. Her Father (Papa) taught her in secret. After his death, she hatched a plan to conceal her female identity and was accepted into a religious school to study the Talmud. Her song, "Papa can you hear me?" represents well the heart cry of those who are crying out to be heard, to know and to be touched by God.

This passion to cry out to God is seen in the Bible in the story of blind Bartimaeus in Mark 10:46-52 NLT. *Then they reached Jericho, and as Jesus and his disciples left town, a large crowd followed him. A blind beggar named Bartimaeus (son of Timaeus) was sitting beside the road. When Bartimaeus heard that Jesus of Nazareth was nearby, he began to shout, "Jesus, Son of David, have mercy on me!" "Be quiet!" many of the people yelled at him. But he only shouted louder, "Son of David, have mercy on me!" When Jesus heard him, he stopped and said, "Tell him to come here." So, they called the blind man. "Cheer up," they said. "Come on, he's calling you!" Bartimaeus threw aside his coat, jumped up, and came to Jesus. "What do you want me to do for you?" Jesus asked. "My Rabbi," the blind man said, "I want to see!" And Jesus said to him, "Go, for your faith has healed you." Instantly the man could see, and he followed Jesus down the road.*

In this short passage we can learn so much about relating to and crying out to God in our time of need. Please let me share nine points from this beautiful interaction.

1.   The beggar was recorded by name......probably because he followed Jesus and became his disciple. Many miracles occurred but most of those who received them were unnamed. When we choose to be a disciple and follower of Jesus, he knows us by name! We are never lost in the crowd.

2.   He called Jesus, "Son of David" declaring publicly for the first time that Jesus was the Messiah. Privately Peter had

declared, "You are the Christ, the son of the Living God". But this was the first public declaration. I often tell people to be successful as a Christian you only must know two things – who you are and who God is.

3.   The crowd told the blind beggar to be quiet. He got louder!! Again, declaring Jesus as Messiah and asking for mercy. There will be people in your life who discourage your passion. Don't listen to them. Seek God with your whole heart!

4.   Jesus stood still. He always stops when we cry out to him in faith. Then Jesus said, "call him and tell him to come me." When Jesus hears our cry, he stands still. He listens for every nuance of our petition. Many times, we want him to come to us, when the admonition is for us to go to him. Don't be lazy in your relationship with God. Get up and go!

5.   The beggar threw off his coat. He left the past behind and came to Jesus. This was a bold statement by Bartimaeus. His coat was issued by the government and it gave him legitimacy and qualified him to collect alms. When Bartimaeus threw off his coat he was declaring his healing and his dependency on Jesus and not the government or the help of other people. He seemed to be saying "goodbye" to all he had known and "hello" to a new life in Christ. He didn't gently lay it down, so he could come back for it. He threw it off as if he would never need it again. He had been heard!

6.   Jesus asked Blind Bartimaeus, "What do you want?" (Wasn't it obvious?) Be ready to declare your needs. Know what you need to ask for or discuss when you come into the presence of the Lord. He always has the right to adjust your wishes if they are not in accordance with the word of God. But he wants you to approach him by faith and boldly ask.

7.   "I want to receive my sight" was blind Bartimaeus' simple, non-begging declaration. He was saying, "I'm tired of who I am, and I want to be whole!"

8.   "Your faith has made you whole, go your way" was Jesus' response to Bartimaeus' declaration. No hoops to jump through, just receive. Faith is the substance, the building block of things hoped for according to Hebrews 11:1 AMP "Now faith is the assurance (title deed, confirmation) of things hoped for (divinely guaranteed), and the evidence of things not seen [the conviction of their reality—faith comprehends as fact what cannot be experienced by the physical senses].

9.   Bartimaeus followed Jesus along the road. Once Bartimaeus had been heard by "Papa" and had received his healing, he followed Jesus. Many times, we cry out and bargain with God only to walk away when we receive. We pick up our old life only returning to Jesus when we have a new crisis. Distance causes us to have to cry out again, when walking along the road with Jesus allows for normal conversation.

Be encouraged in your faith today! Let's learn about approaching "Papa" and walking with him where ever he goes.

Parents are life models

Have you ever yelled at your children saying, "You're just like your mother!" or "you're just like your father!" None of us want to admit it but we can all recognize characteristics in our children that we find annoying in our spouses. It's easy to notice a child's strengths and take pride in the son who is athletic like his father or the daughter who is musical like her mother. However, it's not so exciting when our offspring begin to show signs of our personal negative traits or habits. It's easy to speculate that Betty's critical attitude must come from our husband's side of the family! And surely Johnny's laziness must come from our wife's side of the family!

One of the most difficult parenting lessons I have ever learned came from a long-distance friendship many years ago with another couple. Larry and I absolutely loved our friends. We both had children the same age. We would fellowship as families every opportunity we had because we had so much fun together. Distance and travel did not keep us from spending time together — we were friends! As our children grew into their teenage years, our friends began to have difficulties with their children. This family we loved so much became engulfed in rebellion, alcohol, poor academics, and pregnancy before marriage. To tell you the truth, I was so mad at "those children" I wanted to "take them to the wood shed" for some old fashion attitude adjustment! I was heartbroken for our friends and the difficulties they were facing as parents. Secretly, I was mad at God for allowing this to happen to my friends. As I was praying one day, I was led to a passage of scripture in Luke 6:39-42 KJV, Verse 40 says, "A disciple is not above his teacher, but everyone who is perfectly trained will be like his teacher." I knew God was gently adjusting my perspective. My mind drifted back to the times our friends had shared funny stories of their rebellious years, of their pre-marital sexual experiences and how they almost flunked out of college because of alcohol and drugs. Looking through the eyes of reality instead of friendship, I could see many of those traits still working in this couple's life. I began to see they had made disciples like themselves.

The most difficult parenting lesson became a revelation to me: my children would act like me because I was their teacher. They would do what I did, instead of doing what I said. I had blamed those children and God for hurting my friends. But I was wrong. I asked God for forgiveness and asked Him to show me the things in my life that I was replicating in my children. The self-examination was painful, but it was necessary if I was to be the parent I wanted to be. It's easy to see an alcoholic reproducing an alcoholic or a con-artist reproducing a con-artist, but it's not so easy to see the simple bad attitudes and actions in our lives that we instill in our children. It's much easier to blame worldliness, our in-laws, the church or the media for the way our children behave.

There is no guarantee that a child will not choose a different path when he is out from under his parents' leadership. I've been in many counseling sessions where a son or daughter will admit, "Mom and Dad, you taught me better than this. I chose the wrong thing to do on my own." We all have free will; it is a gift from God and not even He will override it. Just as good Christian training impacts our lives and helps us make wise choices, so will the good moral training of a loving parent impact a child's life forever. The upside of this parenting revelation is this: you can also share all the good attributes you possess with your children and train them in wisdom and godly character. Repeatedly, studies reveal the most important influence in a child's life is their parents. With God's help we can parent in humility and be the teacher who produces great disciples. Parenting is a great privilege and an amazing opportunity!

Planet Romance or Planet Reality?

Larry and I had just finished dinner when we decided to catch the last few minutes of *Wheel of Fortune.* A delighted young lady squealed as she solved the puzzle and won the trip to Barbados. Across the big screen flashed a beautiful beach with the wind gently blowing in the palm trees. The sun perfectly illuminated a thatched hut nestled in the tree line. My heart was beating fast as I thought of the perfect romantic get-a-way. In my mind, I was not decidedly old, but I was a bikini-clad beauty on the most wonderful beach in the Caribbean. Then Larry said, "A big snake could get into that hut without any trouble!" My romantic fantasy came crashing down like a brain concussion. He looked at me and we laughed. Then he said, "Another cruise ship moment?" I said, "Yes" remembering our very first cruise.

One night after a sumptuous candlelight dinner we walked out on the deck of the cruise ship. The weather was perfect, and the gentle wind brought back memories of all the romantic movies I had seen of couples passionately embracing on the cruise deck while the moonlight shimmered across the ocean. I was lost in the moment when Larry looking over the deck railing said, "Someone could fall overboard and never be found!" In shock, I began to back away from the railing and search for the nearest exit.

In both instances, Larry was on "Planet Reality" and I was on "Planet Romance". Many couples struggle in their marriage because the two planets never meet in the same orbit. Larry encouraged me to share our experiences in this article because we have both learned to laugh at one another and we have both learned the value of sharing the orbit.

After forty-eight years of marriage we have learned that men and women are different, and those differences must be understood and valued. In courtship, what we love about the other person often becomes what we despise in marriage. We fail to value the differences and allow our spouse to be the person God created them to be. We forget that He is the author of change not us!

With Valentine's Day approaching, there will be many "romantic" versus "reality" happenings as men and women seek to express their love for one another. In 2015, 18.9 billion dollars was spent on this day of love. We purchased $189 million roses, and $277 million on Valentine cards. Six million people are expecting a marriage proposal this year on Valentine's Day. Not to mention jewelry sales, stuffed animals and chocolate sales, you could say that Americans believe in love!

A Valentine gift icon at our house is a bodacious stuffed monkey, about three feet long, with a heart on his chest and a stuffed velvet rose in his mouth. It was Larry's gift to me several years ago, and he still laughs at it and gives it a place of honor in his office. I generously allow him to keep it as I waited for something a little more "Ann". The "Muen-key" as we call him, is a reminder to not take life so seriously.

On Valentine's Day, there are those who will quietly suffer through the abandonment of divorce, the pain of the death of a spouse and the unrequited love of the single man and woman. There will be no roses, candy, or cards. They have my thoughts and prayers as they process the day.

February 14th is an emotional, expensive day expressing our search for real and lasting love. However, our deepest desires and our fulfillment of value and self-worth can only come through a relationship with Jesus Christ as Lord and Savior. John 3:16 – 17 NKJV, reminds us of the greatness of God's love. "For God so loved the world that He gave His only begotten Son, that whoever believes in Him should not perish but have everlasting life. For God, did not send His Son into the world to condemn the world, but that the world through Him might be saved."

God's love cost more than a few billion dollars. It cost the life of his only son. His love was the ultimate expression of love and sacrifice and with Christ's resurrection, an everlasting covenant of love between God and man was established. We have the answer to our greatest desires of love and fulfillment. It's not reserved for one day a year. It is a constant, unfailing love and friendship relationship between God and mankind.

As men and women seek relationships, there will be those "Planet Romance" and "Planet Reality" moments to laugh about. But our value, our ability to love and forgive, our joy and our security will always be found in Christ.

Pretty is as pretty does!

My husband has a Siamese cat named Bear. He's beautiful and knows it as most Siamese do. I am his secondary master, or should I say secondary servant. Bear has been a member of our household since 2013 and he continues to amaze me with his sneaky ability to do what he wants to do instead of honoring the house rules.

Bear can wow me with extravagant love – kiddie kisses, purring, head bumping and kneading my leg to show his affection. But when it's over, it's over. He is on to doing what he wants to do, the way he wants to do it.

Bear meticulously grooms himself several times a day. It's hard to find a smudge of any kind on his beautiful Seal Point body. He gets his beauty rest as needed and eats precisely according to his internal hunger alarm. In many ways, he is very disciplined. He is pretty, even beautiful but what he does is not!

For almost seven years, Bear has been taught not to scratch the sofa and chairs, not to jump on kitchen counters and not to bring fully alive lizards into the house to play with. Does he observe these boundaries? Of course not! As soon as my back is turned, he involves himself in one of his "NO N0" activities. When I rebuke him, he scampers off uttering guttural noises I can only guess to be kiddy cussing!

His outside disobedience is more dangerous as he has learned to jump the six-foot-high backyard fence. Set up for his protection from other neighborhood dogs and cats, the fence worked fine for a while. Recently, I was sitting on the screen porch and a I heard a loud thud. I knew intuitively it was the sound of Bear throwing his body up against the fence. I peeked around the corner just in time to see him use his paws to scale the last few inches of the fence. He positioned himself on top of the fence and proudly looked over his kingdom. We had tried every way to keep Bear safe within the boundaries of our love, but he wanted to do his own thing.

Several nights later we called Bear to come inside for bed. We repeated the calls through the screen porch to no avail. As we walked back inside to get shoes and a flash light to search for Bear, we heard a yowl at the front door. As we opened the door, Bear scooted past us as if to say, "What took you so long?"

I see in Bear some of my own disobedience to God. It is easy for me to worship and pledge my love on Sunday morning, but when the Lord ask me to stay in some of the boundaries he has set up, it is harder. I think I am like most Christians who commit to being well groomed on the outside like Bear is but are willful and defiant on the inside. We think, "Why would God tell me no? There is nothing wrong with what I want to do!" We don't see what dangers are on the other side of the fence or how our action could hurt or destroy an important part of the household of faith.

Isaiah 1:19-20 (NLT) says "If you will only obey me, you will have plenty to eat. But if you turn away and refuse to listen, you will be devoured by the sword of your enemies. I, the Lord, have spoken!"

James 1:21-22 (NLT) says, "So get rid of all the filth and evil in your lives, and humbly accept the word God has planted in your hearts, for it has the power to save your souls. But don't just listen to God's word. You must do what it says. Otherwise, you are only fooling yourselves. "

There are many other scriptures that caution us about outward and convenient holiness. God wants our whole heart, our love and obedience when it is easy and when it is not. He wants our love and obedience when it makes sense and when it does not. His boundaries are for our good!

Growing up I heard the saying, "Pretty is as pretty does". It is more than a colloquial adage, it is the truth that our outward appearance as a Christian is important, but our actions are equally important.

Remembering Easter as a child

It was Easter weekend fifty-six years ago that I gave my heart to Jesus Christ. Notice I didn't say I joined the church, got some religion or talked to the man upstairs. I simply gave my heart, my young love, to a man named Jesus who died on a cross. It is a decision I have never regretted.

 The gospel message didn't come through a theologian or church evangelist but from my Mom as we dyed Easter eggs. She knew little about the Bible and did not attend church. She simply repeated the account of the crucifixion as it had been told to her. The power of the love of God in the story of the cross pierced my heart and started a lifelong adoration of the one who loved me and gave himself for me.

A few months after that experience, I was invited to attend a Girls' Auxiliary group at the little Baptist church down the road from my house. I started going faithfully and also began attending church on Sunday's. No one else in my family attended church, but I never wanted to miss it. Studying God's word and being with the family of God caused my life decisions to be made with the big picture of eternity in mind.

It wasn't until I was in the sixth grade that I joined the church and was baptized. I never thought I was worthy nor had anything to give to the Lord. The poverty, emotional and physical abuse and turmoil that I lived in caused me to have little confidence that I could be of much value in the kingdom of God. During a spring revival I finally got it. After the message, during the invitation song, "Just as I am", I realized He meant "just as I am" – all He wanted was me. I walked down the aisle and joined the church that had loved and nurtured me through some of life's most horrendous experiences. That night I was baptized. I proudly told my sixth-grade teacher on Monday morning of my decision to follow Christ wherever He led me.

Through the years, the word of God has truly been a lamp to my feet and a light to my path. I think often of the grace I had as a child to give my heart to Jesus. I think of the power of a shared testimony. I think of a life that was totally changed by the amazing love of God. I think and I am thankful.

I would like to share a portion of my story as published in 2007 by Bethany Press in a compilation book entitled, "A Light Along the Way". Please enjoy and be encouraged to share your faith and your testimony with others who are hungry for hope.

In my mind's eye I can see her – a pretty, little girl who looks a great deal like young Jennie in the movie, Forrest Gump. Dishwater blonde hair, green eyes and a compassionate smile describes the little girl I see and know.

Her summer sandals and white socks provide some protection for her feet during the cold, winter walk to elementary school. As they laugh at her less than fashionable attire, the snickers of other children bring a blush to her olive skin. The humiliation of poverty and the rejection of being unwanted and uncared for are ever present invisible garments. The daily walk is worth the trip because at school there will be warmth and safety. There will be hope and relationships that outshine the darkness in this young life.

In a few moments the scene changes, the little girl is once again walking; only this time she is alone. Her path winds up the hill and down a busy street to the local church where she attends services. They are singing her favorite hymn, Holy, Holy, Holy, as she slips into the general assembly preceding Sunday school. She has come to meet with the one person she knows loves her unconditionally. His name is Jesus.

Once again, the scene will change. An excited teen is thinking about beginning the year at a new school. Establishing new friendships without a family history to explain is going to be awesome! The bruising evidence of domestic violence, the unpaid bills, and the familiar hand-me-downs would be neatly covered up in a new beginning.

She still has green eyes, brownish-blonde hair and olive skin but puberty is turning her into a young woman with expectant dreams of love and life. A dark cloud displaces the smile on her face as the telephone rings. The news of her grandfather's death at the hand of her father causes time to stand still. The painful and hopeless expressions of her Mom and brothers leave her speechless. All hope of a restored family or a new beginning is gone. The humiliation is a thousand times greater than ever before. Death would be a sweet escape from the misery she feels. "Is that the answer?" she wonders. In a split second she drops to her knees and cries out to the one who has never let her down. Could there be enough mercy and grace for such a time as this? In the quietness of the moment the answer comes and grace without measure is poured out. Healed in the midst of tragedy, she rises with the peace of God and the courage to live. Infinite, matchless grace has set another prisoner free.

As I consciously return to the present, I close my Bible, and smile as I think of the many times, I have sought for the grace to live in the presence of Jesus. I'm not that little girl anymore. She is a memory that challenges me to encourage others in the truth of God's love. Today I'm an ordained minister, co-founder of a local church, happily married for forty-one years, the mother of two wonderful sons and daughters-in-grace, and grandmother to seven precious grandchildren.

I know I could never have the life I have now, if it was not for that "unmerited favor from the throne room of God" that flowed down to a pitiful, little child who was willing to believe in the unseen and hope in the impossible. His grace truly is amazing!

This Easter on Resurrection Sunday morning, I will be ministering in South Africa. I will be sharing the power of the love of God! I invite you to join me on my Facebook group page, *An Encouraging Word with Ann Nunnally* for photos and updates on the trip.

Revenge is best served cold – or not at all

I stayed up into the wee hours of the morning watching one of my favorite movies, "The Count of Monte Cristo". It is a classic story of an innocent man, Edmond Dantes (Jim Caviezel) who has been betrayed by his friend, separated from the love of his life and falsely imprisoned. His entire mission during his imprisonment is to escape the island of death, *Chateau d'ft,* find the hidden treasure that will make him the wealthiest man alive and then, skillfully enact revenge on those who betrayed him. The compelling story written by Alexandre Dumas has been portrayed on the big screen and on television a dozen times since 1934. The message is always the same. Revenge is best served "not at all".

I was reminded of the actions of Jesus during the crucifixion. Falsely accused by the people he had come to redeem, abandoned by those who had called him friend, Jesus chose to bear all the shame, so we would not have to. He could have appealed to his Father for his freedom and revenge upon those who wanted his death. Matthew 26:52-54 NIV, gives us this insight into Jesus' betrayal and arrest in the Garden of Gethsemane, "Put your sword back in its place," Jesus said to him, "for all who draw the sword will die by the sword. Do you think I cannot call on my Father, and he will at once put at my disposal more than twelve legions of angels? But how then would the Scriptures be fulfilled that say it must happen in this way?"

A legion is approximately 6,000 soldiers. Twelve legions of angels are roughly 72,000. Wow! Talk about revenge! Jesus could have stopped the betrayal and crucifixion before it even started good. But he knew revenge was only the temporary answer to the eternal problem of sin and death. He chose not to use his wealth of angels and position with the Father to dish out revenge.

To tell you the truth, there have been times when I thought revenge was justified. There have been times when I felt "pay back" would be so sweet. But in many cases, I chose the biblical resolution for betrayal found in Galatians 6:7-9 NKJV, "Do not be deceived, God is not mocked; for whatever a man sows, that he will also reap. For he who sows to his flesh will of the flesh reap corruption, but he who sows to the Spirit will of the Spirit reap everlasting life. And let us not grow weary while doing good, for in due season we shall reap if we do not lose heart." God's justice system is unfailing. Those who sow betrayal and harm will themselves reap betrayal and harm. We must not grow weary but wait on due season. Our forgiveness of the individual who has harmed us predicates due season.

It's not easy to let go of the desire for revenge. In many classic works, authors have written about this driving force called revenge and the conclusion is always the same. Only God can extract the justice needed. Man's revenge is never enough.

In the story of the Count of Monte Cristo, God sent several people - the priest, the indebted servant, the lost love to Edmond Dantes to challenge him to forgive and let go of his hate. Only in the end, when his revenge almost cost him everything, did he let go of his right to persecute his betrayers.

We have the choice to react early with love and forgiveness when we are offended or betrayed. As Jesus challenged us in Matthew 26, we can "Put your sword back in its place" and allow God to bring our justice. It's a spiritually healthy and wonderful way to live. Let God be on your side and let him be your vindicator!

Running on empty

It was my first adventure outside the house after the birth of my second child. I was so proud of myself. Getting a two-year-old, a newborn baby and myself ready in time for church was nothing short of a miracle. As our little family started down Highway 84, everything seemed right in the world – until the car coasted to a stop.

I asked my husband, "What's wrong with the car?" Momentarily, he replied, "You forgot to fill up. We are out of gas!" You can image my dismay. It was Sunday morning and thirty-eight years ago most service stations were closed. A passerby came to our rescue and took my husband to buy some gasoline while I occupied a two-year-old and a newborn in a car on the side of the road. How could I have been so dumb? I had prepared for everything except putting gas in the car. I had not noticed I was "running on empty".

That embarrassing experience taught me a lesson that I still live by. Although I now have a car that gives me a yellow caution light reminder when I reach my last 45 miles of fuel, I try to fill up when I reach the half empty mark. Because I travel a good bit, I know I could get caught on the interstate for hours because of an accident and a full tank of gas is a necessity. I don't wait till the last minute to find a service station no matter how pre-occupied I might be.

The embarrassing experience of running out of gas taught me a spiritual lesson also. The effectiveness of my spiritual life depends on fueling up with the word of God and prayer regularly. I've learned to monitor my spiritual fuel tank and actually take action early before I run out of spiritual energy. I've taken note of Bible characters who knew the importance of taking in as well as giving out. Jesus is probably the best example of this re-fueling lifestyle.

In Luke 5:15-17 NLT, we read "But despite Jesus' instructions, the report of his power spread even faster, and vast crowds came to hear him preach and to be healed of their diseases. But Jesus often withdrew to the wilderness for prayer." Although there were many people who needed Jesus' attention, he knew there had to be times alone for re-fueling.

In the Old Testament, King David would often leave his duties and retreat into the presence of the Lord where he gave thanks and questioned God. 2 Samuel 7:17-19 KJV, "Then King David went in and sat before the LORD and prayed, "Who am I, O Sovereign LORD, and what is my family, that you have brought me this far? And now, Sovereign LORD, in addition to everything else, you speak of giving your servant a lasting dynasty! Do you deal with everyone this way, O Sovereign LORD?"

Each month, 1,700 or so pastors leave the ministry. Most just simply run out of spiritual gas because of the demands on their time and their families. According to expastors.com, 90% of pastors report working from 55 to 75 hours per week. 50% feel unable to meet the demands of the job. 70% of pastors constantly fight depression and 50% feel so discouraged they would leave the ministry if they had any other way of making a living. 80% believe pastoral ministry has negatively affected their families. 80% of spouses feel left out and underappreciated. 70% of pastors do not have someone they consider a close friend. 50% of the ministers starting out will not last 5 years. Only 1 out of every 10 ministers will actually retire as a minister.

If pastors are struggling to re-fuel, what is happening to the members of the congregation? We all need to follow the example of Jesus, the busiest minister ever and retreat into the wilderness often to refuel. Don't let the urgent get in the way of the important! Don't run out of spiritual fuel simply because you didn't pull into the presence of the Lord for refueling. The amazing thing is this, "The fuel is free – no charge at the pump". Jesus bought and paid for everything you will ever need in this life when he gave his life on Calvary.

Next month I will become a statistic. I will retire as a minister. Through the past 23 years I have felt all the things listed at expastor.com but I have made it a point to live in my inheritance instead of my circumstances. I have determined that my time of refueling with the Lord is the most important thing in my life. Without him, I have nothing to give and I would simply be an empty tank without potential or power.

I love the invitation in Isaiah 55: 1-3 NLT, "Is anyone thirsty drink— even if you have no money! Come, take your choice of wine or milk—

it's all free! Why spend your money on food that does not give you strength? Why pay for food that does you no good? Listen to me, and you will eat what is good. You will enjoy the finest food. Come to me with your ears wide open. Listen, and you will find life. I will make an everlasting covenant with you. I will give you all the unfailing love I promised to David".

Fill up! It's already paid for and his presence is always open. No need to be "running on empty"!

She said "yes"

Through the years there have been many commercials that end with the phrase "she said yes". In addition to the wedding proposals, books, songs and bridal stores bearing this phrase, last year's credit card commercial featuring Jimmy Fallon and the cutest little girl ever remains a favorite. "She said yes" is a life changing phrase in all its uses. It's simple but always represents joy and change.

At Christmas time, I am always thankful for a young Jewish girl named Mary who said yes. In the details and pageantry of the manger, we often overlook how the story started. It begins when an angel appeared to Mary and asked her to be the mother of Jesus. She said yes! Joy and change began for us all that special day.

Luke 1:27-38 KJV, "And in the sixth month the angel Gabriel was sent from God unto a city of Galilee, named Nazareth, to a virgin espoused to a man whose name was Joseph, of the house of David; and the virgin's name was Mary. And the angel came in unto her, and said, Hail, thou that art highly favored, the Lord is with thee: blessed art thou among women. And when she saw him, she was troubled at his saying, and cast in her mind what manner of salutation this should be. And the angel said unto her, Fear not, Mary: for thou hast found favor with God. And, behold, thou shalt conceive in thy womb, and bring forth a son, and shalt call his name Jesus. He shall be great and shall be called the Son of the Highest: and the Lord God shall give unto him the throne of his father David: And he shall reign over the house of Jacob forever; and of his kingdom there shall be no end. Then said Mary unto the angel, how shall this be, seeing I know not a man? And the angel answered and said unto her, The Holy Ghost shall come upon thee, and the power of the Highest shall overshadow thee: therefore, also that holy thing which shall be born of thee shall be called the Son of God. And, behold, thy cousin Elisabeth, she hath also conceived a son in her old age: and this is the sixth month with her, who was called barren. For with God nothing shall be impossible. And Mary said, Behold the handmaid of the Lord; be it unto me according to thy word. And the angel departed from her." She said yes.

Later in the scripture we find what is called as Mary's song. In her song she rejoices concerning the decision she made and expresses her joy with being chosen to give birth to the Messiah. Luke 1:46-49 KJV, "And Mary said, My soul doth magnify the Lord, And my spirit hath rejoiced in God my Savior. For he hath regarded the low estate of his handmaiden: for, behold, from henceforth all generations shall call me blessed. For he that is mighty hath done to me great things; and holy is his name."

We don't often consider what would have happened had Mary said no. I believe she had the freedom to say no but chose to say yes to God's invitation to be the mother of Christ. Would God have found another way to introduce Jesus to the word? Yes, he would have, but Mary received the blessing because she said yes.

Daily God is looking for an obedient heart open to his will and plan. He is daily looking for those who will answer yes to his request to help further the kingdom of God on this earth. He is looking for those who will overcome their fear of the unknown and who will say yes to his invitation. Let's be like Mary and say yes to God's will in our life. Great joy and change will come when we do!

Are you standing on the promises or sitting on the premises?

I have recently finished a study of the book of Acts. I have been inspired particularly by the second half of Acts which chronicles the three ministry journeys of Paul. Through the years I have studied Acts giving more attention to the first half of the book which deals with the establishment of the church in Jerusalem. This time my love and respect for the apostle Paul has grown as I have seen him "standing on the promises of God" instead of "sitting on the premises of suffering".

None of us like to suffer. But to be honest most of our suffering is minor with someone unjustly saying something bad about us or maybe being unfriended on social media. Paul's suffering was more intense. He summarizes his sufferings in 2 Corinthians 11:22-33, NKJV, [22] Are they Hebrews? So am I. Are they Israelites? So am I. Are they the seed of Abraham? So, am I. [23] Are they ministers of Christ? —I speak as a fool—I am more: in labors more abundant, in stripes above measure, in prisons more frequently, in deaths often. [24] From the Jews five times I received forty stripes minus one. [25] Three times I was beaten with rods; once I was stoned; three times I was shipwrecked; a night and a day I have been in the deep; [26] in journeys often, in perils of waters, in perils of robbers, in perils of my own countrymen, in perils of the Gentiles, in perils in the city, in perils in the wilderness, in perils in the sea, in perils among false brethren; [27] in weariness and toil, in sleeplessness often, in hunger and thirst, in fasting's often, in cold and nakedness— [28] besides the other things, what comes upon me daily: my deep concern for all the churches. [29] Who is weak, and I am not weak? Who is made to stumble, and I do not burn with indignation? [30] If I must boast, I will boast in the things which concern my infirmity. [31] The God and Father of our Lord Jesus Christ, who is blessed forever, knows that I am not lying. [32] In Damascus the governor, under Aretas the king, was guarding the city of the Damascenes with a garrison, desiring to arrest me; [33] but I was let down in a basket through a window in the wall, and escaped from his hands." Wow! Talk about some bad days!

Yet Paul declares to Timothy in 2 Timothy 4:7 NKJV, "I have fought the good fight, I have finished the race. I have kept the faith." Paul was satisfied that he had completed everything God has entrusted him to do. He had not been content until every promise of God to him and his promises to God had been fulfilled. Paul was not pleased with "siting on the premises"

In the last chapter of Acts, we see the torch of the gospel being passed from the unbelieving Jewish nation to the Gentiles. Paul's labor becomes one of peace and provision. Acts 28:28-31 NKJV says, "Therefore let it be known to you that the salvation of God has been sent to the Gentiles, and they will hear it!" [29] And when he had said these words, the Jews departed and had a great dispute among themselves. [30] Then Paul dwelt two whole years in his own rented house, and received all who came to him, [31] preaching the kingdom of God and teaching the things which concern the Lord Jesus Christ with all confidence, no one forbidding him."

Paul did not die in the Roman prison after his three ministry journeys, but he lived free, in his own house, with confidence and with no persecution! This continued activity is recorded in his letters 1 Timothy and Titus.

Paul's ability to stand on the promises of God is a great example to us. We must never quit until all the promises of God given to us are complete. Don't let a little persecution cause you to sit down and give up on what God has called you to do!

The angels of Christmas

I noticed, as I was decorating my Christmas tree this year, how many angel-ornaments I had collected and received as gifts through the years. It occurred to me that angels were such an important part of the Christmas story. Every fabric and medium available had been used in creating my ornament collection: resin angels, hand-made crochet angels, crystal angels, stuffed fabric angels, ceramic angels, gold and pearl angels, hand-carved angels, a Coke can angel and even a copper angel from Mexico. Through the years, these angel-ornaments have continued to declare the Christmas story as real angels had done at the advent of Christ.

What is a Biblical angel? We all have our ideas about angels, but the Biblical description and definition is well worth examining. According to BibleHub.com, an angel is "a messenger, generally a (supernatural) messenger from God, an angel, conveying news or behests from God to men." The term is a masculine noun and carries with it the concept of spiritual authority. This is quite different than the often-portrayed pictures of cute babies with wings, playing a harp on a cloud!

The study of angels or the doctrine of *angelology* is one of the ten major categories of theology developed in many systematic theological works. The tendency, however, has been to neglect it according to an article entitled, *Angelology: The Doctrine of Angels* found at Bible.org.

Here are a few facts and Biblical references concerning angels for your study during this "angel season".

ANGELS WERE CREATED BY GOD: Genesis 2:1 and Colossians 1:16

ANGELS WERE CREATED TO LIVE FOR ETERNITY: Luke 20:36 and revelation 4:8

ANGELS WERE PRESENT WHEN GOD CREATED THE WORLD: Job 38:1-7

ANGELS DO NOT MARRY: Matthew 22:30

ANGELS ARE WISE AND INTELLIGENT: 2 Samuel 14:17 and Daniel 9:22

 ANGELS TAKE AN INTEREST IN THE AFFAIRS OF MEN: Daniel 10:14 and Luke 15:10

ANGELS ARE SUPERNATURALLY FAST: Daniel 9:21 and Revelation 14:6

ANGELS ARE SPIRITUAL BEINGS: Psalm 104:4

ANGELS ARE NOT MEANT TO BE WORSHIPED: Revelation 19:10

ANGELS ARE SUBJECT TO CHRIST: 1 Peter 3:22

ANGELS HAVE A WILL: Isaiah 14:12-14 and Jude 1:6

ANGELS EXPRESS EMOTIONS LIKE JOY AND LONGING: Job 38:7 and 1 Peter 1:12

ANGELS ARE NOT OMNIPRESENT, OMNIPOTENT OR OMNISCIENT: Daniel 10:12-13 and Jude 1:9

ANGELS ARE TOO NUMEROUS TO COUNT: Psalm 68:17 and Hebrews 12:22

MOST ANGELS REMAINED FAITHFUL TO GOD: Revelation 5:11-12

ANGELS WERE CREATED TO GLORIFY AND WORSHIP GOD THE FATHER AND GOD THE SON: Revelation 4:8 and Hebrews 1:6

ANGELS REPORT TO GOD: Job 1:6 and Job 2:1

ANGELS OBSERVE GOD'S PEOPLE: Luke 12:8-9, 1 Corinthians 4:9, 1 Timothy 5:21

ANGELS ANNOUNCED THE BIRTH OF JESUS: Luke 2:10-14

ANGELS PERFORM THE WILL OF GOD: Psalm 104:4

ANGELS MINISTERED TO JESUS: Matthew 4:11 and Luke 22:43

ANGELS HELP AND MINISTER TO HUMANS: Hebrews 1:14

ANGELS REJOICE IN GOD'S WORK OF CREATION: Job 38:1-7 and Revelation 4:11

ANGELS REJOICE IN GOD'S WORK OF SALVATION: Luke 15:10

ANGELS WILL JOIN ALL BELIEVERS IN THE HEAVENLY KINGDOM: Hebrews 12:22-23

SOME ANGELS ARE CALLED CHERUBIM: Ezekiel 10:20

SOME ANGELS ARE CALLED SERAPHIM: Isaiah 6:1-8

THREE ANGELS HAVE NAMES IN THE BIBLE: Daniel 8:16, Luke 1:19 and Luke 1:26

ONLY ONE ANGEL IN THE BIBLE IS CALLED AN ARCHANGEL: Daniel 10:13, Daniel 12:1, Jude 9 and Revelation 12:7

In addition to these interesting facts and references, angels are also referred to as messengers, watchers, supervisors for God, military hosts, sons of the mighty, sons of God and chariots in the Bible.

Christmas began thousands of years ago when God sent an angel to Mary and ask her to become the mother of the Messiah. In her willingness and obedience, Mary wrote the first verse in a love story that has been sung through the ages. A story of a baby born in Bethlehem who would be named Jesus, for he would save his people from their sins.

No wonder I love my Christmas angel-ornaments! They represent that love story that is being shared in word and deed every Christmas. "Hark! the herald angels sing, glory to the newborn king!"

The bill paying ritual

As a teen, I watched a television show called, "The Bob Newhart Show". It was one of my favorites as the comedian, Bob Newhart, played a Chicago psychologist, Bob Hartley, married to Emily. Their high-rise apartment was filled with crazy antics concerning marriage, Bob's patients, their friends and neighbors. One of my all-time favorites in the series was Bob's bill paying routine. He had a certain day, a certain time and he wore the same drab, plaid shirt every time he paid bills. Emily played by Suzanne Pleshette dreaded "bill paying night" for she knew Bob would be at his lowest before and after the last check was written. Through humor, I learned about the pain of owing a debt you could not pay.

Several years later, I heard a Christian song written in 1977 by Ellis J. Crum, that remined me of a debt that I owed and could not pay on my own. Here are the lyrics.

He paid a debt He did not owe
I owed a debt I could not pay
I needed someone to wash my sins away
And now I sing a brand-new song
Amazing Grace
Christ Jesus paid a debt that I could never pay

My debt He paid upon the cross
He cleansed my soul from all its dross
I thought that no one could all my sins erase
But now I sing a brand-new song
Amazing Grace
Christ Jesus paid a debt that I could never pay

O such great pain my Lord endured
When He my sinful soul secured
I should have died there but Jesus took my place
So now I sing a brand-new song
Amazing Grace
Christ Jesus paid a debt that I could never pay

He didn't give to me a loan
He gave Himself now He's my own
He's gone to Heaven to make for me a place
And now I sing a brand-new song
Amazing Grace
Christ Jesus paid a debt that I could never pay

The debt I owed for my righteousness - right standing with God, was so astronomical I could never pay it. But Jesus Christ stepped in and wrote the check in His flesh and signed it with His blood so I could be debt-free in the economy of God! Now that is good news! It's like winning the eternal lottery! Our responsibility is to receive the gift that is ours in Christ. 1 John 1:9 AMP, says, "If we [freely] admit that we have sinned *and* confess our sins, He is faithful and just [true to His own nature and promises], and will forgive our sins and cleanse us *continually* from all unrighteousness [our wrongdoing, everything not in conformity with His will and purpose]."

A relationship with Christ Jesus will assure us that no "account past due" bills will torment us, causing fear and condemnation. A relationship with Christ guarantees us freedom from a bill paying ritual filled with distress and disapproval. Indebtedness is over, having been paid by the grace and mercy of God. We no longer must be "sin conscious" but we can be "righteousness conscious" as adopted children of God.

Do you need "debt counseling"? Talk to a local pastor or friend who can help you settle that account you owe. The price has already been paid and the covenant is waiting for your acceptance!

The centerpiece of the Bible is trust

The middle verse of the Bible is Psalm 118:8 NKJV, which states, "It is better to trust in the Lord than to put confidence in man". How much grief and sadness could you eliminate from your life by believing this scripture?

Personally, I have found a lot of disappointment comes from trusting, putting my confidence in mankind instead of the Lord. It's easy to do because we want the relate to a tangible person who we feel understands us and can have immediate input in our lives. A person we can text or call and get an instant response from. Relating to an unseen God who knows us by faith and spiritual communion is a lot harder. For some people it seems like an impossible task to trust God.

The Hebrew verb for trust, "chasah" meaning "to trust, to hope, to make someone a refuge" occurs thirty-six times in the old testament. The Greek verb for trust "elpizó" meaning "I hope, hope for, expect, trust" occurs thirty-one times in the new testament. The concept of trust is interwoven with other words like faith, hope and expectation throughout the Bible. It is an inseparable concept to the faith walk of a Christian.

Psalm 57:1-3 NKJV, beautifully illustrates trust in King David's life. "Be merciful to me, O God, be merciful to me! For my soul trusts in You; And in the shadow of Your wings I will make my refuge, until *these* calamities have passed by. I will cry out to God Most High, To God who performs *all things* for me. He shall send from heaven and save me; He reproaches the one who would swallow me up. *Selah* God shall send forth His mercy and His truth."

This passage pictures David nestling under God's wings for refuge, in the same way a defenseless, trusting baby bird hides itself under its parents' wings. This is the essence of trust - waiting out the storms of life under the protective wings of God's love and grace while expecting His protection, safety and deliverance. This illustration is also used the old testament in Ruth 2:12, 2 Samuel 22:3, and Psalm 91:4.

Jesus uses it in his lamentation over Jerusalem in Matthew 23:37 NKJV, "O Jerusalem, Jerusalem, the one who kills the prophets and stones those who are sent to her! How often I wanted to gather your children together, as a hen gathers her chicks under *her* wings, but you were not willing!"

The desire to love and protect is an attribute of the Godhead throughout the Bible. Allowing the trinity to do that is our decision. We must learn to nestle in the arms of a capable and willing Savior in order to trust. This concept of trust is the centerpiece of the Bible and our walk of faith.

As a young child I memorized Proverbs 3:5-6 and it became a foundational scripture in my life. "Trust in the Lord with all your heart and lean not on your own understanding; In all your ways acknowledge Him, And He shall direct your paths." In my more mature life, it is still foundational for everything I do. I want to be under His wings every moment of every day.

I like to share what I call "relationship wisdom" daily on social media. Yesterday I shared a video by *FaithPanda* that said, "Sometimes God closes doors because it's time to move forward. He knows you won't move unless your circumstances force you. Trust God always." Many people responded and said they needed to be reminded to trust God.

When life isn't going the way we planned, our first replied should be, "Lord I trust you!". Nestle under the Lord's wings, safe and protected in His love! He's got this!

The force of time in our lives

In the classic movie, *Casablanca* (1942), the world was given a song that has endured almost a century. Only recently did I watch the movie, but through the years I have always loved the lead song, "As Time Goes By". It somehow comforts and assures me that love and relationships will prevail against the calendar of time.

Just this morning I thought, "where has the time gone"? How can it be the end of March? What happened to January and February? I'm still struggling to write 2019 instead of 2018 and a quarter of the year has passed. Have I been a good steward of these past three months, seeking as Frank Sinatra crooned, "the fundamental things apply, as time goes by".

Identifying the fundamental things of life and applying them is a monumental task. We have so many choices and distractions that vie for our time and attention. It's very easy to get caught up in the urgent instead of the important. The nature of time is forward motion and unless we insert the important issues of life in that forward motion, we will come to the end of 2019 without accomplishing the fundamentals. I would like to suggest three fundamentals of life that deserve a place in the forward motion of time.

Our relationship with God should always be number one or the center of our life. Out of the understanding of God's love and grace toward us, flows the ability to give love and grace to those around us. A twenty-four-hour day should not pass without our making an investment in our relationship with God. Bible study, prayer, praise and worship and contemplative meditation are the basics of a vibrant relationship with God. Knowing Him will help you develop your life on a strong, immoveable, eternal foundation that will endure the force of time. Matthew 22:37 NKJV, challenges us to a total love experience with God instead of a Sunday morning visit. "Jesus said to him, 'You shall love the LORD your God with all your heart, with all your soul, and with all your mind. This is *the* first and great commandment."

Secondly, nurturing our relationship with our spouse is fundamental. If we don't invest in the person we married, time and activities will cause us to drift apart and eventually lose sight of the fundamental love that brought us together. In marriage counseling, I always ask, "Are you treating one another the way you did when you were dating?" Is the passion to put one another above everything else still there? Often because of time pressure, the answer is no. Loving your spouse is an example of the spiritual relationship between Christ, the bridegroom and the church, the bride. Ephesians 5:25-33 "Husbands, love your wives, just as Christ also loved the church and gave Himself for her, that He might sanctify and cleanse her with the washing of water by the word, that He might present her to Himself a glorious church, not having spot or wrinkle or any such thing, but that she should be holy and without blemish. So husbands ought to love their own wives as their own bodies; he who loves his wife loves himself. For no one ever hated his own flesh, but nourishes and cherishes it, just as the Lord *does* the church. For we are members of His body, of His flesh and of His bones. "For this reason, a man shall leave his father and mother and be joined to his wife, and the two shall become one flesh. "This is a great mystery, but I speak concerning Christ and the church. Nevertheless, let each one of you in particular so love his own wife as himself, and let the wife *see* that she respects *her* husband."

Finally, our children should be a fundamental, important investment of our time and focus. Although the training and development stage of loving children garners the first eighteen years of their life, the relationship continues, as long as the calendar flips from month to month and year to year. The Bible teaches extensively about training and developing children. They deserve a fundamental place in our life and their fair share of our time. Ephesians 6:1-4 NKJV, states "Children, obey your parents in the Lord, for this is right. "Honor your father and mother," which is the first commandment with promise: "that it may be well with you and you may live long on the earth." And you, fathers, do not provoke your children to wrath, but bring them up in the training and admonition of the Lord."

As I look back over the first three months of 2019, I must ask myself, "Have I taken care of the fundamental things in life as time has gone by?" Have I lived at the tyranny of the urgent or have I made my relationship with God, my spouse, and my children the most important thing in my life? Have I given my job, my ministry, other relationships and possessions a place of lesser importance and focused on these three fundamentals?

Time will continue its forward motion. Value what is important and fill each moment with the fundamentals as time goes by!

The Gift

This is the season for gift giving. Christmas giving is a tradition that started to mimic the greatest gift ever given, the babe of Bethlehem. God's love gave us a Savior, so our love gives during the Christmas season to those we care about. The gifts don't have to be large or costly, but they do need to flow from a heart of love.

Growing up in a broken home, riddled by poverty and sin, my gift giving and receiving experiences had to be redeemed. The experiences I had as a child and young adult were negative to say the least. Yet I somehow fell in love with Christmas and developed the mindset that it was not about what I received but about those I could give to. Shopping with my Mom for Christmas meant I would buy and wrap all the socks and underwear to be given to the family, including my own. Christmas morning was not a "wake-up and be surprised" event as my gifts were necessities which I had bought and wrapped!

My best gifts came from members of my church family who wanted to bless me. I remember one year a dear family lost a child in a car accident a few months before Christmas. They spent the money they would have spent on their son on me. The three-foot-tall, walking doll they gave me stayed by my side through the years and followed me to my dorm room at the University of Alabama. Agreeably this was not a cool thing to do, but the doll always reminded me that someone unselfishly loved me.

Most of the early gifts I gave were homemade but created with lots of love. My list was long because I wanted everyone in my sphere of influence to feel the joy of appreciation and love. That is still the approach I take to the season. It's all about loving others not about getting what I want. It's about relationships, friendships and caring.

My only detour from this mindset came a couple of years after I married. My mother-in-law asked me what I wanted for Christmas. She said, "Anything you want, cost doesn't matter". Larry and I had moved into our first home in a neighborhood of shady, curving roads. It was the perfect, low traffic place to enjoy long bike rides and the beauty of being outside in South Georgia. The only problem was I didn't have a bike – had never had one all my life! So, when the question was posed, I said, "I want a bicycle"! I anxiously awaited the Christmas gathering where I would have my first ever bicycle. I would be able to cycle without borrowing someone else's bicycle. Even though I was in my early twenties, I felt like a child anticipating Christmas for the first time.

When Christmas dinner was over and the presents under the living room tree were opened, my mother-in-law said to me and my sister-in-law, "I have something else for you two downstairs in the closet". We ran down the stairs. I didn't know what Cathy had asked for, but I knew my first-ever bicycle was waiting for me just a few steps away! We swung open the big walk-in closet door to find two sets of luggage, one for me and one for Cathy. Major disappointment swept over me. While I could certainly use the luggage, my heart was filled with dreams of a new bike. Somehow Christmas had become about me and not about others and the pain was unbearable. I recovered enough to make it through the visit, but I knew my "what I want" detour had ended. I recommitted to the true meaning of Christmas and I have never been disappointed since.

This Christmas guard your heart as Proverbs 4:2-23 NKJV, says, "My son, give attention to my words; Incline your ear to my sayings. Do not let them depart from your eyes; Keep them in the midst of your heart; for they *are* life to those who find them, and health to all their flesh. Keep your heart with all diligence, for out of it *spring* the issues of life."

Let your self-image be determined by your relationship with Christ not by the gift you might or might not receive. Make Christmas about the joy you can give others. Trust God to provide for your needs and wants because he knows, and he cares. Remember the essence of Christmas is the coming of a Savior. "For unto us a Child is born, unto us a Son is given; and the government will be upon His shoulder. And His name will be called Wonderful, Counselor, Mighty God, Everlasting Father, Prince of Peace. Of the increase of *His* government and peace *there will be* no end". Isaiah 9:6-7 NKJV.

The heavens and the earth declare His glory

A friend of mine in Minnesota posted a beautiful photo last night of the Harvest Moon reflecting on one the 10,000 lakes the state is known for. It was breathtaking. A kiss from heaven and a reminder of the changing seasons of life. It prompted memories of some of the other spiritual lessons I had learned during my ministry trips to Minnesota. It brought a smile to my face and reminded me of the scripture in Psalms 19:1-4 NLT, "The heavens proclaim the glory of God. The skies display his craftsmanship. Day after day they continue to speak; night after night they make him known. They speak without a sound or word; their voice is never heard. Yet their message has gone throughout the earth, and their words to all the world."

Another friend in Alabama mentioned the early morning Harvest Moon and it's wonder. Although the approaching hurricane may obscure it's view for a few days, it can never dethrone the majesty of God declared by His creation. The storms of life may hide His glory for a season, but they can never destroy who He is and His message of love to mankind. He's shouting "I love you and I made this beautiful world for you to enjoy! Trust me!"

According to National Geographic News, "In the Northern Hemisphere, the harvest moon is the closest full moon to the fall equinox, usually on or around September 22. That means the harvest moon usually occurs in September. But this year the September full moon appeared on the 6th, separating it from the fall equinox by 16 days. The October 5th full moon arrived only 13 days after the fall equinox, making it a closer pairing."

When we put down our cell phones, turn off the television and listen to the hum of creation, the song that's being sung is always a declaration of God's glory and love. Don't miss His song over you!

Another lesson I learned from my trips to Minnesota involved the great Mississippi River. Growing up in the south, I had always assumed the Mississippi River originated below the Mason Dixon Line. I had flown over the massive river and all its tributaries many times heading westward. I always booked a window seat on the airline and I anxiously waited for the first sighting of the mighty Mississippi. My amazement was always without words. On a ground level trip to New Orleans, LA I had stood inches from the retaining wall that held back the 200 feet deep and 11-mile-wide Mississippi River. Little did I know that one day I would visit the natural spring in Minnesota that births the enormous river that flows 2,300 miles draining 31 US states and 2 Canadian provinces.

USA Today shares this report about the origin of the Mississippi at Lake Itasca, MN "Kneel at the water's edge and you can hear it; a whispery gurgle as the water moves across the rocks that delineate the river from the lake. A downstream riffle is barely discernible, but it is clearly the beginning point. "

Having knelt at the headwaters of the Mississippi, less than 3 feet deep, I can see how God takes our trickle of faith and turns it into a mighty force for the kingdom of God. His creation declares the baby steps of faith have the potential to become a deep current watering, feeding and providing for the multitude of people in its path. His creation declares His glory.

It's easy to fill our hearts and minds with fear and anxiety especially if you watch television or use internet services for news. Nothing good is usually at the top of the reporting cycle. But if we look and listen to the ever-unfolding revelation of God in creation then we can have peace and rest knowing that God is greater than any problem sinful man is able to conjure up. His order and design are for His children to have an abundant life. Believe!

 His promise and perspective are proclaimed by Jesus in Matthew 6: 25-33 NLT, ""That is why I tell you not to worry about everyday life—whether you have enough food and drink, or enough clothes to wear. Isn't life more than food, and your body more than clothing? Look at the birds. They don't plant or harvest or store food in barns, for your heavenly Father feeds them. And aren't you far more valuable to him than they are? Can all your worries add a single moment to your life? "And why worry about your clothing? Look at the lilies of the field and how they grow. They don't work or make their clothing, yet Solomon in all his glory was not dressed as beautifully as they are. And if God cares so wonderfully for wildflowers that are here today and thrown into the fire tomorrow, he will certainly care for you. Why do you have so little faith? "So, don't worry about these things, saying, 'What will we eat? What will we drink? What will we wear?' These things dominate the thoughts of unbelievers, but your heavenly Father already knows all your needs. Seek the Kingdom of God above all else, and live righteously, and he will give you everything you need."

The holidays require adaptability

My brother lost his battle with cancer in October 2009. During the last six months of his life we talked every day. He was six years older than me and I grew up thinking he hung the moon. His outgoing personality and his service during the Viet Nam war set him apart from all others in my mind. He never met a stranger and he loved life recklessly. He defined his faith in God as being "a whosoever" from John 3:16 KJV, "For God so loved the world, that he gave His only begotten son that whosoever believeth in Him should not perish but have everlasting life." He knew it was not what he could do but what God had done through Jesus Christ that made the eternal difference.

I was speaking at women's conference in St. Louis, Missouri the first weekend in October. I had ridden the shuttle from the airport and settled into my hotel. The onsite restaurant would be the location of my evening meal and after I placed my order, I called my brother. The conversation lasted the entire meal and proved to be the tête-à-tête that changed the last days of his life and mine. He shared his hope of enjoying one last Thanksgiving with his family and friends before death called his name. I knew that he was weak and very sick, and I didn't see how he could possibly enjoy Thanksgiving a full two months out. I began to pray and as I started the weekend of ministry, I asked the Lord to show me what I could do for my brother to make his wish for a final family Thanksgiving come true.

The women's weekend was amazing, but I flew home without an answer to my prayer. I knew God had heard me and in the right moment the wisdom would come. It did in a still, small idea that said, "Declare Thanksgiving as October 12 and have it early". Delighted with the idea, I checked with my family and all were available to have early Thanksgiving in honor of my brother. We would adapt, adjust to the new conditions, be versatile, changeable and make a final wish come true.

I called my brother and told him we would be having Thanksgiving early and he was to invite fifty friends and family members for the celebration. I began preparing the food and set the party in motion.

Everyone rallied around this brother, uncle, dad, spouse and friend to fulfill his wish.

Little did I know the morning after I arrived with Thanksgiving goodies, a pain event would cause me to watch my brother being loaded in the back of an ambulance and taken to hospice. I wondered if I had heard the Lord correctly and if my timing was too late. Hospice kindly offered a meeting room and allowed the feast to happen as planned. My brother sat with family and friends and enjoyed Thanksgiving one last time. A few days later he stepped into eternity as a "whosoever".

The holidays require adaptability. To navigate life successfully, you must be willing to adjust to new conditions and be able to modify for a new use or purpose. Unhappy people are those who are inflexible and must do it the way it's always been done. This attitude can make the holidays unbearable. In counseling, I often encourage divorced parents, or disassociated family members to realize it's not the day on the calendar but the relationship that matters the most. Recently, I shared with a young man who will be having December 25 for the first time without his children, that Christmas is everyday your children wake up and gaze into your eyes, the eyes of a loving father. It's not a day but a relationship. Birthdays, Thanksgiving and Christmas can be celebrated anytime you agree to the details and plan accordingly. Too many times bitterness and resentment take root in our hearts when loved ones don't perform the way we want them to.

One of the greatest miracles in the Bible occurred when Jesus and the disciples were adaptable. The feeding of the five thousand, recorded in all four gospels, is an example of great adaptability. The disciples wanted to send the people away because it was late, they were hungry and there was no food. Jesus said, "What do you have?" Adaptability often appears in what you have, not in what you want or in what you have always done. God's endless supply is always ready as you pray and believe for His wisdom. He can take two fish and five loaves of bread and feed the multitudes if you will allow him too!

Make the decision to be adaptable and you will experience miracles and have real holiday joy this year!

The Honor of Your Name

"I face your Temple as I worship, giving thanks to you for all your loving-kindness and your faithfulness, for your promises are backed by all the honor of your name." TLB Psalm 138:2

As I read this scripture this morning, I couldn't help but contemplate the portion that says, "your promises are backed by all the honor of your name".

So many times, in my life my promises have lacked sound backing. It's so easy to make promises to my children and my spouse and never follow through. Or at best use some excuse to wiggle out of my promise when it becomes inconvenient. It seems that I am not alone.

The news cycle is full of broken promises in the political arena. The names of those seeking leadership in our country are tainted by years of broken promises. It's not a Democrat problem, a Republican problem or an Independent problem but a sin problem.

The scriptural definition of sin is to "miss the mark" or to "fall short of the intended target". The intended target for us as Christians is to back our promises with the honor of our name. Part of the brokenness of society is to produce homes where a child's inherited name means nothing - where fathers and mothers pass on names associated with drugs, alcohol, abuse, financial ruin, unforgiveness and failure on all levels. This is the deepest of poverty and it can never be fixed by government legislation. It can only be fixed by a life-changing experience where our spiritual poverty and shame is replaced as we are adopted, given a new name by the loving-kindness and faithfulness of a Savior whose promises are backed by the honor of His name.

As children of God, we have a responsibility to carry the name of 'Christian" with honor. Christian literally means "little anointed one". We are to look and act like our big brother, Jesus. When the world and those in relationship with us, see us they should not see promise breakers but promise keepers. For strife and division to permeate the Christian church is to our shame. It can only happen when are representing ourselves and not the family name. God is not the God of strife and division but of peace and unity.

When my two sons were growing up, I used to tell them that their actions represented not only themselves but the family name. I challenged them to consider their actions at school and in the community and to represent the Nunnally name with honor. I wanted them to understand that they had all the privileges and inheritance of being a Nunnally but also all the responsibility of carrying the name with honor. As Christians we have all the blessings and inheritance of the kingdom of God, but we also have the responsibility to represent well the name of the Father, the Son and the Holy Spirit.

The scripture states in Proverbs 22:1 NAS, "A good name is to be more desired than great wealth. Favor is better than silver and gold." I challenge you to begin to build a good name for yourself and for your family. If you do, the wealth will take care of itself as you seek the kingdom of God first!

The Importance of Friendship

I walked into the church foyer on Sunday and was greeted by a young, twenty-something friend.   After cooing over her new baby, exchanging hugs and laughter, she said, "Let's have lunch and catch up!" My heart smiled as I thought of time with my exuberant friend. I proceeded through the entrance to the sanctuary and was met by another friend and ministry partner of twenty-five years. We quickly began to share and concluded with 'Let's do lunch or coffee this week and catch up!" Friendships are very important.

On Monday, I was led in counseling to advise a young woman who was lonely and struggling, to develop Godly friendships. Also, on Monday, a call from Texas confirmed that a friend and ministry partner of forty-five years would be traveling to Mexico with me to hold a woman's conference. On Tuesday, a friend from Alabama called and said, "Let's go to the beach for a few days in May!" Chronologically new and old friendships need to be cared for and valued.

I have been working since February on setting up a 'Girls Weekend Get-away Cruise" so moms, daughters, sisters and friends could enjoy three days away from the responsibilities of life. Three days to nurture those relationships and friendships that refresh and heal our female souls.

The philosopher Aristotle said, "In poverty and other misfortunes of life, true friends are a sure refuge."

The Mayo Clinic published an article as part of its "Healthy Lifestyle-Adult Health" division, which headlined "Friendships: Enrich your life and improve your health". It addressed the benefits and the difficulties of friendships and some ways to meet new friends.

It seems to me the Holy Spirit's spotlight has been on friendships this entire year! As I have been cultivating my friendship garden, I have also been investing in my friendship with Jesus. I don't say that to minimize the deity of Christ or bring Him down to my level. I write this in faith because of Jesus's declaration to His disciples in John

15:15 NIV, "I no longer call you servants, because a servant does not know his master's business. Instead, I have called you friends, for everything that I learned from my Father I have made known to you." Jesus has called me and you His friend. Think about that! He is willing to spend time with us, walk and talk with us about the plans, desires and relationships of the Kingdom of God. What an amazing friendship we have been given to develop and nurture!

Throughout the Old and New Testament, the theme of friendship is governing. We have missed this at times for we have boiled down our relationship with God to mean "salvation" when God has always wanted friendship and an active relationship with mankind.

Please consider these passages from the Bible that spotlight friendship between God and man.

Genesis 3:8 NKJV, "And they heard the sound of the Lord God walking in the garden in the cool of the day, and Adam and his wife hid themselves from the presence of the Lord God among the trees of the garden". Adam and Eve were used to the sound of God's friendship but hid after their disobedience to His commands.

Genesis 5:24 NKJV, "Enoch walked with God; and he *was* not, for God took him."

Genesis 6:9 NKJV, "This is the genealogy of Noah. Noah was a just man, perfect in his generations. Noah walked with God.

James 2:23 NKJV, "And the Scripture was fulfilled which says, "Abraham believed God, and it was accounted to him for righteousness." And he was called the friend of God."

Friendship in both the Old and New Testament is a strong, covenant word. It is not a flighty, inconsistent term but one that is explained in John 15:13 NKJV, "Greater love has no one than this, than to lay down one's life for his friends." A true friend loves when it's not convenient.

Is it time for us to work on our natural friendships? Is it time for us to work on our friendship with God? I think it is!

The Marriage Map

We did it again! Larry and I went on vacation and got lost. It's not that we didn't plan, print out a map and get verbal directions. We thought we knew everything we needed to know about getting to the cabin on the Tennessee mountaintop. But alas, we were missing a few very important details.

As I drove west, watching the sun go down, I prayed that I would find my, home away from home, before darkness settled in. I could only imagine being lost in the dark mountains with no street lights and only bears and Tennessee wildlife to ask directions from. We finally arrived.

After a good night's sleep, I began to think about my experience. In many ways it reminded me of marriage. Caring for all the known details, most couples drive off from their wedding ceremony sure of their destination. After all, "How hard could it be to find Happily-Ever-After? Others may have lost their way, but *we know* what we are doing." Years later in confusion, frustration, and disappointment a couple may abandon the search for Happily-Ever-After, get stuck in traffic on Boring Boulevard or drive straight to Divorce-land.

When we discovered that we were lost on our vacation trip, we did two things—we stopped and asked for directions and we bought a detailed map. We had to stop wandering and come up with a plan that would get us to our destination. It's funny but the directions we received were all different. Some said, "Take Hwy 8 until you run into Hwy 11, then follow it to Hwy 30 and you'll see it on the right." Others said, "Just take Hwy 27 to Hwy 127, then left on Hwy 30 and it will be on the left." It was frustrating to hear so many options when we didn't have someone we trusted personally to guide us. One grocery store clerk said, "I've never been there, but I think you..." I wanted to faint!

It's easy to get marital advice from someone at work or from a family member. You can quickly get several options on how to fix your marriage by mentioning your need. Those directions might get you to Happily-Ever-After or they might cause you to become more confused and lost than ever. You should ask yourself if the person giving the advice has ever been there. Does this person know the Creator of all marriages?

We looked at the map we bought and began to analyze where we had missed our first turn. It took precious time to retrace our route, but it was the only option if we wanted to get back on track. At one point we had to go back down the interstate for several miles and take an exit that we had passed. Then we had to climb one mountain and go back down it in order to climb the mountain we were looking for. It was slightly humiliating to think we had been so dumb.

Getting your marriage back on track will take time and a concerted effort. Examining the mistakes, you have made will be humiliating and you will, no doubt, feel dumb. But that is not the issue. The outcome of a sound marriage will be well worth the time you invest and the uncomfortable feelings you endure. The following advice may be helpful to those looking for direction in their marriage:

- Go to the Wonderful Counselor (Isaiah 9:6). Pray together and ask God to give you direction for making your marriage what you want it to be. God gives grace to the humble (James 4:4-10)
- Seek wisdom from a natural counselor that you both trust. (Proverbs 11:14)
- Set aside the time to study your marriage map. Discuss where you took wrong turns, being careful not to blame one another, but sharing the responsibility for your situation. This will mean time without the children. It may mean simplifying your schedule, so you can have time to discuss your marriage map.
- Commit to the destination of Happily-Ever-After, your original choice, and determine that no other destination will do. (Mark 10:2-9)
- Fast and pray, using your spiritual weapons. (Ephesians 6:10-18)

It's never too late to redeem a marriage if both the husband and wife are willing to make corrections, forgive one another and seek God's love as the glue that holds a marriage together. Don't stay "lost" and don't give up on "Happily-Ever-After"!

The Original Green-eyed Monster

Hollywood has become very adept, skilled and proficient at creating monsters and aliens. When I was a child the scariest thing on the movie screen was King Kong, a rattling skeleton over a vat of acid or some green slime that oozed under the door to attack you! Now with the advent of computer generated –CG, we have a myriad of monster and alien possibilities.

I'm not a sci-fi fan but my husband is. He thrives on the creative imagination of aliens with glowing red eyes, mechanical body parts like the Borg Queen and mutant abilities to transform from a normal looking human being into a supernatural, powerful villain. I watch with him through the lattice-work of my fingers across my eyes. Ugh.... I need a drama or a chick-flick!

In ministry I have encountered some of the fiercest of monsters living within beautiful human beings, controlling and destroying their lives and their relationships. The green-eyed monster of jealousy and envy are always the worst and sometimes the hardest to uproot.

Our society encourages the development and growth of comparison, envy, strife and jealousy. Social media enables us to know what others have and to want it. Marketing tells us we will be happy, sexy, and young again if we purchase certain products. We live in a very discontented world even though we have more resources at hand than any former generation. We have perfected the lust for more and buried the peace of contentment.

There are many scriptures that address this spiritual problem, but I would like to share just a few from the Old and New Testament. All are from the King James Version of the Bible.

Psalms 37:1 Fret not yourself because of evildoers, neither be you envious against the workers of iniquity.

Proverbs 14:30 A sound heart is the life of the flesh: but envy the rottenness of the bones.

Proverbs 27:4 Wrath is cruel, and anger is outrageous; but who is able to stand before envy.

Song of Solomon 8:6 Set me as a seal on your heart, as a seal on your arm: for love is strong as death; jealousy is cruel as the grave: the coals thereof are coals of fire, which has a most vehement flame.

Romans 13:13 Let us walk honestly, as in the day; not in rioting and drunkenness, not in chambering and wantonness, not in strife and envying.

1 Corinthians 3:3 For you are yet carnal: for whereas there is among you envying, and strife, and divisions, are you not carnal, and walk as men?

1 Corinthians 13:4 Charity suffers long, and is kind; charity envies not; charity brags not itself, is not puffed up,

Philippians 2:3 Let nothing be done through strife or vainglory; but in lowliness of mind let each esteem other better than themselves.

James 3:14 But if you have bitter envying and strife in your hearts, glory not, and lie not against the truth.

James 3:15 This wisdom descends not from above, but is earthly, sensual, devilish.

James 3:16 For where envying and strife is, there is confusion and every evil work.

Many a marriage has suffocated a slow death because of jealousy and envy. Many a prisoner has awakened incarcerated after a binge of jealously and envy. Many a life has ended in suicide because of the lies of jealous and envy. Many a relationship with a friend has ended abruptly because of jealousy and envy. There is no happiness in a life engulfed with jealousy and envy.

The antidote for this poison is love. Not the love we associate with cookies and pets but the Godly love that lays down its life for another. This kind of love can only flow from a person who knows who they are in Christ; a person who is safe in the presence of God and needs little more. The very act of loving another uproots the monster of jealousy and causes freedom to come. Just suppose what would happen in your life if you wrote down the things you were jealous for and envious of and set about to make them happen in someone else's life? Are you always wanting a new dress? Buy one for someone who has lost everything in a flood. Are you always wanting a new tool? Buy one for the hardworking laborer who needs a new tool to continue to provide for his family. Are you always wanting to have a bigger house? Use what you have and provide a place for a small group Bible study. Laying-down-your-life love will break the bondage of jealousy and envy every time! Let's kill those green-eyed monsters and walk free in peace and joy!

The rest of the story concerning Job

Paul Harvey was an American radio broadcaster who was famous for a segment called "The Rest of the Story". During his Monday through Friday programs, Harvey would present a story on a variety of topics, holding back the key element until the very end. He would conclude with "and now you know the rest of the story". His broadcasts reached as many as 24 million people a week.

Today I would like to share with you a key element, the rest of the story concerning Job. We have all heard sermons concerning the problems Job had. We have all identified with his loss and misfortune. We have all recognized the poor judgement and input Job received from his friends during the tragedies and hardships he experienced. We know his wife, in her own pain and loss advised Job to curse God and die. We have often been advised that God sent the calamity to Job to test him and his faithfulness. But what is the rest of the story?

Job is the oldest book in the Bible. It predates the Pentateuch; the first five books of the Old Testament and it is an example of a Gentile in covenant with God before Abraham's covenant. Its authorship is often attributed to Moses but there is some speculation that likely it was written by another unknown author. Job is a book that must be studied in its entirety, in the context of one man's relationship with God that precedes the cross of Calvary or it becomes easy to misunderstand God.

In Job chapter 1:1-3 NLT, we are introduced to Job, "There once was a man named Job who lived in the land of Uz. He was blameless—a man of complete integrity. He feared God and stayed away from evil. He had seven sons and three daughters. He owned 7,000 sheep, 3,000 camels, 500 teams of oxen, and 500 female donkeys. He also had many servants. He was, in fact, the richest person in that entire area."

Later scriptures speak of the tragedies, anguish, pain and that overtook the life and family of Job. But the end of the story occurs in the final chapter of Job. It is a testimony to the power of forgiveness and the extravagant redemption of God.

Job 42:7-16 NLT, "After the Lord had finished speaking to Job, he said to Eliphaz the Temanite: "I am angry with you and your two friends, for you have not spoken accurately about me, as my servant Job has. So take seven bulls and seven rams and go to my servant Job and offer a burnt offering for yourselves. My servant Job will pray for you, and I will accept his prayer on your behalf. I will not treat you as you deserve, for you have not spoken accurately about me, as my servant Job has." So Eliphaz the Temanite, Bildad the Shuhite, and Zophar the Naamathite did as the Lord commanded them, and the Lord accepted Job's prayer. When Job prayed for his friends, the Lord restored his fortunes. In fact, the Lord gave him twice as much as before! Then all his brothers, sisters, and former friends came and feasted with him in his home. And they consoled him and comforted him because of all the trials the Lord had brought against him. And each of them brought him a gift of money and a gold ring.

So, the Lord blessed Job in the second half of his life even more than in the beginning. For now, he had 14,000 sheep, 6,000 camels, 1,000 teams of oxen, and 1,000 female donkeys. He also gave Job seven more sons and three more daughters. He named his first daughter Jemimah, the second Keziah, and the third Keren-happuch. In all the land no women were as lovely as the daughters of Job. And their father put them into his will along with their brothers. Job lived 140 years after that, living to see four generations of his children and grandchildren. Then he died, an old man who had lived a long, full life."

Although Satan may test us and bring loss and suffering, God is the redeemer, liberator, rescuer, savior! When we humble ourselves before him, resist the temptation to walk in unforgiveness and doubt, he restores our loss plus more! And that is the rest of the story concerning Job.

The Sin Cycle

Why do I do the things I know I shouldn't do? Why do others fail when it comes to being obedient to God's will in their life? Why is it so easy to end up at the wrong place, at the wrong time doing something that will only bring disaster in my life?

These have been valid questions through the ages as Christians and non-Christians alike struggle with sin. I believe even the mightiest among us struggle with sin and its consequences.

Even the apostle Paul in the book of Romans laments this question. Romans 7:14-24 NLT, "So the trouble is not with the law, for it is spiritual and good. The trouble is with me, for I am all too human, a slave to sin. I don't really understand myself, for I want to do what is right, but I don't do it. Instead, I do what I hate. But if I know that what I am doing is wrong, this shows that I agree that the law is good. So, I am not the one doing wrong; it is sin living in me that does it. And I know that nothing good lives in me, that is, in my sinful nature. I want to do what is right, but I can't. I want to do what is good, but I don't. I don't want to do what is wrong, but I do it anyway. But if I do what I don't want to do, I am not really the one doing wrong; it is sin living in me that does it. I have discovered this principle of life—that when I want to do what is right, I inevitably do what is wrong. I love God's law with all my heart. But there is another power within me that is at war with my mind. This power makes me a slave to the sin that is still within me. Oh, what a miserable person I am! Who will free me from this life that is dominated by sin and death?" Thankfully in the next chapter, Romans 8, Paul gives us the answer and the essence of our new covenant in Christ Jesus.

Understanding the sin cycle in our life is paramount to walking in victory. There are four stages of the sin cycle and at any point our forward motion toward sin, missing God's perfect will in our lives, can be halted. Pride, rebellion, deception and perversion are the four stages.

- The origin of sin is pride. The Greek word for pride, is "huperephania *–to appear over.* It means haughtiness, arrogance, ostentatious pride bordering on insolence and a disdainful attitude toward others. It is used in Mark 7: 14-23 as Jesus challenges the Pharisees concerning the sin in their hearts.

- Rebellion follows pride in the sin cycle. The Greek words for rebellion are "antilogia - *a contradiction* and apeithes – *unbelieving or disobedient*." While we often see rebellion as a person's outward appearance or outward actions, the scripture explains rebellion as a matter of the heart. When we walk in pride and appear to know more than God, we easily move into contradiction, unbelieving and disobedient behavior.

- Deception in the Greek "exapatao – *to seduce wholly, deceive.*" This stage in the sin cycle describes someone taken in, and enslaved by Satan, sin and darkness. While we use the term "deception" lightly, the scripture assigns great force to it using terms like completely and wholly.

- Perversion is the final stage of the sin cycle. It is the Greek word, "diastrepho – *opposite from the shape/form it should be, twisted.* At this point in the sin cycle we have become someone we were never intended to be. We are shaped by sin and twisted.

There are many individual examples in the Bible of this sin cycle but for this article I would like to point you to the book of Judges and the sin cycle of an entire nation. Please take time to read the whole book of Judges and note the cycle of apostasy, oppression, repentance and deliverance experienced by the nation of Israel. The key to the plight of the nation is found in the repeated verses of Judges 17:6, 18:1, 19: 1, and 21:25 "In those days there was no king in Israel; everyone did what was right in his own eyes."

When we live, without making Jesus Christ our Lord and king – doing what is right in our own eyes – we enter the sin cycle and live the defeated life. At any stage along the way we can repent of our pride, humbly ask Jesus to become the "the boss, the king" and live a victorious life led by the Holy Spirit.

The acceptable sin of offense

There are several stories in the Bible about offense. In the Old Testament we find the story of Naaman in 2 Kings chapter 5 who needed healing from leprosy. He heard that Elisha the prophet could heal him, so he traveled from Syria to Israel seeking freedom from his dreaded disease. Elisha sent his servant to meet Naaman and told him to dip seven times in the Jordon River and he would be healed. Naaman was highly offended! After all, he was an important commander in the Syria army and was used to being given much respect. Elisha didn't even come to the door upon Naaman's arrival and then had the gall to ask Naaman to wash in the dirty Jordon River. Only at the urging of his servant did Naaman carry out Elisha's request. He rose out of the Jordon River completely healed! Offense almost stole Naaman's provision for healing!

In the New Testament we find a sad story of offense that wasn't repented from and left many in the town of Nazareth unhealed. Jesus had been teaching the parables on the kingdom of God to multitudes for many days as recorded in Matthew 13. With great wisdom and power, he had explained the mysteries of his father's kingdom. At the end of the chapter we find this story of offense.

Matthew 13: 53-58 NLT, "When Jesus had finished telling these stories and illustrations, he left that part of the country. He returned to Nazareth, his hometown. When he taught there in the synagogue, everyone was amazed and said, "Where does he get this wisdom and the power to do miracles?" Then they scoffed, "He's just the carpenter's son, and we know Mary, his mother, and his brothers—James, Joseph, Simon, and Judas. All his sisters live right here among us. Where did he learn all these things?" And they were deeply offended and refused to believe in him. Then Jesus told them, "A prophet is honored everywhere except in his own hometown and among his own family." And so, he did only a few miracles there because of their unbelief."

It's easy to note three key words in this passage - offense, honor and unbelief. Although the people in Nazareth heard Jesus's wisdom and saw his miracles they couldn't get beyond their natural reasoning and knowledge. They were offended and took what is often called the bait of Satan. In the Geek language the noun for offense is "skandalon". It refers to the bait stick of a trap. When we become offended, we take the bait from the trap, springing the lever that's designed to kill the prey. It's kind of like the cheese on the mouse trap! Once the mouse nibbles on the cheese, the trap-stick is released and well, you know the results. In the New Testament this word, "skandalon" is always used metaphorically of "that which hinders right thought or conduct".

The second notable word in this passage is honor. The word for honor is "hadar" and it means splendor, glory, adornment, magnificence and beauty. The verb form means "to make splendid". The people of Nazareth had the opportunity to honor, make splendid their native son, Jesus. But instead they dishonored him. They made the son of God illegitimate, a mere local family member. When we are in offense against someone, we dishonor them with our words and our actions. Instead of making them splendid we tear them down, often publicly.

The third word in this passage is unbelief. Offense steals faith. It stops your offense, forward motion and it keeps you in status quo, unfulfilled and without the miracle you need. You cannot believe in a person, a spouse, a child or even a God you are offended with.

If I had to give you a basic reason as to why we get offended I would say it is because someone didn't do what we wanted the way, we wanted it done. Offense is an acceptable sin today because we feel like we have the right to "have it our way".

Let's be like Naaman who repented and received not like the citizenry of Nazareth who chose offense over their miracles! It's easy to eat the cheese but remember it's a trap!

The Supernatural Gift of Giving

The feeding of the five thousand is probably the most well know miracle in the Bible. It is recorded in all four gospels: Matthew 14:13-21, Mark 6:30-44, Luke 9:10-19, and John 6:1-14. It is immortalized in books, tapestries and various art expressions. It comforts all of us as it declares God's supernatural provision in our lives.

One ingredient in this miracle of provision is the gift of giving by a young boy with five loaves and two fish. There have been many messages preached on this young boy's willingness to share but I think we have often missed the fact that his actions were motivated by a supernatural, God-given gift listed in Romans 12.

Romans 12: 3-8 NKJV, "For I say, through the grace given to me, to everyone who is among you, not to think *of himself* more highly than he ought to think, but to think soberly, as God has dealt to each one a measure of faith. For as we have many members in one body, but all the members do not have the same function, so we, *being* many, are one body in Christ, and individually members of one another. Having then gifts differing according to the grace that is given to us, *let us use them:* if prophecy, *let us prophesy* in proportion to our faith; or ministry, *let us use it* in *our* ministering; he who teaches, in teaching; he who exhorts, in exhortation; he who gives, with liberality; he who leads, with diligence; he who shows mercy, with cheerfulness."

The seven gifts listed in this passage are the motivational gifts given by God to individuals. I believe this passage explains an old testament passage in Jeremiah 1:4 - 5 NKJV, "Then the word of the Lord came to me, saying: "Before I formed you in the womb I knew you; Before you were born I sanctified you; I ordained you a prophet to the nations." God's plan, and purpose in our lives is set in motion before we are born. His calling in our lives is rooted in one of these seven gifts. Out of that gift will flow our ministry in the kingdom of God.

The young boy provided through the gift of giving with liberality, the catalyst for this most famous miracle of Jesus. I'm sure there were others in the multitude of people who had prepared lunch for the day, but it was this little boy who gave supernaturally.

Another Biblical example of someone who gave supernaturally is connected to the resurrection of Jesus. In all four gospels, this miracle is recorded, and it is foundational for the establishment of the New Covenant. The supernatural gift giver in these passages is a man named Joseph of Arimathea.

Mark 15:42-46 NKJV, "Now when evening had come, because it was the Preparation Day, that is, the day before the Sabbath, Joseph of Arimathea, a prominent council member, who was himself waiting for the kingdom of God, coming and taking courage, went in to Pilate and asked for the body of Jesus. Pilate marveled that He was already dead; and summoning the centurion, he asked him if He had been dead for some time. So, when he found out from the centurion, he granted the body to Joseph. Then he bought fine linen, took Him down, and wrapped Him in the linen. And he laid Him in a tomb which had been hewn out of the rock and rolled a stone against the door of the tomb."

According to the Jewish historian, Josephus, the traditional burial for a person who had been crucified was an open grave with all others receiving the capital punishment of crucifixion. For the Jews, it was important to bury the dead before the Sabbath, thus the petition of Joseph of Arimathea for Jesus' body.

In Luke, Joseph of Arimathea is called "a good and upright man." In Matthew, he is called "a rich man". We know Joseph's giving fulfilled the prophetic passage in Isaiah 53:9 AMP, "His grave was assigned with the wicked, But He was with a rich man in His death, Because He had done no violence, nor was there any deceit in His mouth."

The supernatural gift of giving provided the location for the resurrection of Jesus Christ! I doubt Joseph of Arimathea really understood what he was providing. He was simply moving in the spiritual gift of giving, imparted to him by God and activated at this moment in history. Many undocumented stories are recorded of Joseph's generosity but this gift of the tomb for Jesus' burial is forever noted.

The gift of giving, whether in the life of a young boy with a picnic lunch or a wealthy, respected man of community statue, is integral to the miracles, past and present in the kingdom of God.

The Unexamined life is Mediocre

I had a lot of goals for my children in their developing years. They had to learn to eat with a fork, tie their shoes, read and write, develop social skills and learn how to enjoy life. But the most important development, preservation and growth skill I taught them was "how to think". This is not a skill that can be measured by visual examination but by the results of the choices they would make in life.

I didn't want to give them a list of "do this, don't do this" but I wanted to give them the ability to use their God given intelligence. I wanted them to be able to "think" instead of just responding to a list of acceptable behavior and achievement. I wanted them to understand that God had given them an incredible brain that could work for them in making choices and having a life of hope and fulfillment.

One of my favorite quotes says, ""The unexamined life is not worth living." -Socrates. It is a wise person who lives a life of self-examination and choice-making based on contemplative thought and prayer.

I recently attended the *American Association of Christian Counselors World Conference* where Dr. Caroline Leaf was a plenary speaker. Her work on faith and the power of the brain has been revolutionary in Christian circles for several decades. I was reminded in her presentation that the brain gives us the ability to "self-examine" every ten seconds. Six times a minute our brain gives a pause to reflect and consider our forward motion. I had to ask myself, "Do I take advantage of this gift of self-evaluation, or do I go with the flow of life not thinking beyond my nose?" Also, I had to ask myself "Does this concept appear in scripture and is it something that strengthens my faith?"

So many times, in the Bible we hear Godly leaders challenging the nation of Israel in the Old Testament and the church in the New Testament to "choose"; elect to use their God given intelligence to make a decision that will produce life and health.

Deuteronomy 30:15- 20 NLT, "Now listen! Today I am giving you a choice between life and death, between prosperity and disaster. For I command you this day to love the Lord your God and to keep his commands, decrees, and regulations by walking in his ways. If you do this, you will live and multiply, and the Lord your God will bless you and the land you are about to enter and occupy. "But if your heart turns away and you refuse to listen, and if you are drawn away to serve and worship other gods, then I warn you now that you will certainly be destroyed. You will not live a long, good life in the land you are crossing the Jordan to occupy. "Today I have given you the choice between life and death, between blessings and curses. Now I call on heaven and earth to witness the choice you make. Oh, that you would choose life, so that you and your descendants might live! You can make this choice by loving the Lord your God, obeying him, and committing yourself firmly to him. This is the key to your life. And if you love and obey the Lord, you will live long in the land the Lord swore to give your ancestors Abraham, Isaac, and Jacob."

Matthew 7:13 NLT, "You can enter God's Kingdom only through the narrow gate. The highway to hell is broad, and its gate is wide for the many who choose that way." Even eternity is a choice for the individual.

Romans 6:15-16 NLT, "Well then, since God's grace has set us free from the law, does that mean we can go on sinning? Of course not! Don't you realize that you become the slave of whatever you choose to obey? You can be a slave to sin, which leads to death, or you can choose to obey God, which leads to righteous living."

In I Corinthians 4:20-21 NLT, the apostle Paul challenges the Corinthian church to make a choice. "For the Kingdom of God is not just a lot of talk; it is living by God's power. Which do you choose? Should I come with a rod to punish you, or should I come with love and a gentle spirit?" Paul was certain the believers at Corinth had the God-give ability to pause, reflect and make the right choice.

In closing, I would like to ask you as I did my children many years ago to "think". Consider your life, your eternity and the results of the decisions you have made and through this self-examination "choose life"!

The value of a human life

The events of this week have caused me to ponder the value of human life. On several fronts, human life has been defined and measured, but I believe God's perspective is the most important. Let's explore this together for a few moments.

According to a *Bloomberg*, article written in October of 2017 by Dave Merrill, the following statistical values have been assigned to a human life when the government calculates a cost-benefit analysis of an imposed regulation.

The Environmental Protection Agency - $10 M

Food and Drug Administration/Health and Human Services - $9.5 M

Department of Agriculture - $8.9 M

Every government agency develops a VSL, Value of Statistical Life, to use to rate the benefits of a proposed regulation. Other studies vary, but the current assumed value of a human life is about $9.6 M.

The lost of life this week in the Broward County school shooting of seventeen students and teachers amounts to a staggering 163.2 M using government statistics. This is not to mention the potential within these students to solve problems like a cure for cancer or aids, the race to Mars or the Middle-East conflict. The wasted potential is immeasurable. The pain and suffering of parents, siblings and friends is vast. The shock to our American culture is incalculable. We were all reminded that human life is a precious commodity.

In the spiritual analysis of this horrific event, we must consider God's perspective and value of human life. In Genesis 1:26-27 NLT, we find out that the creation of mankind was God's idea. "Then God said, "Let us make human beings in our image, to be like us. They will reign over the fish in the sea, the birds in the sky, the livestock, all the wild animals on the earth, and the small animals that scurry along the ground." So, God created human beings in his own image. In the image of God, he created them; male and female he created them."

In Genesis 2:7 NLT says, "Then the Lord God formed the man from the dust of the ground. He breathed the breath of life into the man's nostrils, and the man became a living person." Our breath came from the breath of God! We were intentional, created with a purpose and a plan, created from the heart of God. Our value was determined by God himself when he gave us his breath! We have shared eternal value which cannot be measure in dollars and cents.

In the commandments given to Moses on Mt. Sinai, God specifically said in Exodus 20:13 NLT, "You must not murder". The Hebrew word used here for murder is "ratsach". It means "to dash to pieces, manslayer, murder." The word carries the implication of premeditation and does not refer to killing in general but refers to murder. This would be different from legal or acceptable forms of killing like execution, war or self-defense. The word carries the concept of illegal or premediated murder.

God spoke to the prophet Jeremiah and said, "For I know the plans I have for you," says the Lord. "They are plans for good and not for disaster, to give you a future and a hope." God never intended for his creation to experience disaster like we witnessed this week in the school premeditated slayings. God's plan for all his children is an abundant life in Christ Jesus.

According to Wikipedia, "Abundant life" is a term used to refer to Christian teachings on fullness of life. It is not an organized movement or a unique doctrine, but a name applied to the teachings and expectations of the groups and people who follow the teachings. Abundant life teachings may include expectations of prosperity and health but may also include other forms of fullness of life when faced with adverse circumstances. The term "abundant life "comes from the Bible verse in John 10:10, "I am come that they might have life, and that they might have it more abundantly." Abundant life refers to life in its abounding fullness of joy and strength for mind, body and soul.

The word of God teaches over and over about God's great love, value and provision for his children. He sets an eternal value on my life and yours. I believe not only did earth grieve over the school shootings, but heaven also mourned as Biblical laws were broken.

It's our responsibility to teach every man, woman, boy and girl on this earth that premediated murder is wrong, life is precious, and life is a gift from God. Let's champion the Biblical value of life – it is priceless!

The Veil of Calvary

There are many facets to the story of the cross of Calvary. Volumes could be written on each detail of the passion of Christ and his resurrection. Each facet has multiple meaning and purpose in the life of a Christian.

A look at the torn veil of Calvary is well worth the study for its meaning is profound in a person's relationship to God. The scripture in Luke 27:45-54 NKJV, gives this account of the mid-Friday afternoon events of the crucifixion.

"Now from the sixth hour until the ninth hour there was darkness over all the land. And about the ninth hour Jesus cried out with a loud voice, saying, "Eli, Eli, lama sabachthani?" that is, "My God, My God, why have You forsaken Me?" Some of those who stood there, when they heard that, said, "This Man is calling for Elijah!" Immediately one of them ran and took a sponge, filled it with sour wine and put it on a reed, and offered it to Him to drink. The rest said, "Let Him alone; let us see if Elijah will come to save Him." And Jesus cried out again with a loud voice and yielded up His spirit. Then, behold, the veil of the temple was torn in two from top to bottom; and the earth quaked, and the rocks were split, and the graves were opened; and many bodies of the saints who had fallen asleep were raised; and coming out of the graves after His resurrection, they went into the holy city and appeared to many. So, when the centurion and those with him, who were guarding Jesus, saw the earthquake and the things that had happened, they feared greatly, saying, "Truly this was the Son of God!"

From noon until three in the afternoon, darkness covered the entire geographic area around the cross. When the natural sun should have been the brightest, it was blotted out and separation between God and mankind was at its greatest. When Jesus breathed his last breath, the earth trembled, quaked and erupted opening graves and destroying buildings and natural habitats. Inside the temple of the Jews, the veil that separated the holy of holies, the dwelling place of God, from the other chambers of the temple was torn vertically from top to bottom.

The tearing was a divine act from heaven downward by God himself. Why is this important? Because it meant from this moment forward mankind would not be separated from the presence of God.

In Exodus 26:31, 33 NKJV, the priests were commanded, "You shall make a veil woven of blue, purple, and scarlet thread, and fine woven linen. It shall be woven with an artistic design of cherubim. And you shall hang the veil from the clasps. Then you shall bring the ark of the Testimony in there, behind the veil. The veil shall be a divider for you between the holy place and the Most Holy."

In Leviticus 16:2 NKJV, "and the LORD said to Moses: "Tell Aaron your brother not to come at just any time into the Holy Place inside the veil, before the mercy seat which is on the ark, lest he die; for I will appear in the cloud above the mercy seat" The priest could not come inside the veil because the presence of God would be hovering over the mercy seat and face to face confrontation with God would mean death.

The work of the cross gives us access to the presence of God; life not death. It gives us the privilege of a relationship with God through Christ who was the final sacrifice for sin. When Jesus appeared to Mary at the resurrection on Sunday morning, he said this, "Woman, why weepest thou? Whom seekest thou? She, supposing him to be the gardener saith unto him, "Sir, if thou have borne him hence, tell me where thou hast laid him, and I will take him away." Jesus saith unto her," Mary." She turned herself, and saith unto him, Rabboni; which is to say, Master. Jesus saith unto her, "Touch me not; for I am not yet ascended to my Father: but go to my brethren, and say unto them, I ascend unto my Father, and your Father; and to my God, and your God." John 20:15-17 KJV

Jesus' message to Mary, the disciples and all of mankind was inclusion. I go to my Father and now, your Father. I go to my God and now, your God. The veil has been torn from top to bottom as an act of God for the inclusion of "whosoever will" into the family of God. Don't stand on the outside wishing you could go into his presence. The door is wide open!

There is power in your testimony

Last September I attended the American Association of Christian Counselors International Convention. I learned many interesting things, but a bit of information has kept me anxiously waiting for six months. The Christian band, *MercyMe,* was in concert and announced the March 2018 release of the movie, *I Can Only Imagine.* The movie is the testimony of band leader Bart Millard and the story behind the bestselling, triple platinum Christian song, *I Can Only Imagine.* I saw the movie last night and quietly wept as the redemptive power of the gospel unfolded before my eyes. It is a testimony of God's forgiveness and love for sinful mankind and our freedom to participate in that process.

I think, like most Christians I minimize the power of a personal testimony. Because we have become accustomed to preaching on Sunday mornings and on television and radio, we often miss the power of a personal testimony. A testimony is simply the story of how your life was changed when you encountered Jesus Christ as your Savior. It is a story of grace and the love of a heavenly Father who sent his son to pay the penalty for sin and death in your life.

For many years I didn't share my testimony because it was not sensational like the other testimonies I had heard. I was not delivered from drugs, alcohol, prison, the occult or a life of "bad sin". I was simply delivered from "my sin" as a little girl. I realized my testimony was one of the keeping power of God.

The apostle Paul who was a great orator, teacher and evangelist shared his testimony before King Agrippa in Acts 26 1-31 NLT, "Then Agrippa said to Paul, "You may speak in your defense." So Paul, gesturing with his hand, started his defense: "I am fortunate, King Agrippa, that you are the one hearing my defense today against all these accusations made by the Jewish leaders, for I know you are an expert on all Jewish customs and controversies. Now please listen to me patiently!

"As the Jewish leaders are well aware, I was given a thorough Jewish training from my earliest childhood among my own people and in

Jerusalem. If they would admit it, they know that I have been a member of the Pharisees, the strictest sect of our religion. Now I am on trial because of my hope in the fulfillment of God's promise made to our ancestors. In fact, that is why the twelve tribes of Israel zealously worship God night and day, and they share the same hope I have. Yet, Your Majesty, they accuse me for having this hope! Why does it seem incredible to any of you that God can raise the dead?

"I used to believe that I ought to do everything I could to oppose the very name of Jesus the Nazarene. Indeed, I did just that in Jerusalem. Authorized by the leading priests, I caused many believers there to be sent to prison. And I cast my vote against them when they were condemned to death. Many times, I had them punished in the synagogues to get them to curse Jesus. I was so violently opposed to them that I even chased them down in foreign cities.

"One day I was on such a mission to Damascus, armed with the authority and commission of the leading priests. About noon, Your Majesty, as I was on the road, a light from heaven brighter than the sun shone down on me and my companions. We all fell down, and I heard a voice saying to me in Aramaic, 'Saul, Saul, why are you persecuting me? It is useless for you to fight against my will.

"'Who are you, lord?' I asked.

"And the Lord replied, 'I am Jesus, the one you are persecuting. Now get to your feet! For I have appeared to you to appoint you as my servant and witness. Tell people that you have seen me and tell them what I will show you in the future. And I will rescue you from both your own people and the Gentiles. Yes, I am sending you to the Gentiles to open their eyes, so they may turn from darkness to light and from the power of Satan to God. Then they will receive forgiveness for their sins and be given a place among God's people, who are set apart by faith in me.'

"And so, King Agrippa, I obeyed that vision from heaven. I preached first to those in Damascus, then in Jerusalem and throughout all Judea, and also to the Gentiles, that all must repent of their sins and turn to God—and prove they have changed by the good things they do. Some

Jews arrested me in the Temple for preaching this, and they tried to kill me. But God has protected me right up to this present time so I can testify to everyone, from the least to the greatest. I teach nothing except what the prophets and Moses said would happen—that the Messiah would suffer and be the first to rise from the dead, and in this way announce God's light to Jews and Gentiles alike."

Suddenly, Festus shouted, "Paul, you are insane. Too much study has made you crazy!"

But Paul replied, "I am not insane, Most Excellent Festus. What I am saying is the sober truth. And King Agrippa knows about these things. I speak boldly, for I am sure these events are all familiar to him, for they were not done in a corner! King Agrippa, do you believe the prophets? I know you do—"

Agrippa interrupted him. "Do you think you can persuade me to become a Christian so quickly?"

Paul replied, "Whether quickly or not, I pray to God that both you and everyone here in this audience might become the same as I am, except for these chains."

Then the king, the governor, Bernice, and all the others stood and left. As they went out, they talked it over and agreed, "This man hasn't done anything to deserve death or imprisonment."

Paul used his audience with the King and his court to share his personal testimony. He could have taught history, the scriptures or doctrine but he chose to simply tell about his encounter with Christ.

Do you share your testimony? It is a powerful method of introducing others to Christ. If you need help in preparation, please visit my website: AnnNunnally.org for a preparation outline.

There's nothing too dirty!

I was having lunch with a friend yesterday and enjoying the laughter when it happened. I spilled the last bite of loaded potato soup down the front of my blouse! I hate doing that! I feel so klutzy when I spill, drop food and drink on my clothes. Especially since I intended to wear that blouse into the evening meeting I had scheduled. All I could think about was the stain I was wearing; it began to define me.

At home I changed blouses and dropped the soiled, dirty blouse into the laundry. I have plenty of products for stain removal and spot cleaning laundry. It has been part of my regimen for a long time. In fact, I am not alone. The average family spends $854 a year on cleaning products. The grocery store shelves are lined with cleaning products for every imaginable need. There is a desire within all of us to deal with the stains, the dirt and the mistakes that define us. We want to be clean and we cling to the hope that there is a way to redeem the mess we have made.

Spiritually this is true also. Sometimes we don't have as much hope for a spiritual cleansing as we do for a natural cleansing. We think the stain is too deep and the dirt is to ground in. Often when I share God's forgiveness with a person they reply, "But you don't know what I've done". They have become defined by the sin stains of life and they have little hope that cleansing can be realized.

This is a wrong mindset because the scripture clearly states otherwise. Consider the following passages that reference cleansing and restoration.

Psalm 51:7-10 NLT, "Purify me from my sins, and I will be clean; wash me, and I will be whiter than snow. Oh, give me back my joy again; you have broken me - now let me rejoice. Don't keep looking at my sins. Remove the stain of my guilt. Create in me a clean heart, O God. Renew a loyal spirit within me." King David cried out to God for forgiveness and cleansing from adultery and murder. God answered.

Isaiah 1:18 NLT, "Come now, let's settle this," says the Lord. "Though your sins are like scarlet, I will make them as white as snow. Though they are red like crimson, I will make them as white as wool."

I John 1:7-9 NLT, "But if we are living in the light, as God is in the light, then we have fellowship with each other, and the blood of Jesus, his Son, cleanses us from all sin. If we claim we have no sin, we are only fooling ourselves and not living in the truth. But if we confess our sins to him, he is faithful and just to forgive us our sins and to cleanse us from all wickedness."

These are but a few of the scriptures that share the hope and the certainty of spiritual cleansing. The gospel, "good news" is synonymous with stain removal and restoration. It is the reason Jesus came to this earth; to be the final sacrifice for our sins.

Natalie Grant, one of my favorite contemporary Christian artists explains it this way in her song, "Clean".

I see a shatter, you see whole
I see it broken, but you see beautiful
and you're helping me to believe
you're restoring me, piece by piece.
There's nothing too dirty, that you can't make worthy,
you wash me in mercy I am clean
there's nothing too dirty, that you can't make worthy,
you wash me in mercy
I am clean
What was dead now lives again
my hearts beating, beating inside my chest
oh, I'm coming alive with joy and destiny
oh, cause you're restoring me piece by piece,
oh, there's nothing too dirty, that you can't make worthy
you wash me in mercy
I am clean,
oh, yeah there's nothing too dirty, that you can't make worthy
you wash me in mercy
I am clean
Washed in the blood of your sacrifice
your blood flowed red and made me white

my dirty rags are purified,
I am clean
Washed in the blood of your sacrifice
your blood flowed red and made me white
my dirty rags are purified
I am clean, I am clean,
oh, washed in the blood of your sacrifice
your blood flowed red and made me white
my dirty rags are purified
I am clean, I am clean, I'm clean
Oh, You made me, You washed me clean. You made me clean.

There's no better way to start the new year than with the revelation that the blood of Jesus cleanses our sin stains. We have a new joy and a new destiny in Christ!

Turkey and Stressing

I must begin by giving credit for this title to my son, Jamie. He was preparing for his Sunday morning message and the title seemed to be the perfect fit. I asked to borrow it for this article because I want to encourage everyone to enjoy the upcoming Thanksgiving weekend and not be stressed out over things that don't quite work out.

Stress seems to be a part of our modern life. Even when we plan, overthinking every detail, there's always something that goes wrong during the holidays. A cherished recipe doesn't turn out right, a family member arrives a little tipsy, an invited guest brings their horse-size dog who promptly uses the bathroom in the kitchen floor, one family comes with sick children causing the other families with children to hide, and the stories go on and on.

Could our expectations be too high? Are we looking for the Hallmark holiday or the Publix perfect dinner as seen on TV? What is Thanksgiving all about anyway?

I'm all in favor of special moments and family gatherings but the foundation for Thanksgiving is thanks and giving. Thanks for all the big and little blessings we have during the year. Giving love, respect, friendship and honor to those people who are the fabric of our lives. Thanks to a Savior who redeemed us with his life and giving praise for his unending love. Thanksgiving in its proper perspective brings a smile to our face and joy to our heart.

Stress is defined as a state of mental or emotional strain or tension resulting from adverse or very demanding circumstances. Stress is often the culprit in ten major health problems. They are heart disease, asthma, obesity, diabetes, headaches, depression and anxiety, gastrointestinal problems, Alzheimer's disease, accelerated aging and premature death. Our bodies were not designed to shoulder the mental and emotional strain many of us live under. When we accelerate stress during the holidays, we end up sick and depressed.

What can you do to help deal with the stress of the upcoming holidays? Four suggestions are widely used in stress management. First breathe deeply. This can be done anywhere with no preparation or expense. Deep breathing can tame the physiologic stress response and comfort your body that feels like it's under attack.

Secondly, focus on the moment. Most stress comes from living in the future or the past. Worrying about what might happen or regretting what has already happened. This mentality does nothing for you. It's the old hamster on the wheel mentality – working but going nowhere!

The third suggestion for stress management is to reframe the situation. Put a positive spin on your negative situation and laugh out loud at the circumstances.

Finally, keep your problems in perspective. Instead of focusing on the little things that are wrong, focus on the many blessings you have. Perspective is everything when dealing with stress.

Beyond the natural suggestions listed above, we have the ultimate stress reliever in our relationship with Jesus Christ. In Matthew 11:28 NLT, we find this invitation, "Then Jesus said, "Come to me, all of you who are weary and carry heavy burdens, and I will give you rest. Take my yoke upon you. Let me teach you, because I am humble and gentle at heart, and you will find rest for your souls." Casting the cares of life over on the Lord makes our life so much better. Relinquishing control to the Lord is a wise thing to do because we can't change our circumstances or others. Only God can do that!

As we approach all the variables of the upcoming Thanksgiving weekend, let's keep our eyes fixed on the Lord, our hearts set on loving and our declared purpose to be at peace with all. If we do these things we will not have "Turkey and Stressing" but "Turkey and Blessing"!

Two Life Principles to Live By

Age has its advantages and disadvantages. I can't play tennis like I use to. I don't run distances anymore - walking is just fine and I can't go non-stop 24/7 for months at a time. One of the advantages is the wisdom life has provided, and the opportunity to share it with others who are looking for a shortcut through the crises of life. As I pondered today's article I decided to share two of the spiritual principles I have built my life upon in the hopes that this wisdom will encourage you and make life easier to navigate. The treacherous world we live in makes it easy to fall off a cliff and not know it until we are close to the crash point at the bottom! We all need wisdom.

The first principle is trust. As a child I learned about trust in God through Proverbs 3:5-6 NKJV,

> "Trust in the LORD with all your heart,
> And lean not on your own understanding;
> In all your ways acknowledge Him,
> And He shall direct your paths"

I had very little parental guidance as a child, so finding wisdom to live by was a welcomed acquisition. These two simple verses instructed me to trust God with everything within me even when His leading didn't seem to make sense. They taught me to acknowledge Him in everything I did – not just on Sunday morning at church. Finally, they gave me the promise that He would give my life direction and He would lead me down life's path with purpose and divine destiny.

Our human default is to trust others and to trust our own intellectual ability. Both bring pain and frustration. By embracing the humility of acknowledging a God whose wisdom is greater than mine, I have enjoyed a good life even during difficult times. It may sound simple, but it really is profound.

The second life principle I want to share is found in Philippians 3: 13-14 NLT, "No, dear brothers and sisters, I have not achieved it, but I focus on this one thing: Forgetting the past and looking forward to what lies ahead, I press on to reach the end of the race and receive the heavenly prize for which God, through Christ Jesus, is calling us."

The Apostle Paul says I haven't completely gotten this yet, but I focus and make this one thing a priority – forgetting the past. So many of us hold on to the past events in life and it keeps us from moving forward. Those past events can be hurtful memories or situations, or they can be good, self-fulfilling events that stop our forward motion. If it's in the past, that's where it should stay. Agonizing over it, rehearsing and nursing it will never change the fact that it happened. Let go and begin to press on into a destiny and future designed by a loving God for you His child.

I know that it takes time to let go of the past especially if it is a crushing experience like divorce, financial ruin or the death of a loved one. It takes time to let go of the accomplishments of the past as seasons change and someone else trumps our legacy. But there is wisdom in pivoting from the past to the future and looking forward to tomorrow. Camping out in the past never changes it. It only stops you from the joy of today and hope of tomorrow. These two principles are unfailing and eternal. Trust God and forget the past!

Understanding relapse

Have you ever found yourself doing so good in an area of recovery only to turn around and find yourself in complete failure? How does that happen? Most of the time you feel blindsided, not expecting the failure and feeling rather dumb for walking down the same treacherous path.

Having spent the last three years helping men and women in recovery from hurts, habits or hang-ups through the nationally known program, "Celebrate Recovery", I have learned much about the predictable patterns of relapse. While we often perceive relapse as sudden and without warning, it is a process of four key self-defeating patterns. I would like to share all four with you today.

The first step in relapse is complacency. Relapse can come in a diet, a relationship that's not so good for you, an addiction to drugs or alcohol or in finances to name a few areas. Initially in all these areas you are diligent even desperate to deal with the problem. Once a little victory is yours and the pain level of failure is reduced, it is easy to get comfortable. You stop doing the things that brought you victory, like praying, working with an accountability partner or attending meetings where you are encouraged. You decide you can live with what you have now, and you quietly slip into complacency. You have relief but not change.

The second step in relapse is confusion. You begin to rationalize, even deny the gravity of the problem you had. You find yourself playing mental games and saying things like, "It wasn't really that bad" or "I've got this" or "I'm not like so in so". Your thinking becomes fuzzy, confused and self-gratifying. Your downhill slide has just gained momentum.

The third step in relapse is compromise. This is where you go back to the place of temptation. For the alcoholic it's the bar for "one" drink. For the drug addict it's the street corner for just "one" score. For the dieter it's just "one" donut. For the financial addict it's just "one" new credit card. At the point of temptation, you will most often make a poor choice and end up losing the ground you have gained. You probably assumed this is where it all begins to unravel but it is step one, complacency and step two confusion that has brought you to this place of temptation.

The fourth step in relapse is catastrophe. In this phase you give in to the old habit, hurt or hang-up that you worked so hard to walk away from. The addictions, resentments and relationship failures, conflicts with the authorities and financial pressures return with a vengeance. In 2 Peter 2:20-22 NLT, Peter paints a vivid picture of this situation. "And when people escape from the wickedness of the world by knowing our Lord and Savior Jesus Christ and then get tangled up and enslaved by sin again, they are worse off than before. It would be better if they had never known the way to righteousness than to know it and then reject the command, they were given to live a holy life. They prove the truth of this proverb: "A dog returns to its vomit." And another says, "A washed pig returns to the mud." Verse 22 is quoted from the Old Testament book of Proverbs 26:11 NLT, "As a dog returns to its vomit, so a fool repeats his foolishness".

So what is the best medicine to protect you against relapse? In a word, humility. It is the main character trait that protects you from failure. Take it three times a day with the food of the word of God and your lasting healing from hurts, habits and hang-ups will spring forth!

Consider memorizing these scripture passages to use when you are struggling with relapse.

Proverbs 11:2 NLT, "Pride leads to disgrace, but with humility comes wisdom."

Proverbs 16:18 AMP, "Pride goes before destruction, and a haughty spirit before a fall.

James 4:6-7 NLT, "But he gives even more grace to stand against such evil desires. As the scriptures say, God opposes the proud but favors the humble. So humble yourselves before God. Resist the devil and he will flee from you".

Interrupt the cycle of relapse in your life. You deserve lasting freedom…it is God's plan for you!

Watch out for the cat!

I was sitting on the screen porch yesterday morning when I witnessed the perfect visual of mankind's struggle with Satan. My kitty cat, Rudy, was atop his tower when he froze, glared at the large croton plant on the porch perimeter and began to twitch his tail. He had spotted a lizard who unknowingly had wandered into cat territory. Rudy wasted no time pawing through the leaves of the plant trying to locate the lizard.

Once found, the cat became aggressive in his treatment of the tender, green lizard. He maimed him and then laid down on the porch floor and watch as the lizard struggled with pain and became paralyzed with fear. The cat loved exercising his dominance over the tiny lizard.

Several times the lizard tried to escape, hiding once again in the croton, then trying to climb the screen to be out of reach from his cat predator. He opened his mouth, to bite Rudy, but he was not successful in biting or scaring his monstrous enemy.

I waited to see what the outcome of the conflict would be. To my surprise, Rudy did not want to kill the lizard, nor did he not want to have him for breakfast. Rudy's game was intimidation and dominance.

I couldn't watch any longer. I got up, shooed the cat away, gently picked the lizard off the screen and carried him to safety. I placed him on the dew-drenched leaf of a large hydrangea where his green was perfectly matched, and he would be camouflaged from the eyes of his predatory as he healed. I had rescued the lizard from the cat and had given him the gift of life.

The parallel between this story and the story of Jesus Christ becoming our rescue is clear. Our enemy is watching and waiting for us to wander into his territory so he can pounce. He wants to intimidate and dominate with fear, so we become unproductive in life. John 10:10 NLT, states "The thief's purpose is to steal and kill and destroy. My purpose is to give them a rich and satisfying life." A great contrast in purpose between Satan and our savior, Jesus Christ.

Last weekend we celebrated Easter, the story of the crucifixion and resurrection of Jesus. His death and rebirth ushered in Jesus' purpose on this earth and the victory that would secure His dominance over our enemy Satan. The Easter story continues daily, producing freedom and hope over our predator, Satan, who would try to toy with us, intimidate us and paralyze us with fear and eventually kill us.

Consider what the Apostle Peter wrote in 1 Peter 5:8 NLT, "Stay alert! Watch out for your great enemy, the devil. He prowls around like a roaring lion, looking for someone to devour." Satan is a real spiritual entity who is looking for a way to discourage, maim and watch you die a slow death. He is your adversary!

So many times, in life we struggle against people and situations. But according to Ephesians 6: 12 NLT, our real battle is with Satan. "For we are not fighting against flesh-and-blood enemies, but against evil rulers and authorities of the unseen world, against mighty powers in this dark world, and against evil spirits in the heavenly places."

We have already been given the victory, and we are being intimidated by a defeated foe.

1 John 3:8 NLT, declares, "But the Son of God came to destroy the works of the devil." Colossians 2: 13-15 states, "You were dead because of your sins and because your sinful nature was not yet cut away. Then God made you alive with Christ, for he forgave all our sins. He canceled the record of the charges against us and took it away by nailing it to the cross. In this way, he disarmed the spiritual rulers and authorities. He shamed them publicly by his victory over them on the cross."

As I quietly watched the interaction between Bear and the lizard, I knew the only way the lizard would gain life and victory was if I were to rise from my chair and involve myself in the conflict. So, it was with Jesus, he arose from His heavenly throne, came to earth, involved himself in the conflict between mankind and Satan and evened out the playing field. He came to grant us victory over sin, death and our adversary, Satan. He gently picked up those who had been wounded, intimidated and who were paralyzed with fear and declared "you are free!"

Luke 1:17-19 NKJV, states the impartation of authority we have over the enemy. "Then the seventy returned with joy, saying, "Lord, even the demons are subject to us in Your name." And He said to them, "I saw Satan fall like lightning from heaven. Behold, I give you the authority to trample on serpents and scorpions, and over all the power of the enemy, and nothing shall by any means hurt you."

You are on the winning team. The enemy Satan has been defeated and you have the authority to walk free from his tyranny. A great and gentle Savior has rescued you!

Put on the Belt of Truth

I recently watched a heavy-weight boxing title fight. Surprised? Me too! I only watched because the title defender was from my hometown and many of my high school and college friends were talking about the fight. My boxing interest has pretty much been limited to the "Rocky" movies I have watched through the years. I guess I'm just not a fan of broken noses, blood and eyes that are swollen shut because of the pounding received from the opponent.

But one thing I did love about the fight was the championship belt. That may sound like a "girl-take" on the fight but it really is a "God-take". When I saw the heavyweight championship belt, I could only compare it to the belt of truth written about in Ephesians chapter 6. The part of the whole armor of God that cradles the middle of the body of the believer is called the belt of truth.

Ephesians 6:10-17 NLT, "A final word: Be strong in the Lord and in his mighty power. Put on all of God's armor so that you will be able to stand firm against all strategies of the devil. For we are not fighting against flesh-and-blood enemies, but against evil rulers and authorities of the unseen world, against mighty powers in this dark world, and against evil spirits in the heavenly places. Therefore, put on every piece of God's armor so you will be able to resist the enemy in the time of evil. Then after the battle you will still be standing firm. Stand your ground, putting on the belt of truth and the body armor of God's righteousness. For shoes, put on the peace that comes from the Good News so that you will be fully prepared. In addition to all of these, hold up the shield of faith to stop the fiery arrows of the devil. Put on salvation as your helmet, and take the sword of the Spirit, which is the word of God."

Most of us think of a belt as a small accessory used to hold up our pants. Basically, created in leather or a synthetic material, the normal belt is about two inches wide. It is not a very impressive or large part of the armor of God if it is perceived by the modern description but if perceived as the belt of a champion it's another story!

In today's culture, most accomplishment is rewarded with certificates and trophies of various sizes and descriptions. In combat sports like boxing, martial arts and wrestling where opponents are pitted one on one, the champion is awarded a large, bold, often jewel-embellished belt. The belt belongs to him forever. A new belt is created for every new champion so there is an elite fraternity of championship belt holders. Since the official Marquess of Queensberry rules established in 1895, there have been approximately 128 heavy-weight champions including names like George Foreman, Muhammad Ali, Ken Norton, Joe Frazier and current champion Deontay Wilder.

God has given every believer the championship belt of truth. The belt was purchased by the sacrificial death, burial and resurrection of Jesus Christ. He is the ultimate, eternal champion and he has shared his victory with everyone who will believe in their heart and confess with their mouth that Jesus is Lord.

Hebrew 12:1-3 NLT, "Therefore, since we are surrounded by such a huge crowd of witnesses to the life of faith, let us strip off every weight that slows us down, especially the sin that so easily trips us up. And let us run with endurance the race God has set before us. We do this by keeping our eyes on Jesus, the champion who initiates and perfects our faith. Because of the joy awaiting him, he endured the cross, disregarding its shame. Now he is seated in the place of honor beside God's throne. Think of all the hostility he endured from sinful people; then you won't become weary and give up."

You can lay aside the belt of truth and live your life outside of the truth of God's word, but you won't be a champion! You will be pounded, bloodied and defeat by Satan, the enemy of your faith. Or you can strap on the belt of truth and all the other parts of the armor of God and live the abundant life Christ purchased for you. Show up to every fight dressed to win and thankfully raise the championship belt of truth as your victory prize!

Welcome to Thomasville

Zinhle Nxumalo sat clutching her hot pink suitcase, scanning the baggage claim area for a familiar face. It was her first visit to America. She didn't know me, and I didn't know her. We had "talked" via email and had made our plans by faith. As our eyes met, we both smiled a smile that would continue for the thirteen days she was my "adopted daughter".

The flight from South Africa had been grueling. A full twenty-six hours of flight time and an overnight stay had passed since her Dad had put her on the plane in Johannesburg. She was hungry and sleepy yet wide-eyed and alert as she began her first visit to America. She had exceled in her Fashion Design School back in South Africa and had graduated with honors. Her family had given her the trip as a graduation present and as an investment in her spiritual life. Growing up as a PK-preachers kid, had not been easy.

Zinhle also known as "ZiZi" planned her trip to include a local Christian conference being held in Thomasville at Victory Fellowship Church (VFC). Her father, Pastor Thomas Nxumalo, had attended the "InPower" conference the year before. It had been a life changing event for him, and he intuitively knew it would be for her also. He was right.

ZiZi and I have shared our faith, our fears and our love for the word of God and Christian music for days now. I can't remember not knowing her and loving her. Her visit has also changed my life and ministry. It has given me great vision and expectation for my ministry trip to South Africa next June. I am counting the days already until I can visit ZiZi's family, her church family and the family of God in South Africa. Teaching an encouraging, serving and praying for my brothers and sisters in Africa will be an amazing adventure.

In addition to the church meetings, ZiZi has experienced the love of God through lunch dates at all the Thomasville restaurants, exercise classes, football games, family gatherings and a surprise trip to see the sugar-white beaches and the sunsets in Destin, Florida. There has also been shopping, more shopping and getting her first ever pedicure!

Daily I have been reminded of the Biblical truth to love our brothers and sisters in Christ. Sometimes petty differences cause division and strife in the church, but the answer is for us is to simply love one another. God calls us to unity not uniformity! Consider these scriptures: I John 3:14 NLT, "If we love our brothers and sisters who are believers, it proves that we have passed from death to life. But a person who has no love is still dead."

Hebrews 13:1-3 NLT, "Keep on loving each other as brothers and sisters. Don't forget to show hospitality to strangers, for some who have done this have entertained angels without realizing it! Remember those in prison, as if you were there yourself. Remember also those being mistreated, as if you felt their pain in your own bodies."

Everyone thought ZiZi's visit to Thomasville was a graduation gift to her, but for those of us who have spent the last two weeks with her, we know that it has been a gift to us!

Welcome to spring! Welcome to life!

Spring is the most spiritually active season of the year. I was reminded of this when I saw all the activities scheduled at an area church for the Easter weekend. There was an Easter egg hunt for the children on Saturday, a Palm Sunday Service, an Easter musical on Sunday evening, a Christ in the Passover service on Wednesday, and on Easter Sunday there was a Sunrise/Communion service, an Easter breakfast followed by Easter morning worship service. This church was using every opportunity to declare the story of the crucifixion and resurrection because they intuitively knew that this is the time of the year when old things are passing away and new life is beginning. Spring is the season of great natural and spiritual activity. It is the season when things that are dead come to life!

In 1 Corinthians 15: 3-11 NLT, we find the apostle Paul sharing on the resurrection of the dead. "I passed on to you what was most important and what had also been passed on to me. Christ died for our sins, just as the Scriptures said. He was buried, and he was raised from the dead on the third day, just as the Scriptures said. He was seen by Peter and then by the Twelve. After that, he was seen by more than 500 of his followers at one time, most of whom are still alive, though some have died. Then he was seen by James and later by all the apostles. Last of all, as though I had been born at the wrong time, I also saw him. For I am the least of all the apostles. In fact, I'm not even worthy to be called an apostle after the way I persecuted God's church.   But whatever I am now, it is all because God poured out his special favor on me—and not without results. For I have worked harder than any of the other apostles; yet it was not I but God who was working through me by his grace. So, it makes no difference whether I preach or they preach, for we all preach the same message you have already believed."

Later, in this chapter, Paul continues to share how important the resurrection is to our faith. I Corinthians 15: 12- 23 NLT, "But tell me this—since we preach that Christ rose from the dead, why are some of you saying there will be no resurrection of the dead? For if there is no resurrection of the dead, then Christ has not been raised either. And if

Christ has not been raised, then all our preaching is useless, and your faith is useless. And we apostles would all be lying about God—for we have said that God raised Christ from the grave. But that can't be true if there is no resurrection of the dead. And if there is no resurrection of the dead, then Christ has not been raised. And if Christ has not been raised, then your faith is useless, and you are still guilty of your sins. In that case, all who have died believing in Christ are lost! And if our hope in Christ is only for this life, we are more to be pitied than anyone in the world. But in fact, Christ has been raised from the dead. He is the first of a great harvest of all who have died. So, you see, just as death came into the world through a man, now the resurrection from the dead has begun through another man. Just as everyone dies because we all belong to Adam, everyone who belongs to Christ will be given new life. But there is an order to this resurrection: Christ was raised as the first of the harvest; then all who belong to Christ will be raised when he comes back."

On Passover Sunday, over two thousand years ago, Jesus Christ rose from the dead to become the first born of many brothers and sisters. He ushered in the first "spiritual spring" where new, resurrection life overcame old, decaying life. In the same chapter verses 45- 46 we find this profound statement, "The Scriptures tell us, "The first man, Adam, became a living person. But the last Adam—that is, Christ—is a life-giving Spirit. What comes first is the natural body, then the spiritual body comes later. Adam, the first man, was made from the dust of the earth, while Christ, the second man, came from heaven. Earthly people are like the earthly man, and heavenly people are like the heavenly man. Just as we are now like the earthly man, we will someday be like the heavenly man." What a promise!

As we welcome spring to South Georgia, let's remember that the natural deadness of the trees, plants, grass and flowers is a symbol of our lifelessness without Christ. When the resurrection power of God is permitted to invade our natural lives, we are born again into a spiritual, eternal, fruit-bearing human being with the promise of eternity.

This is the season to share your faith, your hope and your love with someone who doesn't know there is resurrection life freely given to anyone who will call on the name of the Lord. It's a season of strong spiritual activity and power. Tell someone the resurrection story that they may live!

What are you looking for in the Bible?

Have you ever thought about what a condensed Bible would look like? Not sixty-six books, 31,102 verses but fifteen of the most sought after and read verses in the Bible? Please know that I am not advocating this, as I love the history of the Old Testament, and the New Testament with the life of Jesus and the fulfillment of His ministry on the earth. I am a total, whole Bible girl and so much of who I am has come from understanding the totality of God's work through men and women of faith throughout the ages.

But what if we could look at the fifteen most popular Bible verses in online research. Could we discover something about ourselves and our needs as Christians? Well, here goes that challenge as I share with you the top fifteen scripture references from the online study tool called, "Bible Study Tools". What will you learn about yourself?

Jeremiah 29:11 - "For I know the thoughts that I think toward you, says the Lord, thoughts of peace and not of evil, to give you a future and a hope."

Psalm 23 – "The Lord *is* my shepherd; I shall not want. He makes me to lie down in green pastures; He leads me beside the still waters. He restores my soul; He leads me in the paths of righteousness for His name's sake. Yea, though I walk through the valley of the shadow of death, I will fear no evil; For You *are* with me; Your rod and Your staff, they comfort me. You prepare a table before me in the presence of my enemies; You anoint my head with oil; My cup runs over. Surely goodness and mercy shall follow me, All the days of my life; And I will dwell in the house of the Lord Forever."

1 Corinthians 13:4-8 – "Love suffers long *and* is kind; love does not envy; love does not parade itself, is not puffed up; does not behave rudely, does not seek its own, is not provoked, thinks no evil; does not rejoice in iniquity, but rejoices in the truth; bears all things, believes all things, hopes all things, endures all things. Love never fails. But whether *there are* prophecies, they will fail; whether *there are* tongues, they will cease; whether *there is* knowledge, it will vanish away"

Philippians 4:13 – "I can do all things through Christ who strengthens me."

John 3:16 – "For God so loved the world that He gave His only begotten Son, that whoever believes in Him should not perish but have everlasting life."

Romans 8:28 – "And we know that all things work together for good to those who love God, to those who are the called according to *His* purpose."

Isaiah 41:10 – "Fear not, for I *am* with you; Be not dismayed, for I *am* your God. I will strengthen you, Yes, I will help you, I will uphold you with My righteous right hand."

Proverbs 3:5-6 – "Trust in the Lord with all your heart and lean not on your own understanding; In all your ways acknowledge Him, And He shall direct your paths."

Psalm 46:1 – "God *is* our refuge and strength, A very present help in trouble."

Galatians 5:22-23 – "But the fruit of the Spirit is love, joy, peace, longsuffering, kindness, goodness, faithfulness, gentleness, self-control. Against such there is no law."

Hebrews 11:1 – "Now faith is the substance of things hoped for, the evidence of things not seen."

2 Timothy 1:7 – "For God has not given us a spirit of fear, but of power and of love and of a sound mind."

1 Corinthians 10:13 – "No temptation has overtaken you except such as is common to man; but God *is* faithful, who will not allow you to be tempted beyond what you are able, but with the temptation will also make the way of escape, that you may be able to bear *it.*"

Proverbs 22:6 – "Train up a child in the way he should go, and when he is old, he will not depart from it."

Isaiah 40:31 – "But those who wait on the Lord, shall renew *their* strength; They shall mount up with wings like eagles, they shall run and not be weary, they shall walk and not faint."

The continual theme found in these fifteen verses is finding strength, courage, faith, trust, and the assurance that you are not alone in your troubles and temptations. You could call these verses our "spiritual comfort food". How much stronger in the Spirit could we be if we added to our favorites from the 31,102 verses available? Let's add at least fifteen more this year as we study God's word!

What happens when I leave? - Help Wanted!

When we think of the ministry of Jesus we look first to the cross of Calvary and the resurrection. Then we remember the miracles, the teachings and the relationships he had with his disciples. But there is another facet of Jesus ministry that escapes the focus of much of Christendom. The contemplative thoughts of Jesus wondering, "What happens when I leave? – Help wanted!"

In Matthew 9:35-38 NLT, we hear Jesus' petition to his disciples. "Jesus traveled through all the towns and villages of that area, teaching in the synagogues and announcing the Good News about the Kingdom. And he healed every kind of disease and illness. When he saw the crowds, he had compassion on them because they were confused and helpless, like sheep without a shepherd. He said to his disciples, "The harvest is great, but the workers are few. So, pray to the Lord who is in charge of the harvest; ask him to send more workers into his fields."

Also, we find this petition recorded in Luke 10: 1-2 NLT, "The Lord now chose seventy-two (some text says seventy) other disciples and sent them ahead in pairs to all the towns and places he planned to visit. These were his instructions to them: "The harvest is great, but the workers are few. So, pray to the Lord who is in charge of the harvest; ask him to send more workers into his field."

We go even deeper into the compassionate heart of Jesus in John 4:30-35 NLT, "So the people came streaming from the village to see him. Meanwhile, the disciples were urging Jesus, "Rabbi, eat something." But Jesus replied, "I have a kind of food you know nothing about." "Did someone bring him food while we were gone?" the disciples asked each other. Then Jesus explained: "My nourishment comes from doing the will of God, who sent me, and from finishing his work. You know the saying, 'Four months between planting and harvest.' But I say, wake up and look around. The fields are already ripe for harvest."

Preceding this passage, Jesus had ministered to the woman at the well. Her encounter with Jesus and her testimony to her village brought about the above discourse between Jesus and His disciples. Jesus essentially says, "I had rather see people set free and restored to God than to eat!"

Wow! I must ask myself is that my mindset. Is that the mindset of the church? Or would we rather eat than share our faith? What would happen in the world if we ate three times a day and shared our faith in God three times a day? The harvest is ready, but the laborers are few!

I have just returned from a ministry trip to South Africa. Part of my ministry agenda was the graduation and ordination of eleven students who are eager to go out into the harvest and gather fruit for the kingdom of God. Teaching, training and challenging these students over the past five months has been an amazing experience for me. It has satisfied my hunger much like Jesus talked about in John 4.

When the commencement speech was over and the students graduated, the whole church erupted in song, dance and joy! It was like nothing I had ever seen in sixty years of ministry. Hundreds rejoiced as God set apart laborers for the harvest! It was raw, unbridled joy - a taste of heaven on earth!

When Jesus met with his disciples the last time before ascending to the Father, he simply told them, "Go!" His last wish was for laborers to go and receive the harvest, grown and ready to be picked, because he had been sown into the ground and resurrected into a new covenant of grace. The separation between God and man, the veil, had been torn and access to the Father had been given for all, throughout eternity!

Matthew 28:19-20 NLT, is affectionately known as "the great commission". "Therefore, go and make disciples of all the nations, baptizing them in the name of the Father and the Son and the Holy Spirit. Teach these new disciples to obey all the commands I have given you. And be sure of this: I am with you always, even to the end of the age."

There is a "Help Wanted" sign in the spirit. Are you ready to apply for the job? Are you ready to be a laborer in the kingdom of God?

What if we believed?

Recently, I spoke to a group of ladies on the topic of prayer. To tell you the truth, I was hesitant to share for two reasons. First there has been so much published on prayer. Books, movies, methods, journals just to mention a few of the recent ventures concerning prayer. Secondly, prayer has always been very personal to me and I have felt a little "out of step" with mainstream Christianity concerning prayer. Nevertheless, I plunged into preparation for this invitation to speak on prayer.

Looking to the word of God as my foundation for understanding prayer, it revealed a strong basis for prayer theology. Throughout the old and new testaments, mighty miracles have been tied to the practice of prayer. In fact, you could say the entire Biblical narrative is punctuated by God moving in extraordinary ways in response to the prayers of ordinary people like me and you.

 Consider the story of three Hebrew children, Shadrach, Meshach and Abednego in Daniel chapter three. When challenged because they didn't fall and worship the golden idol created by King Nebuchadnezzar, they responded in faith and prayer. Daniel 3:16-18 NLT, "Shadrach, Meshach, and Abednego replied, "O Nebuchadnezzar, we do not need to defend ourselves before you. If we are thrown into the blazing furnace, the God whom we serve is able to save us. He will rescue us from your power, Your Majesty. But even if he doesn't, we want to make it clear to you, Your Majesty that we will never serve your gods or worship the gold statue you have set up." The king in his fury stoked the flames of the fiery furnace and had the young men thrown in. The prayers of three ordinary men brought extraordinary results. Daniel 3: 20-27 NLT, "Then he ordered some of the strongest men of his army to bind Shadrach, Meshach, and Abednego and throw them into the blazing furnace. So, they tied them up and threw them into the furnace, fully dressed in their pants, turbans, robes, and other garments. And because the king, in his anger, had demanded such a hot fire in the furnace, the flames killed the soldiers as they threw the three men in. So, Shadrach, Meshach, and Abednego, securely tied, fell into the roaring flames. But suddenly, Nebuchadnezzar jumped up in amazement and exclaimed to his advisers, "Didn't we tie up three men and throw them into the furnace?" "Yes, Your Majesty, we certainly did," they replied. "Look!" Nebuchadnezzar shouted. "I see four men, unbound, walking around in the fire unharmed! And the fourth looks like a god!" Then Nebuchadnezzar came as close as he could to the door of the flaming furnace and shouted: "Shadrach, Meshach, and Abednego, servants of the Most High God, come out! Come here!" So, Shadrach, Meshach, and Abednego stepped out of the fire. Then the high officers, officials, governors, and advisers crowded around them and saw that the fire had not touched them. Not a hair on their heads was singed, and their clothing was not scorched. They didn't even smell of smoke!" They didn't even smell like they had been persecuted!

When you stand in prayer, the supernatural presence of God joins with you to bring about His will in your life. This is repeated over and over in the old and new testament. Remember the story in Acts 16 when Paul and Silas were thrown into jail for preaching the gospel? Acts 16: 22-29 NLT, "A mob quickly formed against Paul and Silas, and the city officials ordered them stripped and beaten with wooden rods. They were severely beaten, and then they were thrown into prison. The jailer was ordered to make sure they didn't escape. So the jailer put them into the inner dungeon and clamped their feet in the stocks.

Around midnight Paul and Silas were praying and singing hymns to God, and the other prisoners were listening. Suddenly, there was a massive earthquake, and the prison was shaken to its foundations. All the doors immediately flew open, and the chains of every prisoner fell off! The jailer woke up to see the prison doors wide open. He assumed the prisoners had escaped, so he drew his sword to kill himself. But Paul shouted to him, "Stop! Don't kill yourself! We are all here!" The jailer called for lights and ran to the dungeon and fell down trembling before Paul and Silas. Then he brought them out and asked, "Sirs, what must I do to be saved?"

Paul and Silas were in an impossible situation so they prayed and worshiped God. He moved in an extraordinary way in response to their faith and petition.

What if we really believed in the power of prayer? What extraordinary event might happen in our lives? Consider these words from James, the half-brother of Jesus found in James 5:16 NLT, "Confess your sins to each other and pray for each other so that you may be healed. The earnest prayer of a righteous person has great power and produces wonderful results."

Next week I will continue this challenge to pray. Get ready to grow in your prayer life!

Everyday Diamonds

What if we believed? – Cleansing Prayer

In my last article I asked the question, "What if we believed?" Would we pray more if we really thought it would make a difference in our life situations? The Bible is composed of example after example where ordinary people prayed and natural circumstances changed by the supernatural power and intervention of God.

Every great minister throughout history was a man or woman of prayer. You cannot find a single biography of a successful minister who dared to "go it alone" denying prayer time with God. John Wesley, founder of Methodism may have slightly overstated his prayer passion when he said, "God will do nothing but in answer to prayer." Corrie Ten Boom admonished us to "Don't pray when you feel like it. Have an appointment with the Lord and keep it". John Maxwell, author, speaker and pastor said, "Every time I have had a breakthrough in my life, it has been because of prayer." In my opinion, every effective minister of God must be clothed in prayer – it's what we wear!

In ministry training, I always tell my students they must have a "PP ministry". Prayer and Preparation equals great success. Too many of us pray and set back leaving all the responsibility on God. While others work hard preparing and never ask God for the correct plan. It takes both, prayer and preparation for a successful, vibrant ministry.

Prayer-on-the-go has become popular in recent years. You can often hear people say, "I pray all the time, in my car, in the shower, in the grocery store." While that's a good thing to apply the Biblical concept of "pray always" or "pray without ceasing", it's not the kind of prayer that captures the heart of God and moves mountains. Nor does it provide the kind of cleansing that comes from being in the presence of God without distraction or time limits. Jesus left his disciples and all the people that followed him so he and his Father could be alone, face to face in prayer and preparation for every step of his earthly ministry. If Jesus needed to pray certainly we do!

226

Psalm 51 is King David's prayer before the Lord after his adultery with Bathsheba. It's not the car, shower, grocery store kind of prayer. Its fruit was forgiveness, restoration and healing from deep, dark separation from King David and his God.

Psalm 51: 1-17 NLT, "Have mercy on me, O God,
because of your unfailing love.
Because of your great compassion,
blot out the stain of my sins.
Wash me clean from my guilt.
Purify me from my sin.
For I recognize my rebellion;
it haunts me day and night.
Against you, and you alone, have I sinned;
I have done what is evil in your sight.
You will be proved right in what you say,
and your judgment against me is just.
For I was born a sinner—
yes, from the moment my mother conceived me.
But you desire honesty from the womb,
teaching me wisdom even there.

Purify me from my sins, and I will be clean;
wash me, and I will be whiter than snow.
Oh, give me back my joy again;
you have broken me—
now let me rejoice.
Don't keep looking at my sins.
Remove the stain of my guilt.
Create in me a clean heart, O God.
Renew a loyal spirit within me.
Do not banish me from your presence,
and don't take your Holy Spirit from me.

Restore to me the joy of your salvation,
and make me willing to obey you.
Then I will teach your ways to rebels,
and they will return to you.
Forgive me for shedding blood, O God who saves;
then I will joyfully sing of your forgiveness.

Unseal my lips, O Lord,
that my mouth may praise you.

You do not desire a sacrifice, or I would offer one.
You do not want a burnt offering. The sacrifice you desire is a
broken spirit.
You will not reject a broken and repentant heart, O God."

Cleansing from King David's horrendous sins came in real, passionate, and purposeful prayer.

Prayer breeds confidence. In my life, prayer is not a place - a devotional chair, a garden or a closet. Prayer is a priority. It's not a matter of where but when, I will find a quality, face-to-face time in conversation with the Lord. I challenge you to make real prayer a priority in your life. The healing, cleansing and restoration you desire will meet you there! What if we believed?

What is a spouse looking for?

I have been a pastoral counselor for twenty-five years. Marital relationships, finances, youth, and children are the main topics a pastoral counselor is called upon to address. Every situation is different and there are no pat answers. It takes prayer and wisdom to help families navigate life's difficulties.

Many books have been written on marriage and family, expounding the scriptures and the latest studies on what it takes to have a great marriage and family. Yet we still struggle to stay married and have good family relationships. Statistics show the divorce rate for first marriages at 41%, second marriages at 60% and third marriages at 73%. Important also is the statistic of 100 divorces every hour. Wow! So, what is a spouse looking for?

A problem with marriage and family is that it is always changing. Just when you think you have all the dynamics figured out something changes! There is a financial crisis, a child leaves home, aging parents need help, a job change occurs, health issues surface, there is an endless flow of events that pressure your marriage and family.

Underneath all of this, there are two basic ingredients that keep a marriage strong; the desire to have someone to love and the desire to have someone to play with. These two desires propel couples to march down the aisle at a rate of 2, 077, 000 marriages per year in the US. It is these two basic desires, someone to love and someone to play with, that get buried in the annoyances of life.

I was reminded of these two basic needs recently when I adopted a puppy for a short season. He was so cute and fluffy, and he adored seeing me every morning. He jumped up and down and made puppy noises inviting me to hold him and snuggle with him. He ate his breakfast quickly so we could play. He would chase his miniature tennis balls and bring them back to me every time I threw them. He never tired of playing. He never tired of licking my face and sitting in my lap. He wanted to love and be loved. I found myself giggling at these same antics daily and I found myself being excited to throw a ball to a puppy. He mirrored the needs we all have - to love and play.

No wonder the pet industry boasted a whopping $62.75 billion in 2016! Someone to love and someone to play with is part of our human DNA and the foundation for all long-lasting, great marriages.

Most couples major on these two desires during courtship. As love blooms in a relationship, spending time together, loving one another and playing together are paramount. During the dating season, there is no end to the time and money we will spend to be with the person we love. We put all other relationships on hold as we get to know our future spouse. But when we get married we begin to conquer life, achieve success and juggle family, forgetting to love, and play with the spouse we have married. How could we be so distracted? How could we forget that what brought us together as husband and wife would be the thing that keeps us together?

Marriage counselors often suggest a weekly date night to couples who are struggling in their marriage. This suggestion is so time will be scheduled for loving and playing. The husband who is too busy at work, hunting or playing sports to spend time with his wife will open the door of temptation for another man who is looking for someone to love and play with. The wife who is too busy with the children, her parents or her social activities will open the door of temptation for another woman who is looking for somebody to love and play with. Separate lives that don't overlap in love and fun time are destined to become "separate lives".

Marriage is not something you conquer and set on a shelf or mount on your wall. It is a living relationship that grows with care and attention. You can't set marriage in motion and hope that it will sustain itself. Like everything else in this world, it will follow the second law of thermodynamics which says, "the state of entropy (disorder) within a system will increase over time." Just as an ice cube at room temperature begins to melt, we always get older not younger, and clean rooms always get messy again, marriages unnurtured will lose their vitality, strength, and purpose and will die a slow death. You often hear couples say, 'We just grew apart". But what really happened is two people who were once madly in love forgot how to love and play.

So, what is your spouse looking for? It is time to talk and shore up your marriage relationship with love and playtime!

What to do about the Christmas tree

A friend of mine recently shared about her teenage boys and husband not wanting to decorate the Christmas tree this year. Her frustration was evident, and her conundrum reminded me of the year my husband and sons mutinied about decorating the tree and the lesson I learned.

Years ago, when my two sons were teen-agers, I had arranged for a local nursery to deliver and set up a fresh Christmas tree for our living room. The 10-foot-tall ceilings would barely accommodate the beautiful, full, and fragrant tree. I was so excited about decorating it the coming Saturday and about all the presents it would canopy during the holiday season. The hard work was done, now it would be the fun time of adding the hundreds of ornaments, lights and garland I had collected over the years. Of course, there would be hot chocolate in Christmas mugs and the music of the season to guide us along the tree decorating experience.

To my surprise, my husband and both boys declared they didn't want to decorate the tree this year. There were ballgames and other activities on Saturday that they wanted to do instead of the tree decorating tradition on the first Saturday in December. I was speechless! They graciously – a little sarcasm here – told me I could do it this year. My traditional world crumbled, and I responded the way I often do when major change comes, with perplexity and confusion.

I spent the next several days trying to figure out the next step. I knew I couldn't "decorate as usual" and pretend nothing had changed. The family tradition had become "a job" for me to do. Being the only girl in the household, I had shied away from the frilly, designer trees that were being presented in all the magazines. Was this my opportunity to do something different? Yes, it was!

I began to shop for pink, silk poinsettias, pearl garland and organdy ribbon for the hundreds of bows I planned to make for the new look. There would be silver and pink, shiny ornaments – not those handmade kindergarten relics of the past. I even made a new tree skirt of pink felt overlaid with lace and bordered with more lace. It was going to be a creative masterpiece!

Saturday came and I was ready for the task before me. I issued one last invitation to my husband and sons to help decorated the tree and it was declined as the game of the day was about to start. As I stood before the tree a wave of loneliness washed over me. I smiled and a wave of creativity overtook the loneliness and a new tree was about to be born! The result was spectacular! I'm sure Martha Stewart or Southern Living would have broken down my door for a glimpse if only they had known!

I had taken a disappointing situation of change and made it into a fresh, new experience. Instead of harboring resentment, nagging my way into what I wanted and making life miserable for my husband and sons, I had given them the first gift of the season – the freedom to do what they wanted to do. In return I had receive the freedom and inspiration to do something totally creative and new. I was thankful God had given me the grace to respond with love and freedom. He had once again opened my eyes to the truth that people are more important than things. My relationship with my husband and sons was much more valuable than a tradition.

When the game ended that day, the guys emerged from the den to say "Hello" and to see the tree. They gasped when they saw the untraditional, decidedly feminine ten-foot creation. They were shocked. The traditional tree had meant more to them than I thought.

There was not much conservation about the tree among the four of us that year but every visitor to the house was amazed and took pictures. The next year the guys approached me about decorating the tree. We set up a mutually beneficial time to decorate. We returned to the traditional tree with all the memories, kindergarten ornaments and life-saver garland. There was once again Christmas music, hot chocolate in seasonal mugs and a family decorating the tree. The pink poinsettias and pearl garland where never to be seen again.

Romans 12:18 NKJV, says this, "If it is possible, as much as depends on you, live peaceably with all men." The NLT makes it even clearer. "Do all that you can to live in peace with everyone." We can choose to demand our way, or we can choose to walk in love this Christmas. The peace that comes from walking in love far exceeds the joy of having it our way. Our way is temporal but peace with those we live, work and play with is eternal. On December 26, the calendar will indicate that Christmas is over for this year but our relationship with family and friends continues. Make the love choice in your relationships and peace and joy will follow.

When it doesn't feel like Christmas

Christmas is a sensory experience! Seeing the lights, hearing the sounds, smelling all the goodies baking, touching the presents, and tasting the recipes of Christmas makes for a full month of sensory overload. We look forward to the intoxication of the season for months before it happens. The problem arises when the circumstances of life are such that we hear ourselves say, "It doesn't feel like Christmas".

The world is still decorated, the option of sensory overload is still here but life events have buffered our intake of it. Personal health problems, the death of a loved one, financial crisis, broken relationships, and divorce often cause us to say, "It doesn't feel like Christmas".

I remember my first Christmas after my mother died unexpectedly on December 2. The travel, the funeral and all the emotions blocked many of the sensory delights of that Christmas. Three years later my oldest brother died three days before Christmas. Traveling home from his funeral on Christmas Eve was one of my saddest Christmas memories. There was no "feeling" of Christmas. Three years later I would face the death of another brother only a few days after Christmas.   What I remember about those Christmas seasons was not the sensory overload of a decorated world, but the unfailing love of God. Although life circumstances had separated me from the feelings of Christmas, it could never separate me from God's love and provision.

In Romans 8:31-39 NLT, we find this comfort. "What shall we say about such wonderful things as these? If God is for us, who can ever be against us? Since he did not spare even his own Son but gave him up for us all, won't he also give us everything else? Who dares accuse us whom God has chosen for his own? No one—for God himself has given us right standing with himself. Who then will condemn us? No one—for Christ Jesus died for us and was raised to life for us, and he is sitting in the place of honor at God's right hand, pleading for us. Can anything ever separate us from Christ's love? Does it mean he no longer loves us if we have trouble or calamity, or are persecuted, or hungry, or destitute, or in danger, or threatened with death? (As the

Scriptures say, "For your sake we are killed every day; we are being slaughtered like sheep.") No, despite all these things, overwhelming victory is ours through Christ, who loved us. And I am convinced that nothing can ever separate us from God's love. Neither death nor life, neither angels nor demons, neither our fears for today nor our worries about tomorrow—not even the powers of hell can separate us from God's love. No power in the sky above or in the earth below—indeed, nothing in all creation will ever be able to separate us from the love of God that is revealed in Christ Jesus our Lord. "

Often, I say to myself "nothing – NO THING" can separate me from the love of God. This revealed truth from the word of God is always a comfort in life's difficulties.

If Christmas doesn't "feel right" this year, celebrate your faith in a Savior that was born in Bethlehem as a gift from your Heavenly Father. Celebrate the eternal truth that no crisis in life can ever separate you from God's love. Celebrate the understanding that Jesus Christ died for us and was raised to life and is now at the right hand of the Father interceding for us. Celebrate your victory over the fears of today and the worries of tomorrow. The love of God in Christ Jesus is greater than anything we experience in life!

Why are children so important in God's kingdom?

I have just completed a week of training with the teachers, program directors and para pros for a ministry my church is launching for children and families. This past year has been dedicated to building a new building that is totally kid-friendly, working with banks for financing and the state of Georgia for licensure. The man hours for this project have been off the chart and the prayer required to keep my peace and my "cool" has been endless. As I approach the one-year mark on this project I am amazed at what God has done and what will be accomplished through this ministry to children and families.

Recently, I found myself in the wee hours of the morning asking, "why are children so important in God's kingdom?" I know from personal experience that often churches must place the children's ministry low on the funding and attention list. It's easy to justify because the children don't tithe and are basically consumers of time, energy and money. They give little and demand much in the church arena. Yet in the scripture, children seem to be integral in the establishment of the kingdom of God on this earth. Consider the following examples of children who impacted the kingdom of God in the old and new testaments.

In the Old Testament, Joseph as a young boy was given a dream about his place in the economy of God. He was called not as a seminary graduate, mature and established in his theology but as a young boy. He would endure years of hardship but eventually would be the leader who saved the nations of the world from starvation through his relationship, wisdom and ability to hear from God.

Moses began his ministry in the kingdom of God as an infant floating down the river. His rescue by an Egyptian princess positioned him to understand the plight of his captive brethren. He would grow up in luxury watching the nation he would one day lead from slavery into the promise land of Israel. This loved and dedicated child set apart before he was able to speak would someday be known as "the deliverer" of Israel.

Hannah presented her three-year-old son, Samuel to Eli for service in the temple. She said, "Oh my lord, I prayed for this child as a gift from God, and God gave me my desire; and now I give him again to God as long as he shall live". Samuel grew up in the temple in the presence of God. He was known by the people as a "friend of God". His wisdom and understanding positioned him to become the chief prophet, the ruler and the judge of Israel.

In the New Testament, there are many examples of children called as infants to positions of authority and influence. John the Baptist was ordained from birth to prepare the way for the Messiah. Timothy, an apostle alongside Paul was taught the scripture in his infancy according to 2 Timothy 3:14-15.

Jesus, the babe of Bethlehem was born destined to die for the sins of the world. He taught the spiritual leaders in the temple at the age of twelve and they marveled at his wisdom. Jesus's growth pattern is expressed in this conversation passage with his parents in Luke 2:49-52 AMP, "And He answered, "Why did you have to look for Me? Did you not know that I had to be in My Father's *house*?" But they did not understand what He had said to them. He went down to Nazareth with them and was continually submissive *and* obedient to them; and His mother treasured all these things in her heart. And Jesus kept increasing in wisdom and in stature, and in favor with God and men."

As an adult minister, Jesus rebuked his disciples when he saw them preventing the children from coming to him during a time of ministry. In Mark 10: 13-16 NKJ, we find this account. "Then they brought little children to Him, that He might touch them; but the disciples rebuked those who brought *them*. But when Jesus saw *it*, He was greatly displeased and said to them, "Let the little children come to Me, and do not forbid them; for of such is the kingdom of God. Assuredly, I say to you, whoever does not receive the kingdom of God as a little child will by no means enter it." And He took them up in His arms, laid *His* hands on them, and blessed them."

As I look back at a year of labor and toil, and as I look forward to the opening of the learning center, I know God is pleased that children will grow naturally, emotionally and spiritually in this dedicated place of care. I am thankful for my church and their commitment to the call of God on the lives of children. I am humbled to be a part of the preparation of the next generation of men and women who will lead the church and declare the goodness of God!

Why are people so contentious?

I am a peacemaker and a peace lover. Contention and strife have never made a lot of sense to me. Too much energy expended for too little lasting results!

I have known people who live their entire lives moving from one conflict to another. As a minister, I have laughed with them, cried with them, and sat with them during the logical consequences of their actions.

Several years ago, I happened upon a single verse in Proverbs that opened my understanding as to why people live and die in a contentious, strife-filled lifestyle. Proverbs 13:10 NKJV, "By pride comes nothing but strife, but with the well-advised *is* wisdom." Could it be that simple? Does our pride usher us into every situation of strife and contention? I began to search alternate translations and other verses to see if this profound truth could possibly be confirmed in other scriptures. These are a few of the scriptures I found that reveal the pathway to contention and strife via pride. All of them are from the New King James Version -NKJV of the Bible.

Proverbs 16:18
Pride goes before destruction, And a haughty spirit before a fall

1 Samuel 17:28
Now Eliab his oldest brother heard when he spoke to the men; and Eliab's anger was aroused against David, and he said, "Why did you come down here? And with whom have you left those few sheep in the wilderness? I know your pride and the insolence of your heart, for you have come down to see the battle."

2 Chronicles 32:26
Then Hezekiah humbled himself for the pride of his heart, he and the inhabitants of Jerusalem, so that the wrath of the Lord did not come upon them in the days of Hezekiah

Job 35:12
There they cry out, but He does not answer, Because of the pride of evil men.

Psalm 10:2
The wicked in his pride persecutes the poor; Let them be caught in the plots which they have devised.

Psalm 59:12
For the sin of their mouth and the words of their lips, Let them even be taken in their pride, And for the cursing and lying which they speak.

Proverbs 8:13
The fear of the Lord is to hate evil; Pride and arrogance and the evil way And the perverse mouth I hate.

Proverbs 11:2
When pride comes, then comes shame; But with the humble is wisdom.
Proverbs 14:3
In the mouth of a fool is a rod of pride, But the lips of the wise will preserve them.

Proverbs 21:24
A proud and haughty man— "Scoffer" is his name; He acts with arrogant pride.

Proverbs 29:23
A man's pride will bring him low, But the humble in spirit will retain honor.

Isaiah 16:6
We have heard of the pride of Moab— He is very proud— Of his haughtiness and his pride and his wrath; But his lies shall not be so.

Isaiah 25:11 *And He will spread out His hands in their midst as a swimmer reaches out to swim, And He will bring down their pride, together with the trickery of their hands.*

Pride, contention, and strife have separated brothers, sisters, parents and children, spouses, business partners, churches, and every relationship, including our relationship with God. Pride and arrogance is currently ripping at the very fabric of our nation trying to destroy us. News reports hourly show how much strife and contention permeates our government and our relationships.

Pride exalts itself above reason and love. You can't walk in pride and love at the same time because pride blinds you to the needs of others. It captivates your imagination and focuses on how great you are.

If you want peace and favor with God and mankind, you must repent of pride and voluntarily humble yourself. Humility will preserve you and honor you at the same time. The choice is yours!

Why are you cast down?

The Psalmist speaks about being cast down several times in the Book of Psalms. He speaks of it being an issue in the soul that produces an issue in the natural for sheep. Not being sheep herders or people even near a flock of sheep, we totally miss the figurative language and the profound meaning of being "cast down".

"Why are you cast down, O my soul? And *why* are you disquieted within me? Hope in God, for I shall yet praise Him *For* the help of His countenance." NKJV   This scripture is found in chapter 42:5, 11 and in chapter 43:5. A variation is found in 42:6.

 In the New Testament, there are two very important references to being "cast down". One applies to temptation in 2 Corinthians 10:4-6 NKJV, "For the weapons of our warfare *are* not carnal but mighty in God for pulling down strongholds, casting down arguments and every high thing that exalts itself against the knowledge of God, bringing every thought into captivity to the obedience of Christ, and being ready to punish all disobedience when your obedience is fulfilled."

The second, found in Revelation 12:10 NKJV, applies to Satan's demise. "Then I heard a loud voice saying in heaven, 'Now salvation, and strength, and the kingdom of our God, and the power of His Christ have come, for the accuser of our brethren, who accused them before our God day and night, has been cast down. "

So, what does it mean to be "cast down"? In the dictionary definition, it is an adjective defined as "experiencing feelings of dejection, depression, or sadness". This is a mere shadow of what the Biblical term means and what the writers of the Bible were trying to express.

In his classic book *A Shepherd Looks at Psalm 23*, W. Phillip Keller gives a complete picture of the care and gentleness of a shepherd and what it means to be cast down. "Sheep are built in such a way that if they fall over on their side and then onto their back, it is very difficult for them to get up again. They flail their legs in the air, bleat, and cry. After a few hours on their backs, gas begins to collect in their stomachs, the stomach hardens, the air passage is cut off, and the sheep will eventually suffocate. This is referred to as a "cast down" position. When a shepherd restores a cast down sheep, he reassures it, massages its legs to restore circulation, gently turns the sheep over, lifts it up, and holds it so it can regain its equilibrium."

Being "cast down" literally means being on your back with no ability to get up, suffocating in the circumstances and having the life flow of blood drain from you. It is a serious life threating position. In reference to temptation and Satan it is an applicable position for the two to be in. In reference to the believer it is a position to be rescued from!

Once a sheep is upside down, there are only two chances for his survival. The first is for other sheep to discover his predicament, gather around him and work together to "nudge" him back to his side and up again. The second is for the shepherd who is always guarding his sheep to discover the cast down sheep and restore him. Without one of these two scenarios occurring, the cast down sheep is sure to perish. We need one another and the Lord's presence during difficult, cast down periods to survive!

Why does a sheep lose its equilibrium and fall over? In my studies, I have discovered two reasons, fear and fat. When a sheep becomes fearful it loses its balance and begins to struggle to stay upright. When a sheep becomes "wool-heavy" it's more likely to lose its balance.

Fear and fat are two conditions we as human sheep must guard against, so we don't become "cast down". Fear is not from God and it disrupts our balance in life. Only taking in and never giving out is not of God and makes us spiritually fat and naturally at risk.

But thank God, we have one another to hold us accountable and we have the "Good Shepherd" who watches day and night over his beloved sheep to keep them safe.

I challenge you to repent of fear, shear off the fat by helping others, build relationships with other sheep and get to know the good shepherd of your soul so you don't live a 'cast down" life.

Why do you lose your faith?

This week I have had four people share with me about losing their faith. A doctor, a friend, a pastor and a youth pastor all experienced a lapse in their faith in God for different reasons. It started me thinking about the "why" and it challenged me to study this all too common problem. Why do we have periods when we lose our faith? What are the reasons? How hard is it to renew our faith? Does God understand this feeling of separation?

Even the strongest faith can be a fragile thing. Faith by its nature is not supported by the obvious but is sustained by a powerful narrative that helps define who we are and gives us place and significance in the world. When it comes under attack by circumstances, evil influence, doubt, lack of understanding and pain, our faith identity can be damaged. Faith, however, is supernatural and while it may be influenced by natural circumstances it recovers with just a little bit of nurturing.

I believe there are five basic reasons we lose faith. I'm sure there are other causes, but I think these are the fundamentals from my study this week. It is through understanding that restoration and renewal can occur. Faith can once again help define and influence our goals and motivations for life.

A crisis that cannot be reconciled with a person's faith is probably the number one reason people lose their faith. It could be the loss of a child, sibling or parent, financial devastation, a weather-related catastrophe, war, divorce and abandonment, sexual abuse, false imprisonment or even the hypocrisy within the secular church. These painful and emotionally charged crises often bury our faith under an avalanche of questions with no answers. On the other hand, they often draw people to God for healing, hope and restoration. Navigating the "why" of a crisis, determines whether or faith shatters or strengthens.

The second reason we lose our faith is a poor foundation in the word of God - a foundation which can easily be shaken by unbelievers at college, in the work place or in new friendships. It's easy to lose something you don't strongly identify with. If your faith is the faith

245

of your parents, then it is readily shaken by challenge. I always stress the importance of a personal relationship with Christ. Your faith is not inherited but received through a one on one knowledge of God's love for you. There are no grandchildren in the kingdom of God, only children! Faith is personal and shaped by your individual knowledge and understanding of God.

Another reason we lose our faith is through involvement in an occupation that leads you away from God and the moral standards of faith. According to research, these are the ten occupations that lead people to become atheists: anthropologist, biologist, neurologist, physicist, zoologist, cosmologist, psychiatrist/psychologist, archaeologist, pastors, and Bible scholars. In his article, "The top ten occupations that lead to people becoming atheists", John W. Lotus states his personal faith fall came as a pastor of a church where the actions of people defied the character of God. We must be careful to have faith in God, not people. Love people with all their shortcomings but have your faith centered on God.

The fourth reason we lose our faith is by traveling the world and becoming indoctrinated by other religions. It's eye-opening to see good, kind people of other cultures who believe in a different God. An honest look at the tenants of faith for many world religions will reveal the lofty goal of treating others with kindness and respect. The Christian "Golden Rule" a.k.a. Ethics of Reciprocity is found in every major world religion. But the foundation of faith is not about relationship with others and treatment of mankind but about relationship with God. Out of that God relationship all others flow. Consider what Jesus said in Luke 10:27, "So he answered and said, "'You shall love the Lord your God with all your heart, with all your soul, with all your strength, and with all your mind,' and 'your neighbor as yourself.'" Our relationship with God and our passion to make him first will enable us to treat others with love and respect. God is the source of love and honor. Any religion that proposes otherwise will be filled with rules and standards that no one can live up to and will create faith failure.

Finally, the fifth reason a person loses their faith is when they embark on an intellectual journey to "know the truth". I'm not opposed to study and understanding, and I think every Christian should be well read and challenged. However, God is a spirit and to know him is not solely an intellectual revelation but a spiritual journey of faith. As Jesus shared with the woman at the well in John 4, "But the hour is coming, and now is, when the true worshipers will worship the Father in spirit and truth; for the Father is seeking such to worship Him. God *is* Spirit, and those who worship Him must worship in spirit and truth." Religion and places of worship will never illuminate the character of God for He is a spirit.

If you have lost your faith, here are some important things to consider on your journey back.

*Don't be mad at yourself

*Know that a lapse in faith doesn't make you an atheist

* Talk to someone whose faith you admire and trust

* Go to a Bible believing church

* Begin to study the Bible

* Pray even if you wonder if God is listening

* and finally take communion

Fix what is broken in your spiritual life and experience the joy of your salvation!

You have been adopted!

When Jesus came, he came so you could be born again. And he came not only for you to be born again but so you could become a child of God. Now that sounds too good to be true, but that was the reason that Jesus came. Let me show you in Galatians 3: 26-29; 4:3-5 NKJV, "For you are all sons of God through faith in Christ Jesus. For as many of you as were baptized into Christ have put on Christ. There is neither Jew nor Greek, there is neither slave nor free, there is neither male nor female; for you are all one in Christ Jesus. And if you are Christ's, then you are Abraham's seed, and heirs according to the promise." "Even so we, when we were children, were in bondage under the elements of the world. But when the fullness of the time had come, God sent forth His Son, born of a woman, born under the law, to redeem those who were under the law, that we might receive the adoption as sons."

So, what happened to you when you were born again was much more than just walking down to the front of the church and saying, "I'm sorry for my sins" and filling out a card and becoming a member of the church. What happened to you when you were born again was that adoption papers were signed between you and God the Father in the blood of Jesus Christ and you were adopted! Isn't that amazing? God adopted you.

The world has taught us that there is something wrong with adoption. They have taught us that it is better to be dead than to be adopted. It's better to be aborted than to be adopted and that it so anti-Christ. That mindset is so against the spirit of the living God. Because God loved you so much that he sacrificed His own son so He could take His blood and write a covenant of adoption for you; so that you would be a joint heir with Jesus. That means that everything that Jesus has you have. Romans 8: 14-17 NKJV, says, "For as many as are led by the Spirit of God, these are sons of God. For you did not receive the spirit of bondage again to fear, but you received the Spirit of adoption by whom we cry out, "Abba, Father." The Spirit Himself bears witness with our spirit that we are children of God, and if children, then heirs—heirs of God and joint heirs with Christ."

It doesn't matter what has happened in your natural family. When you asked Jesus Christ to come into your life there was an adoption that took place. God became your father and Jesus became your big brother and your defender. The Holy Spirit became your teacher and your comforter. It's just too marvelous to put into words what happens at the salvation experience, when someone is born again, and they become part of the family of God.

With every privilege comes responsibility. With the privilege of being a child of God you take on the name of Christ. Christian means "little Christ" or "little anointed one". My name is Ann Hocutt Nunnally Christian, because I've been adopted. My last name is so much more than my maiden or married name. It's the name of God Almighty that I carry. It's the name of my big brother who died for me and it represents my inheritance that I have in Christ. And so, I have not only the benefits of being adopted but also the responsibilities.

It's important for you to remember when you go through the Walmart line and that young lady at the cash register can't figure out what to do that your name ends in Christian. You treat people right, just like Jesus would. Others may be rude, impatient and verbally abusive but you cannot. Along with that responsibility of carrying the family name comes great privileges as a child of God.

You will never have victory in your life until you settle without any reasonable doubt what your name is and who your daddy is. What would you think of a parent who adopted a child, who saved the child from the bad situation and then sat them in the corner and said "Now, I saved you. You do the best you can to get by. You have a roof over your head. You have food in the refrigerator and just don't bother me. Leave me alone. I saved you and adopted you but that's it." What would you think about a parent who did that? Not a very good parent, are they? And yet we think that's the way God feels about us. It is not. He sent his son to shed his blood so that you could be adopted. Do you think He is going to quit taking care of you just because He saved you from the fires of hell? Is that the end all of Christianity? No! Christianity should be a life lived to its fullest as part of the family of God.

November is National Adoption Awareness month with the emphasis of placing those in foster care into a loving family. In God's economy, every month is adoption awareness month. God wants to adopt you into a permanent, loving family where you carry the family name. He's looking for children to call his own. He's looking for a family to share the riches and blessings of heaven with. He's looking for you!

Your value is non-negotiable

I entered the drive-thru after a busy day. I quickly ordered and waited on the smiling young lady to give me my food. I had signed the credit card but had forgotten to add a tip. I rummaged through my purse looking for a few dollars to give to the cordial service representative and finally came up with a couple of dollars. One bill looked pristine, but the other dollar looked as if it had been through a war! I hated to offer it as a tip, but it was a smudged, tattered bill or nothing as I was cash poor. My server graciously smiled and thanked me. It didn't matter to her that one of the dollar bills was in sad shape. To her it was money and a gift of appreciation that many working the drive-thru don't receive.

The experience reminded me that our worth and our value is not measured by the experiences of life, but it is set by our creator. Just as the national treasury department sets the value of a dollar bill, so the Lord sets our value no matter how many hard knocks we have received and no matter how wrinkled and smudged we may be.

While teaching at conferences, I have often made this very point using a fifty-dollar bill. I begin by asking the audience, "Who wants this $50 bill?". Every hand raises in the affirmative. Then I slip the bill into a Ziplock bag of dirt. Grinding the dirt into the unspoiled fifty-dollar bill. Again, I ask the same question. All hands go up. Next, I crumple up the dirty fifty-dollar bill, so it is virtually unrecognizable and ask the same question. Every hand still goes up. Finally, I drop, and soccer-style kick the fifty-dollar bill across the stage floor, damaging it from the left and right. Then, it's the same question with the same response. Everyone still wants the fifty-dollar bill even though it has been through tuff times. They seem to understand that value is set, and abuse cannot change it.

We often judge ourselves based on the abuse we have received not on what God's word says about our value. This is an affront to our creator. He sees us and desires us no matter how difficult life has been. He is a redeemer and can clean, uncrumple and heal our lives. He never doubts our value even though we might. Trusting His assigned

251

value to our life is so important. Why should we think ourselves smarter than God? Let me share a few scriptures that demonstrate this point.

"So God created man in His own image; in the image of God He created him; male and female He created them" Genesis 1:27 KJV. Your value begins with the fact that you are made by the hand of the Creator in His very image.

"Can a woman forget her nursing child, and not have compassion on the son of her womb? Surely they may forget, yet I will not forget you" Isaiah 49:15 KJV. Even if you are forsaken by family and friends, you are always cherished in the heart of God.

"For I know the thoughts that I think toward you, says the Lord, thoughts of peace and not of evil, to give you a future and a hope" Jeremiah 29:11 KJV. God's thoughts toward you are wonderful, and He has great plans for your life!

"Yes, I have loved you with an everlasting love; therefore with lovingkindness I have drawn you" Jeremiah 31:3KJV. His love for you is relentless, immeasurable, and infinite.
"But God demonstrates His own love toward us, in that while we were still sinners, Christ died for us" Romans 5:8KJV. The Creator of life loves you so intensely that He allowed His own Son to die in your place before you ever repented.

"Knowing that you were not redeemed with corruptible things, like silver or gold … but with the precious blood of Christ" 1 Peter 1:18, 19.KJV. God was willing to pay the highest price in the universe to redeem you—the blood of His dear Son.

"Therefore, if anyone is in Christ, he is a new creation; old things have passed away; behold, all things have become new" 2 Corinthians 5:17 KJV. If you belong to Jesus, you have a brand new, sparkling-clean life in Him.

"Behold what manner of love the Father has bestowed on us, that we should be called children of God!" 1 John 3:1KJV. God actually considers you His very own precious child.

"But God, who is rich in mercy, because of His great love with which He loved us, even when we were dead in trespasses, made us alive together with Christ ... that in the ages to come He might show the exceeding riches of His grace in His kindness toward us in Christ Jesus" Ephesians 2:4–7 KJV. Your heavenly Father has planned a magnificent, never-ending future for you.

"Now then, we are ambassadors for Christ, as though God were pleading through us" 2 Corinthians 5:20 KJV. God has given you a high calling as an ambassador to share His great love with others.

There are many other verses in the Bible and many stories that verify our worth in God's kingdom. Let's begin to believe them instead of our shame.

Thank you!

I hope you enjoyed reading
"Everyday Diamonds"

For updates on my activities and
information about new book releases,
visit my website at
www.AnnNunnally.org
or join my Facebook page
"An Encouraging Word
with Ann Nunnally"

If you would like for me to share with
your church or Christian group, please
contact me at:
229-221-6944 or
Ann@AnnNunnally.org

Made in the USA
Columbia, SC
19 January 2020

86887629R00148